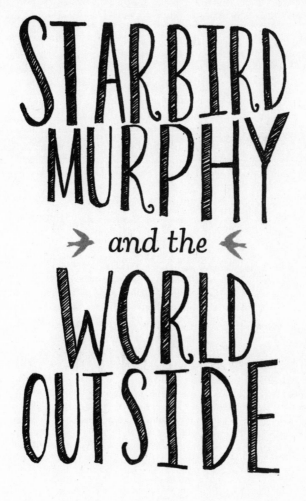

STARBIRD MURPHY
➤ and the ➤
WORLD OUTSIDE

karen finneyfrock

"2" /

VIKING
An Imprint of Penguin Group (USA)

VIKING

Published by the Penguin Group

Penguin Group (USA) LLC

375 Hudson Street, New York, New York 10014

USA ✳ Canada ✳ UK ✳ Ireland ✳ Australia ✳ New Zealand ✳ India ✳ South Africa ✳ China

penguin.com

A Penguin Random House Company

First published by Viking, a member of Penguin Group (USA) LLC, 2014

LIBRARY OF CONGRESS CATALOGING-IN-PUBLICATION DATA

Finneyfrock, Karen.

Starbird Murphy and the world outside / by Karen Finneyfrock.

pages cm

Summary: "Starbird has spent the first sixteen years of her life on a commune in the woods of Washington State. When she gets her Calling to become a waitress at the farm's satellite restaurant in Seattle, it means leaving behind the only place she's ever known and entering the World Outside"—Provided by publisher.

ISBN 978-0-670-01276-3 (hardcover)

[1. Cults—Fiction. 2. Communal living—Fiction. 3. High schools—Fiction. 4. Schools—Fiction. 5. Waiters and waitresses—Fiction. 6. Washington (State)—Fiction.] I. Title.

PZ7.F49835St 2014   [Fic]—dc23   2013027007

Printed in U.S.A.

1   3   5   7   9   10   8   6   4   2

Designed by Nancy Brennan   Set in Berling LT

The publisher does not have any control over and does not assume any responsibility for author or third-party websites or their content.

✳

Dedicated to Louis and Judith Finneyfrock,
my best teachers

✳

1

The owl hooted in a hemlock tree, cornstalks shook their arms in the wind, and Indus Stone's footsteps crunched beside mine on the gravel drive as we walked away from the main house. Summer fell further behind us with each step, and the trees exhaled their autumn breath, making me shiver. Everyone was in bed but the young people, story night had ended hours ago, and my heart raced like something was chasing me.

The moon was as perfect and white as a Buttercup hen's egg. It was visible between the fir trees reaching together over our heads.

"Indus is a southern hemisphere constellation. Why did EARTH name me after something I can't see?"

"Maybe you'll get a Calling to travel south."

The goats bleated as we walked past their pen beyond the cornfield. The September air left a cold mist on my hair and clothes, so I stuffed my hands into the pockets of my wool sweater. In the distance, I could hear frogs croaking by the pond. It was well past midnight, but no part of me felt tired.

"Mom and I were talking in the house last night after dinner," Indus said. Indus joined the Family with his parents when he was a child, so he still called his mother Mom, instead of by her name, Bithiah. "She told me why Dad left when I was a kid."

Most of the big trees on the Farm were on either side of the driveway. The rest had been torn out to create the back lot. But the Douglas firs by the house were old-growth, some over two hundred feet tall.

"I thought he left because he got a Calling," I said.

"So did I." Indus stuffed his hands into the pockets of his jeans. He kicked some gravel on purpose with his boot. At nineteen, Indus stood six inches taller than me and walked gracefully with long strides. "Turns out he couldn't handle Mom sleeping with EARTH."

"Whoa," I said, stopping. The owl hooted again. "Your dad gave in to jealousy?"

Indus kept walking, talking back to me over his shoulder. "That's what Mom accused him of."

I had a flashlight in the pocket of my jeans, but we didn't need it because of the moonlight's glow on the gravel. On either side of the path, though, the trees and ferns held a close, wet darkness. We walked on together until we came to a clearing on our left, and then we climbed a muddy slope to the chicken coop. I checked for signs of predators while the hens made sleepy clucking noises inside the roost.

"The fence looks good," said Indus, leaning against the wood railing of the chicken run, lacing his fingers into the wire covering on top. "You need more corn for the feed this week?"

"Yeah, I already asked your brother. Will you tell him to stop calling me Starchicken? It's not funny."

"It's kind of funny." Indus let his head drop back toward his shoulders and looked at the sky.

"Hilarious for you. You got a real apprenticeship."

"What's wrong with the chickens? It's an important job."

"Oh yeah, critical," I said, testing the door to the coop to make sure it was closed tight. We walked back to the gravel drive.

"So, your dad wanted to own your mom?" I asked, pausing to scrape some mud from my boot off onto the gravel.

"I hate it that everyone uses that word," said Indus. "Is it so crazy to want to be with just one person?"

My chest erupted in red, blotchy spots. I could feel them down there, hidden under my sweater. "Well, it's dangerous." I stole a glance at him. "If you love one person, and that person leaves you or dies, then you're all alone. Your dad left, but you still have lots of dads."

"Yeah, and they keep leaving, too. I think we're down to about six dads now." He laughed darkly.

"You shouldn't joke about that. EARTH will be back soon."

"You say that." Indus kicked a pinecone off the path, looked off into the trees. "But name one person who came back after being gone for years."

My stomach flopped like a dying fish and my mouth went dry.

"I'm sorry. I wasn't thinking about Doug," Indus said. He reached over and gave me an awkward, reassuring pat, the way a person would pat a dog if he didn't really like dogs.

"You think Doug's not coming back?" I kept scraping my boot on the ground.

"Your brother was the smartest guy I ever knew. *Know*. *Is* the smartest guy I know." Indus ran a hand through his shaggy blond hair. I trimmed it for him sometimes, if Bithiah was too busy. It needed to be cut again. "Doug's fine out there."

"But you don't think he's coming back. Or EARTH. You think they both abandoned us?" I asked it forcefully, like an accusation, and I didn't really want to hear the answer. I felt the chilly air through a hole in my sweater.

Indus sighed. "Don't you feel abandoned?"

"Why should EARTH come back if the Farm is full of non-Believers?" I started walking again.

"That's always it with you," he said, following me. "Someone's either a Believer or a non-Believer."

Red blotches spread like fire across my neck and shoulders. "What else is there?"

Indus threw his arms out and looked around. "What if you just don't know? What if you're still figuring the world out? Is that an option?"

"If you don't believe that we were brought together for a reason, then why would you stay?" I said, walking faster. "Why wouldn't you just run off like your dad did?"

"Sure, blame my dad. Because you couldn't possibly blame EARTH for anything, could you?"

"Your dad gave in to jealousy. He acted like an Outsider. That's not EARTH's fault."

Indus grabbed my arm and pulled me to a stop in the gravel. "Do you really think it's so wrong to want to love one person? To love them enough that you don't want to share them with anyone?"

We had reached the fire pit, meaning I was almost back to the yurt I lived in with my mother. The owl hooted again. There was malice in the sound. It was a barred owl known for diving at people when it felt territorial. Its talons had dragged through my hair more than once on a night walk.

I opened my mouth, but nothing came out. It felt like a bird had flown from a fir tree, into my throat and down my chest, flapping its wings where my voice should have been. "You can't doubt EARTH. You have to keep believing in him," I managed to say.

"You didn't answer me," said Indus. "What do you think about loving only one person?"

I had only loved one person my whole life, and he was in front of me talking about love and sex and love in the dark, under the moon. "Jealousy does seem destructive," I said, "but I guess I can't really imagine loving more than one person."

That's when Indus Stone, chest thick as a tree trunk, pulled me into a hug that left only my toes on the ground, his arms around my shoulders so all I could do was snake my hands up to his back. I put my nose into his shirt and inhaled. Nothing existed but the egg moon and the gravel noise and his smell.

Then he did something I'd been dreaming he would do since I was old enough to braid my own hair: He kissed me. Gently at first, so our noses touched and our chins and our lips pressed together. It was sweet. It was so sweet I thought it might kill me the way too much chocolate can kill a puppy. And I don't know how long we kissed like that—a hundred hours?—until something started heating up, like sticks rubbing together to make smoke, and I pulled my arms from under his and wound them around his neck and then we were kissing ferociously, our lips wet and tense. There were some gravel noises and then my back was against a Sitka spruce and the sap was grabbing my hair. Our hands started searching each other's bodies for something. I reached under his sweatshirt and felt the muscles of his chest connect with the muscles in his arms. We gasped and clawed at each other, and I wouldn't have cared if a brown bear was scratching the other side of the tree, or if the owl was flying toward us with his talons out, I wouldn't have stopped. But Indus finally backed away and unwound my body from his. I was sixteen and it was the first time a boy had ever kissed me.

I would have followed him anywhere that night: to the barn, to the orchard, on a deer trail across the border to British Columbia. But Indus said, "Well. Okay. Good night," like we had just been shaking hands, and his boots graveled off toward the Sanctuary and I guess I must have stumbled toward the yurt village because I ended up at my door, but I don't remember opening it or taking off my boots. I do remember my mother rolling over on her cot when I entered, and the sticky sap in my hair getting on the pillow and the raw skin on my lower back where it had rubbed against the bark and trying and trying to get my heart to slow down and go to sleep, thinking of nothing but him.

2

Every Family member's Calling comes in a different way.

When Mercury Ocean got his Calling to build a tree house in a red cedar and refrain from touching the ground, it came to him in a dream.

When Indus's mom got her Calling to have a third child, she said that also came to her in her sleep, but she laughed after she said it.

When a kid called Eagle Feather got his Calling to hitchhike to Alaska, it came in a letter from his Outside father. We haven't heard from Eagle since he left seven years ago. His mother cried for two weeks straight, but she never tried to stop him.

Every child daydreams about her Calling. I imagined mine would include a position in the Farm management, like my brother, Douglas Fir. I hoped it would include having children with Indus Stone. I never dreamed that my Calling would arrive at the Free Family Farm in a refrigerated truck one week after Indus kissed me, at the start of the wettest September anyone could remember, and that it would be cussing up a storm.

"Dumb-ass, stupid-ass, freaking truck."

I was walking down the slope from the chicken coop toward the gravel drive carrying my second egg collection of the day when I heard someone kicking the driver's side door. Not many vehicles came and went from the Farm, so people were emerging from the main house to investigate. I looked around for Indus but didn't see him.

"Does anybody know anything about stupid-ass, freaking refrigerator trucks?" the driver yelled in the direction of the main house. "It's been smoking since Everett."

"Iron John's on the back lot with the tractor," said Fern Moon from the porch, wiping her hands on the flowered apron she wore in the farmhouse kitchen. "Have some lunch and wait for him to come back."

The driver pulled the mass of brown curly hair back from her forehead, sighed, and tossed her keys into the open window of the truck. She walked up the steps and through the screen door.

"Come in for lunch, Starbird," Fern called to me.

If I had been born five years earlier or five years later on the Farm, I might have ended up calling Fern Moon "Mom," but I was raised during the decade when EARTH praised the strengthening of ties to the Communal Family over ties to the maternal and paternal members. I was taught to think of all the women on the Farm as my mom and all the men as my dad. For this reason and others, I've never known the identity of my biological father.

"I can help you package up the eggs for the truck after we eat," Fern said. I walked up to the porch and followed her into the main house.

The kitchen windows were coated with a fine layer of mist, and four iron skillets were steaming from under lids on the stove.

"Why didn't Ephraim come today?" Fern asked the driver, pouring hot water from the kettle and handing her a cup of tea.

"He's sick as a dog and so is Cham. There's a bug going around Beacon House," the newcomer said miserably, pushing her purple sunglasses up to rest on her head. She was wearing a black tank top and jean shorts, and two red bra straps perched visibly on her shoulders.

Just then, eleven-year-old Ursa ran into the kitchen from the long room with her little brother, Pavo, trailing behind her. Pavo was holding up his pants at the waist with one hand. "We tried waving at Iron from the hill, but he didn't see us." Ursa was out of breath.

"He gets lost in his head back there." Fern picked up a metal spoon. "Wash your hands."

Ursa and Pavo went to the deep porcelain sink and put their hands under the faucet. They were both tall enough now to reach the knobs easily, but still young enough to wrestle over the bar of soap. Their birth mother, Eve, walked in behind them, moving slowly because she was six months pregnant. She adjusted the drawstring on Pavo's pants.

"So, this is your first pickup?" Fern said to the driver.

"Yes, and I hate it. What's going to happen if I get pulled over? I don't have a license. We're so short staffed at the restaurant, I can't remember my last day off. Ephraim told me to ask if any of you wants to come work in Seattle. We've got a bed free in Beacon House, and we need a waitress desperately."

Ursa spun around from the sink, letting her wet hands drip on the floor. "A Calling!" she announced to the room, her eyes widening to the size of cherries. Ursa had just turned eleven and had recently become obsessed with Callings the way some girls are with horses. "Who's it for?" The water kept sputtering out of the tap behind her.

"Ursa, don't waste water." Fern motioned for Pavo to turn off the spigot.

"Who's the Calling for?" Ursa asked, as if she hadn't heard Fern, looking from one person to the next.

"It's not necessarily a Calling just because someone has shown up from Beacon House needing something." Fern tightened the string ties on her apron. "Beacon House is full of needs, just like the Farm."

"The Calling is for her," said Ursa, raising her still dripping hand and pointing her finger at me. Three more drops of water fell from her finger to the wooden floor. Everyone turned their heads and stared.

There are lots of rules on the Free Family Farm where I was born. Some rules are posted on the walls as helpful reminders in every common space of the main house, sanctuary, and grounds. For example, above the iron stove in the kitchen is a sign reminding each user never to let the wood box get empty. Hanging on the door to each outhouse in the yurt village, a sign reads, CLEANLINESS IS COSMIC. And inside the front door of the Farm's main house is a sign saying, NEVER ALLOW A POLICE OFFICER INSIDE WITHOUT A WARRANT.

These are the everyday rules, the agreements that help us live together in comfort and security. They're important, but not as important as our true and guiding rules, what we call "The Three Principles."

> One: *The Free Family is chosen by the Cosmos.*
> Two: *The Cosmos provides for us and we share what*
>   *is given equally.*
> Three: *Everyone in the Free Family gets a Calling.*

Our first Principle tells us that we are chosen. There are still Family members who haven't been found yet, so EARTH periodically goes on Missions to collect our missing members. Our second Principle is about sharing.

There is no such thing as personal property in our Family; everything we own, we own together. We share work, too, with each adult Family member filling a job suited to him or her.

The third Principle says that each person in the Family is given a unique purpose, dictated by the Cosmos and translated for us by EARTH, our Family's benevolent leader. At least, he had been translating for us until he left for a Mission three years ago, forcing us to try to understand the will of the Cosmos on our own for a while. Occasional letters would come in the mail, translations from EARTH written on parchment paper, which Eve and I would mount and post in the Sanctuary. They were postmarked from California, but we hadn't received one in over a year. Still, those of us left on the Farm remained committed and confident that EARTH would return any day. Most of us did anyway. I did.

"Starbird is getting her Calling," Ursa repeated, her arm still raised to point at me, specks of water from her hands dotting the hardwood floor around her.

"It's not polite to point," said Fern Moon, pushing Ursa's arm back down to her side. "Dry your hands."

The driver with the red bra straps turned around in her chair, her eyes still focused on me. "Are you looking for a job, Starbird?" she said. "Does this feel like your Calling?"

"I can't see that," Fern answered. "Starbird's a farm

girl, and you're talking about going Outside. She's too young for worldly influences."

"It's tempting for birth mothers to intervene when our children get their Callings," said Eve, walking over to put a hand on Fern's shoulder. "But we can't know how or when someone else will be Called, and we can't interfere with another person's Calling."

Fern visibly bristled, as if Eve's touch had landed on sunburned skin.

"Your Calling, your Calling," Ursa repeated, jumping up and down. Pavo just stood behind her staring.

"You can start tonight, if you want to," the driver said, blowing air over her steaming cup of tea. "It would help the Family, that's for sure."

Before I could say a word, Iron John walked in through the back door, wiping his forehead with a handkerchief and stuffing it into the front pocket of his overalls. "Wettest September I can remember." He looked around the room full of women. "Where's Ephraim and why's the truck smoking?"

"Starbird got her Calling," Ursa said, grabbing a water glass from a shelf behind her and handing it to Fern.

Iron looked at me and raised an eyebrow.

"It's just a job on the Outside," said Fern as she handed Iron the glass.

"Outside," Iron nearly whispered. "Is it your Calling?"

"To be a waitress?" I snapped. "I hope not. Maybe it's Ursa's Calling since she's so excited."

I was joking, but Ursa shook her head at me solemnly. "It's *your* Calling, Starbird."

Her insistence was irritating me, and so were everyone's stares. I could feel the blotches start to blossom on my chest. *They think the best offer the Cosmos is going to give me is becoming a waitress in Seattle? Thanks, Family.* Still, I didn't want to be rude to the driver, so I didn't say anything else.

"The polenta will get dry if we don't start eating, so let's put the talk of Callings on the back burner and have some lunch," Fern said, uncovering one of the iron skillets to reveal polenta and vegetables.

One honest thing you can say about the Free Family is that we respond quickly to instructions. Plates are kept in two stacks to the left of the wood-burning range. Utensils are kept in three wooden divided trays to the right, and cloth napkins are taken from a drawer before a meal and placed on the kitchen table along with salad and home-baked bread. Ceramic cups are kept on a shelf next to the filtered water that fills two glass basins.

At Fern's instruction, we formed a line that started at the plates and placed me right behind the driver with the red bra straps.

"I'm Venus Lake." She offered me her hand to shake.

She was wearing black fingernail polish. "Call me V."

There are clues you can pick up from knowing the name of any Free Family member you meet. If you are introduced to a Family member with a name from the Bible, like Ephraim, then you know that person joined the Family in the early days, when the Cosmos instructed EARTH to name our first babies Adam and Eve. If a member is called something reminiscent of a Native American name, like Eagle Feather, he was born or joined the Family during the short time when EARTH studied Native shamanism in the early 1980s. If your name has a cosmic combination like mine, Starbird, which includes some aspect of the heavens, like a comet, star, or asteroid, and something from the Earth, then you would mostly likely be under nineteen, born in the newest cycle of the Family, or one of the more recent joiners.

There were a few exceptions, like Iron John, who lived on the farm before the Family came, or my brother, Douglas Fir, whose spirit became so linked to the old growth on the property that EARTH never gave him a cosmic name. But, generally, the names fit into one of those three categories.

However, if you are named after one of the planets in our solar system, that marks you as an original member of the Free Family, along with EARTH, a venerated Elder. No way did this Venus with the red bra straps look old enough to be a Planet Elder.

"I know what you're thinking," she said. "My mother was Venus Ocean, but she died giving birth to me, so EARTH gave me her name." She shrugged and took a step closer to the polenta. "Except she was the ocean, and I'm just a lake."

"Where did you grow up?"

"In Beacon House, mostly. I've visited the Farm for Solstice Festivals and the apple pressing, but I usually stay in the tree house with my dad, and I don't really do the Feasts or anything." She chewed on one of her black fingernails and looked out through the back screen door.

It wasn't a total shock that I hadn't met Venus Lake before. Lots of Family members had spread out in the past decade, and even more since EARTH left for his Mission. There were Family communities in Bellingham and on an island in British Columbia, and some members lived in houses in Seattle. It had been years since the entire Family was able to fit into this one farmhouse in rural Washington State.

"So, do you have your birth certificate and Social Security number?" Venus turned back to me. "If you do come work at the café, we need more documented workers to keep names on the books. There are too many of us off-gridders."

"I'm off-grid," I said, annoyed that no one seemed to be listening to me when I said I didn't want to be a waitress. *Typical. This wouldn't be happening if EARTH were here.*

"Oh well." Venus shrugged. "Maybe it's not your Calling then."

A few more Family members showed up and joined the line for lunch. Lyra Hay swept into the kitchen in a long, white cotton dress, finishing the braid in her hair.

"Lyra, no hair fixing in the kitchen," said Fern, as Lyra stood over the bread table twisting an elastic band onto the bottom of her braid.

"My bad, Fern," said Lyra with a tired smile. "Peace," she added, holding up two fingers in a *V* shape.

Fern Moon frowned and answered, "Peace, Lyra."

Lyra was the most recent addition to the Family, and the only person to join our group since EARTH left. She met Caelum and Indus in Bellingham, came back with them to the Farm, and never left. At first everyone called her Joan, and without EARTH around to name her in a ceremony, we weren't sure what to do when she wanted to join the Family officially. In the end, Lyra Hay chose her own name. I still think of her as Joan.

"Peace, Starbird," said Lyra-Joan with a wide smile as she floated past me. "Peace, friend," she said to V. V cocked her head to the side, but then mumbled back, "Peace," at Lyra, who took her place at the end of the line. I didn't respond at all, but I did manage enough generosity to not roll my eyes.

"Lyra, did you stack the firewood in the kitchen box

this morning?" Gamma Lion's voice cut through the room as she walked into the kitchen wearing her reading glasses and holding a stack of papers, her gray hair like a ragged mop. For a short and slender woman, Gamma always had a big presence in the room.

"I just woke up," said Lyra, in a voice a little girl would use.

"Right after lunch, please." Gamma looked over the top of her glasses. "Venus," she said, spotting V in the lunch line. "Did Ephraim remember to give you the check for the pickup today?"

"Gamma!" Eve spun around with both hands on her pregnant belly. "Money should not enter the kitchen."

"Forgive me, Eve." Gamma turned to us so that Eve couldn't see her frown. "V, could you stop by the office before you leave today?"

Venus nodded. Then Gamma cut to the front of the line, grabbed a plate of polenta, and started back toward her office. Tiny as she was, she still had to squeeze through the hall to avoid bumping into Caelum and Indus, whose broad shoulders practically stretched wall to wall. The skin on my face and arms got hot, and I found myself staring hard at my plate.

An awkward and mystifying week had passed since the night Indus kissed me against the spruce tree. When we saw each other at a distance, he would wave, but during meals, he never sat next to me. He had started going to bed early rather than staying up with the young people, and the only conversation we had had in six days was about how much corn they expected to harvest this year. *It's the harvest*, I told myself, *he's just busy*. But I didn't really believe me.

"Hi, guys," I heard Lyra purr from the end of the line. I stared harder at my plate.

More Family members showed up, and the line snaked through the kitchen until all fourteen of us had gotten food. We sat down together at the wooden table in the long room, our largest indoor gathering space besides the Sanctuary.

Adam, our blond-haired, fortysomething master builder, stood and held up his ceramic water cup. "Cosmic Intelligence, I humbly invite your blessings to fall upon us, the Free Family, and upon all the families of the Earth."

"The Family is Free," we responded in chorus, also raising our cups. All of us except for Iron John, sitting next to me, who half raised his glass and did not chant along.

3

I ron John has never been what I would call a full-fledged member of the Family. Iron's mother, Callisto Air, invited EARTH and the Family to move to her farm in 1973, when Iron (who was just called John then) was nine years old. It was a year after John's father had died in a farm accident. Callisto (then called Doris) was in Seattle to see her in-laws when she met EARTH. She told us the story during school one day, the year she served as our history teacher.

Callisto-Doris had just come from an emotional argument with her brother-in-law about how to manage the harvest. He wanted her to sell the farm, telling her she wasn't capable of managing the farmhands and he couldn't keep helping her forever. She couldn't imagine giving up the property, which had been in her husband's family for a hundred years. John's grandparents were babysitting him, so Doris was alone for the afternoon in the city. Deciding to stop at a coffee shop to calm her nerves, she found her-

self sitting in a booth by a window and crying uncontrolla-
bly. That's when she felt a hand on her shoulder, and what
she described as a warm, soothing presence. She looked
up and saw an exceptionally tall man with generous blue
eyes who said to her, "Child of God, why are you crying?"

EARTH sat with Doris for hours in the coffee shop,
listening to her fears about managing the farm on her own,
her anxiety over what would happen to John with no father figure, and her heartbreak about how alone she felt in
the world. One week later, seven of the nine Planet Elders,
including EARTH, left the house they had been sharing
on Beacon Hill and moved to the farm to help their new
member, Callisto, with her harvest. Three years later, Callisto officially signed over the deed for the property to the
Free Family.

Although she gave the Family the main house, barn,
and property, Callisto and John had still lived in a one-
room log cabin, older than the farmhouse and situated
among the fir trees. When she died ten years ago, John
kept living there alone.

According to Callisto, John didn't embrace the Family
the way she did. He refused to go to any of the Translations when he was growing up. The only one I had known
him to attend was the one in memory of his mother, when
EARTH gave him the name Iron.

Being six years old then, I wasn't allowed to attend
that ceremony. Like most kids, I didn't go to a Translation

until I was ten. Until the right age, children play together in the house while the rest of the Family members enter the Sanctuary, located in the barn. When EARTH was with us, Translations happened every Sunday afternoon, right after breakfast, and I will never forget my first one.

My mother and I spent the Saturday before making a wreath for my hair out of sweet peas and pansies. It was late summer and everything on the Farm was ripe. In addition to my first Translation, it would be a special day for us because new apprenticeships would be handed out and my brother, Doug Fir, had recently turned thirteen. He spent the afternoon mending a hole in his shirt and chatting nervously about which apprenticeship he wanted.

"I'm the best at math, so I'll probably get Trader. But I want to work with Iron on the harvest. I hope I don't get animals or the kitchen. As long as I get something important." He was sitting on his cot in our yurt, and he had been trying to thread a needle for several minutes. Fern and I sat on her cot with a pile of flowers.

"Well, we do need some new composting toilets. Maybe the Cosmos needs you there," Fern said, moving to Doug's cot and taking the needle and thread from his hands.

"Gross." Doug crossed his arms as Fern laughed. "That's worse than goats."

"EARTH will put you in the right spot for your talents, my brilliant son." She touched his face. "And all jobs here are important. But Iron did tell me that he would be getting an apprentice this year."

"He did?" Doug uncrossed his arms and sat up. "For real?"

Fern smiled and handed Doug the threaded needle. "I don't mean to get your hopes up, but Iron would love to have you."

Doug took the needle and started sewing too quickly, making several sloppy stitches while Fern came back to her cot and added another flower to my wreath.

I believed Fern about EARTH. He always placed people in the right apprenticeships, probably because he was always listening to the voice of the Cosmos.

It's impossible to describe the feeling of being in the presence of EARTH. If his blue eyes actually looked at you, you felt as if he was looking right into your heart, through your skin and bones and into your talents and your needs. Fern says that when I was a baby, I would always stop crying if EARTH held me. When I was six and fell off the back of the truck onto the gravel drive and skinned both my knees, EARTH put his hands on my legs and all the pain went away. It was my duty to think of all the men in the Family as my father, but I was pretty confident I knew who my birth father was. I knew it was EARTH.

✻   ✻   ✻

That Sunday after breakfast, we walked to the gathering place where two hundred other Family members were waiting. When the Family first moved to the Farm, EARTH held Translations in the living room of the main house. But when the Family grew too big, he moved them into the old gable barn. The Sanctuary was built under a hayloft window and shared space with our tractor, tools, and apple press.

There was lots of talking and laughter. Family members often came on Sundays from Seattle and Bellingham, even British Columbia, to hear the Translations and put in a few hours of work on the Farm. People welcomed me and congratulated me on my first Translation. It felt like everyone wanted to talk to me or put their hands together in front of their hearts and bow. The ring of flowers in my hair dropped pink petals around my feet.

When the door to the Sanctuary finally opened, the Herald began allowing Family members to enter, row by designated row. Since it was my first time at the Translation, and since Doug Fir was scheduled to get his apprenticeship, we were invited, along with Fern Moon, to sit in the Venus orbit, right behind the Planet Elders, one row removed from EARTH.

It was hot and dry inside the Sanctuary that morning, and the sun was streaming through the window in the hayloft and through all the little gaps in the roof. The ceiling seemed to extend miles over my head, and above me particles of dust and hay danced in the sunlight. The plank floor was covered with at least twenty rugs in different patterns, but I could still hear the floor creaking as we walked across it to our seats.

We entered with the rest of our orbit and sat on a rug, each with our own pillow. Family members filed in behind us, forming the other seven consecutive rings, emanating out from a plywood platform just under the window at the north end of the room. After everyone was seated, the chatter dropped to a comfortable silence. Then another door opened at the front corner of the Sanctuary, and EARTH walked in.

Naturally, I had known the tall, blue-eyed EARTH since I was a baby, and had always seen him as our most venerated Elder, our Translator. Day to day, EARTH was soft-spoken and kind, often hidden away in his rooms on the second floor of the main house. At the Summer and Winter Solstices, his voice boomed and his presence filled the Farm as he heard complaints, judged differences among Family members, and gave out names. But when EARTH entered the door to the Sanctuary for my first Translation, I felt like I had never seen him before. In his long robe, tied around the waist with a gold cord, and followed by an adoring Mars Wolf, he looked like a storybook king.

Mars Wolf, EARTH's closest adviser, was the first to

approach the platform, the plywood creaking as he walked across it and kneeled to the left of a stack of pillows. Then came EARTH, stepping onto the stage and walking contemplatively to the place where the cushions and a short table were waiting. He sat down and crossed his legs at the ankles. Light from the window above him fell on his white hair, making it glow like wheat during the harvest.

Then Uranus Peak, dressed in a faded blue robe and purple cord, a scarf holding back her graying blonde hair, stood from the front row and addressed the congregation.

"Our Family was summoned together in 1970 by the Cosmic Imagination that Called the eight principal elders to witness the first Translation by our interpreter, EARTH. In the first Translation, the Cosmos gave EARTH his Calling, and instructed him to name his Planet Elders. In the second Translation, EARTH was told to build his Family and repopulate the Cosmos. And in the third Translation, EARTH was given Three Principles: The Free Family is chosen by the Cosmos; the Cosmos provides for us and we share what is provided equally; and every Family member receives a Calling. We live by these Principles because we are the Family and we are Free."

"The Family is Free," two hundred voices chanted back. Uranus Peak took her seat.

All eyes in the Sanctuary turned to EARTH, who was seated with his hands touching at the palms in front of his chest, his eyes resting on his knees. There was a long silence, during which he did not seem to flinch or blink. Someone coughed, a few people crossed or uncrossed their legs. EARTH sat still as a statue. After a few minutes of this, I glanced up at Fern Moon, who refused to meet my gaze, staring intently at EARTH. Then I turned to look at Doug Fir, who gave me a comforting nod.

Finally, after ten painfully long minutes, EARTH's voice broke the silence like a glass.

"The Cosmic Intelligence is not speaking to me this Sunday afternoon." He took his eyes off his knees and looked up at the congregation. Then he looked directly at me. "It is screaming."

I inhaled sharply. Doug Fir put his hand on my arm.

"The Cosmic Imagination, the Infinite Creator, the Intelligence that lives in everything, has a message for the Family collected here. Are you all well fed?" EARTH raised his hands out to the room, palms facing up.

"Yes," several people sitting in the semicircles responded, including Fern Moon.

"Do you have warm clothes and comfortable places to sleep?"

"Yes," more voices added to the chorus. Doug Fir joined in.

"Are you surrounded by a benevolent circle of people who love you and your planet?"

"Yes," I tentatively said.

"And can this be said for the World Outside? Does the World Outside allow people to starve, homeless in the street?"

"Yes."

"Does the World Outside pollute the air, put poison on the fruits and vegetables, pollute the ocean until the whales can't breathe?"

"Yes."

"Does the World Outside have corrupt politicians, greedy corporations, and people bathing in riches while others die in squalor?"

"Yes."

"Do the Outsiders selfishly divide up the world into tiny pieces and claim, 'I own this piece,' and 'you own that one,' and, 'you can't own any at all'?"

"Yes."

"Let me speak for a moment to the first generation, because our lucky children who were born into the Family will not know what I mean. Do you remember the hardships you faced before hearing your Call to the Family?"

"Yes," Fern Moon said next to me, allowing her head to drop two inches toward her chest. I could guess what she was remembering. She was seventeen years old and pregnant with my brother when her Outside family disowned her. She had told me many times that when the Free Family found her, EARTH had saved her life.

"Do you recall the brutal survival required to exist in a world without your brothers and sisters?"

"Yes," the adults said again. Fern's head still hung down.

"So, then, why would we let our precious young ones, our fertile girls of the second generation, the future of our Family, visit the town for its movie theaters?" He paused and looked again around the room. "For its bakeries and dress shops? Does this not require our children to handle money? We may live beside the Outsiders, feed them in our café, exchange goods and services when necessary. And love them, as the Cosmos commands us to love the Outsiders. We will feed them with good food and make quality goods for exchanging, but be wary. I call to you mother tigresses, and you father tigers, protect your cubs ferociously in the World Outside." He pointed to a handful of men and women in the congregation. "If you agree to this, say yes."

"Yes," said the adults. "Yes," said Fern Moon.

"The Cosmic Intelligence has spoken and I have Translated for you," EARTH finished, taking a deep breath and then retraining his eyes again on his knees.

After a few minutes of silence, Mars Wolf stood. He was a short man, barely taller than I was, and dark in all the ways EARTH was light. Mars's black hair hung to his shoulders and his eyes were brown as the smoke of burning leaves. The sound of his voice was sour to my ears, while EARTH's was always sweet. "New apprentices, please come forward."

My brother took a quick breath and stood up. He stepped between two Planet Elders to the inner circle, and turned to face the congregation, along with the two other kids who had turned thirteen recently, Halley Aspen and Indus Stone. Even when I was ten, I was drawn to the strong, quiet Indus and knew I would miss seeing him in school every morning once his apprenticeship started. All three of them were dressed in clean, if somewhat threadbare, clothes, and Halley was wearing a flower wreath similar to mine. They looked jittery and pale, but Doug Fir still managed the air of confidence he always had, even when he was terrified.

"On instruction from EARTH, I will now assign you each a mentor," Mars Wolf's voice issued sharply through the room. "Halley Aspen, you will apprentice Neptune Fox in the apple orchard." Halley smiled widely and looked at her birth mother, Golden, who smiled back at her.

"Indus Stone, you will work with Iron John on planting and the harvest." Indus's brother, Caelum, jumped up and pumped his fist in the air, hooting and breaking the quiet of the Sanctuary. A few people laughed, and there was light applause. But I noticed Doug's face fall. It was rare that two apprentices got the same mentor, so Doug's hopes of working with Iron seemed lost.

"Douglas Fir," Mars Wolf barked, making Doug visibly

tense, so much that he closed his eyes as if bracing against an anticipated smack. "You will apprentice EARTH."

An electric current shot through the Sanctuary. Although several adults tended to EARTH's rooms and office, EARTH had never taken an apprentice before. It was assumed that he was too busy to be a mentor. Fern Moon clapped a hand over her mouth. Doug opened his eyes and let his lips fall open. EARTH didn't react at all, his eyes still trained intently on his knees, giving no indication that he had even heard the announcement. There was a murmuring in the congregation, and everyone seemed to shift in their seats at once.

"Tonight we will have a feast to celebrate increased prosperity from our new business, the Woodworker's Collective," Mars Wolf went on. "We will prepare dishes from our bounty and everyone will eat on the patio at six o'clock. Until then, workers are needed in the back lot to harvest corn and tomatoes. Please see Iron John."

When Mars Wolf finished, EARTH stood and led the Planet Elders back out through the door at the north end of the hall. Then my row stood and exited through the south door and out into the sunny Sunday afternoon. A circle formed around Doug Fir. People waited their turn to pat him on the shoulder, clasp their hands, and bow. Everywhere Family members stood in groups talking about the apprenticeships, and about Doug being chosen. "Maybe he will replace EARTH one day," I heard someone say. "Maybe EARTH will teach him to Translate," said another. A flower petal fell from the wreath on my head. No one asked me about my first Translation.

Looking back, I think EARTH saw leadership in Doug and wanted to groom him for important Family work. Doug would probably be in Gamma's shoes by now, in charge of managing the whole Farm. But that didn't happen, because my brother ran away in the middle of the night three years after his apprenticeship was announced, right after he turned sixteen.

4

After finishing our lunch of polenta and vegetables, we took our plates outside to the washtub on the back patio behind the main house to clean them. By using biodegradable soap, the Family could save our gray water and use it in the herb and vegetable garden by the kitchen. Iron and V went to work on the truck, so I offered to wash their plates. Then Fern Moon came out to help me load up the cucumbers into crates for V to take back to our restaurant in Seattle.

I had never been to the restaurant; in fact, I had never been to Seattle. I had been to Bellingham on trips to the co-op when Adam or one of the other Traders needed a hand, but that hadn't happened in a year. Still, I knew that our restaurant was called the Free Family Café and had been around since the Family was started. I also knew that it served vegetarian organic food, most of which was grown at the Farm. Twice a week during the growing season, Ephraim or Cham drove up in the refrigerator truck to pick up eggs, fruit, vegetables, and herbs, along with cakes, pies, and cookies we baked in the farmhouse kitchen.

"Did you have a chance to ask Gamma about moving into the main house yet?" Fern asked as she picked two cucumbers out of the wheelbarrow and put them into a wooden crate. When she leaned over, her gray braids were long enough to brush the ground.

"No," I said. "I'll go talk to her after we finish packing these up, and once I put the eggs in the truck."

"I'm sorry that I've been a little hard to live with lately," said Fern, stealing a glance at me as she grabbed two more cucumbers. "It was so easy when you and Doug were growing up, sharing the yurt, but when your children become teenagers, well . . ." Fern's voice broke and then disintegrated.

Even after three years, Fern could barely say Doug's name without crying. She didn't need to finish her sentence anyway. Fern and I had been growing more frustrated with each other daily since my fourteenth solstice. Living in a one-room yurt is fine when you're a child and you don't mind your mother knowing what you're doing every minute of the day. But lately, I had been spending more and more time around the main house after dinner, playing music with the Family or hanging out with

Caelum, Indus, Badger, and now Lyra, the only people close to my age on the Farm. I had only been going to the yurt to sleep. When I got up the nerve to tell Fern that I wanted to move into the main house, she suggested I talk to Gamma, our leader of finances and the informal den mother, since EARTH wasn't around to grant permission.

"It's not that you're hard to live with," I lied. "I just like the rooms in the main house better than the yurt. I'm going to ask her about my placement again, too." I tried to sound casual. "Ursa's old enough to take over the chicken coop now. I'm sixteen and my apprenticeship is supposed be over."

Fern gave me a sad smile as I picked up the last cucumber and added it to the crate. "I think Gamma just wants you to wait until EARTH comes back so you can get your placement properly."

"I didn't get my apprenticeship properly," I said, picking up the arms of the wheelbarrow.

Fern sighed. "I'm not trying to argue."

Eve and Bithiah had already loaded the baked goods, and Caelum was putting in the last of the tomatoes and greens when I got to the refrigerated truck. By the time I finished loading three crates of cucumbers and forty dozen eggs, Iron had fixed the smoking problem. Turned out the truck was low on oil. Iron gave V a lecture about checking the oil and air pressure in her tires before any more trips, and then he walked off in the direction of his cabin.

V gunned the truck's engine and backed down the gravel drive. I was walking toward the main house when she stopped and poked her head out through the driver's side window. "Hey, Starbird!" she yelled, motioning me toward her. "I forgot to give this check to Gamma. Will you do it for me?" She held out a rectangular piece of paper.

Like most of the kids born on the Farm, I had never handled money. Most of us had never even seen it. EARTH translated that money was literally and metaphorically the dirtiest thing on our planet. Only selected Traders, who were identified by EARTH, could handle money, and I wasn't one of them. *It's not actually money, it's just a check*, I reasoned. *Plus, Doug Fir used to handle money, and I'm more responsible than he was. He ran away.*

I reached out and took the piece of paper from V. My hand did not catch on fire.

"Thanks," she yelled, turning up the music in the cab until it was loud enough to make the goats grazing near the cornfield look up. "Peace." She laughed and held up two fingers in imitation of Lyra Hay before driving off toward the road.

I turned from the driveway and headed into the main house to see Gamma. As I neared her office, I could hear her talking on the phone. There aren't any landlines at the Farm, or any other connectivity with the Outside. The Traders brought the mail twice a week from a post office box in Bellingham, and Gamma used a cell phone to connect with our other businesses, like the café, the Woodworker's Collective, and buyers for our farm products, but that was the extent of our communication.

I was just raising my hand to knock on her office door when I heard her say, "How is that possible? I'm telling you that we haven't borrowed against the value of the property in three years."

I stood still in the hall, my hand held in a knocking-shaped fist.

"That's impossible because the property has multiple owners. That is not my understanding of the deed and I demand to see a copy of that paperwork." There was a pause. "Yes, I will come down there tomorrow."

As Gamma stopped talking, I became shamefully aware that I had been eavesdropping. I let my knuckles fall against the door.

"Come in," Gamma said.

In the office, I found tiny Gamma sitting behind EARTH's giant wooden desk, like a child trying on one of her mother's dresses. She was wearing her reading glasses, and papers were spread out before her in five neat stacks. There was another smaller desk to her left facing the wall. That's where Doug Fir used to sit.

"Starbird, hello. How are our chickens doing?" She took off her glasses and rubbed her eyes.

"Chocolate is the nicest rooster we've ever had, and Brittle has eight black chicks following her around. Iron's going to help me patch the roof this week so we'll be ready for more rain in October."

"Is Ursa a good apprentice?"

"The best." I stretched the truth until it said "ouch." "I believe she's ready to take over the coop."

Gamma sighed. "Starbird, I know you don't think running the chicken coop is an important job, and I know you want to work in the office or become a Trader, but Ursa is only eleven. Maybe when EARTH comes back—"

"I'm as good at math as Doug Fir was," I said. "EARTH would have wanted me to do something more . . . necessary than making chicken feed."

"Chicken feed is highly necessary if you're a chicken. And the eggs are necessary to the café, and the income from the café is necessary to all of us. Pluto Storm specifically asked for you as her apprentice."

I wanted to say, *Before she ran off and left me with the whole job*, but I bit my lip instead. I still had another favor to ask from Gamma and I didn't want to make her mad.

"Well, then can I move into the main house? The yurt is too small for me and Fern."

Gamma stood up and walked around her desk to put

an arm over my shoulder. Since she was barely five feet tall, it was an awkward comfort. "I'm sorry, Star, but we're full in the house. With Eve pregnant, three of us sharing EARTH's rooms, and Lyra living in the attic, we're bursting at the seams. Maybe you could join the group that's moving into the Sanctuary?"

"Maybe." I felt my scalp getting hot. Indus and Caelum were moving into the Sanctuary along with Badger. The thought of setting up my bed feet away from Indus Stone, with his tan skin that always smelled like the back lot, made my heart chase its own tail. I couldn't allow Indus Stone to hear me sleep or see me get up at night to go to the outhouse or know how I look in the morning.

"Maybe I could move into the attic with Lyra?" I offered reluctantly, acknowledging my own desperation to get out of the yurt.

"With Adeona up there, too, there just isn't room for another bed. I'm really sorry," Gamma added. "We're . . . stretched thin in a lot of ways right now. Speaking of which, can you handle the math class for Adeona tomorrow? She's not feeling well."

Great. Teaching math class. Again. That's almost as exciting as feeding chickens. Still, I nodded dutifully. It was up to all of us to keep the Family going until EARTH got back, and I planned to work as hard as anyone, no matter how insignificant the work. I wanted EARTH to know who he could count on. "Here's the check from Venus." I handed her the slip of paper.

"Oh." Gamma studied my hand before taking the check. "I'm sorry you had to handle that."

"No big deal." I shrugged.

Gamma walked back around the desk and sat down. "Do me a favor and close that door on your way out. I need to make a phone call."

5

I spent the rest of the day depressed in the chicken coop with Ursa, while a thin rain drizzled on the tin roof. Ursa couldn't officially be called my apprentice since she was only eleven, but with EARTH away on his Mission, all kinds of Family rules were being bent until they were in danger of breaking.

In the early days, Farm kids started their apprenticeships at age ten, but then the Family got hassled by Outsiders in the 1980s, when Washington State police raided us on charges of child labor. They interrogated the children, asking if they went to school and how many hours a day they had to work. Adam and Eve were two of the kids who were questioned, and they told us about it one Story Night. Police threatened to put adults in jail and children in foster homes. If terrifying children was the Outsiders' way of getting us to be more like them, it was a pretty stupid plan. EARTH and Mars Wolf spent months in court fighting for the Family's right to have apprenticeships and eventually won, but they had to agree to start them at thirteen and continue homeschooling through grade twelve. Outsiders will use any excuse to try to demoralize us. Their greed-driven, capitalist system is threatened by our commitment to shared property.

But after EARTH left for his Mission, when non-Believers started abandoning the Farm, we were so short-handed that apprenticeships had to start younger, and school days became inconsistent. Lately, classes happened only when someone was available to teach, and mostly in the winter when there was less work to do on the Farm.

Like most Farm kids, I had had dreams about receiving my apprenticeship, especially after seeing Doug Fir get his. But I didn't get to stand in front of the congregation and get assigned a mentor. EARTH had already left for his Mission before my thirteenth solstice. Instead, Pluto Storm came to my yurt one morning and told Fern that she needed my help. Lucky me.

I begged Fern, Gamma, Iron, anyone who would listen, to give me some assignment other than chickens. But they all said that I had to work where I was needed.

It was a hard job made worse by Pluto's mood swings. Some days she would start early, waking me up before the rooster crowed, insisting we remove all the old pine shavings and scrub every board in the coop before lunch. Other days, she would sleep into the afternoon or avoid showing up to the coop at all, leaving me to collect and store all the eggs on my own, which I did slavishly, intent on proving my value to the Family.

But we could never keep up with the demands from the restaurant and Farm. When I first started, we had seventy-five laying hens and were collecting an average of four hundred and fifty eggs a week. But the farm alone could go through thirty dozen, leaving a measly seven dozen eggs for the restaurant. Gamma put pressure on Pluto to increase production, and soon we were squeezing thirty-five new hens into a coop just large enough for the original seventy. Peckings were brutal, with some of our newer hens bleeding heavily from their combs, and our egg production plummeted.

Maybe the stress was too much for Pluto. Six months after EARTH departed on his Mission, she left, too, packing up all of her belongings one day and standing on the main road with her thumb out. No one tried to convince her to stay.

So before I was even fourteen years old, I became the principal caretaker of a hundred and ten hens, one rooster, and a chicken coop full of mites and strife. I cried every day for a week, and I don't know what I would have done without Iron. Even with the harvest to manage, he met me every morning at dawn to collect eggs and every evening to strategize managing the flock. It took a full year and plenty of planning for us to triple the size of the coop and outdoor run, improve ventilation and watering units, and strengthen the fencing from predators. Now I am the keeper of two hundred healthy laying hens producing nearly eighty-seven dozen eggs a week, six roosters, and a constant crop of chicks.

"No more questions about my Calling," I said to Ursa after ten minutes of her babbling on the subject. We were moving a few of the hens so we could clean out the laying boxes.

"But it's exciting." She was holding White Chocolate, our most productive Delaware hen. With so many chickens, I only let her name a handful.

"It's a job as a waitress." I was using a scrub brush to vigorously clean the corners of a box. "That's even less exciting than making chicken feed."

I put the box down and grabbed another one. What I told Ursa about waitressing was true—it did sound boring and unimportant—but I didn't tell her that there were other reasons I didn't want to leave the Farm. The image of Indus Stone crossed my mind. Specifically, a picture of him, shirt off, bringing us fresh pine from the wood chipper, walked right through my thoughts. "Besides, what if EARTH came back and I was gone? The Believers have to be here to welcome him when his Mission is finished."

Ursa moved Cocoa, one of our Sussex hens, from a box to the yard. When she came back in, she was brushing feathers off of her threadbare pants legs. "Well, *I* want to be a waitress in Seattle. How would you like your eggs?" She pulled an egg from each pocket of her worn corduroys.

"You couldn't be a waitress in those pants," I said. "You can have my blue skirt. Eve made it for me and I can't fit into it anymore."

"Thanks, Starbird." Ursa pulled her loose-fitting pants away from her legs. "There's nothing left in the vintage closet but polyester."

In the earliest days of our Family, members made all their own clothing by hand. According to Fern, there was even a time when they sheared sheep and cleaned and spun the wool for sweaters and hats. But as the Family grew, our demand for clothing was too much for the sewing group. So EARTH befriended a man named Jimmy in Bellingham who owned a vintage clothing store. Jimmy would visit the Farm and bring boxes of old clothes with him to refill the coat closet in our living room. Any Family member who needed something could take it. Whenever the Family needed something, EARTH always seemed to meet a person who would fill the need for us. EARTH called it Divine Receiving. Jimmy stopped coming around after EARTH left, and the closet had slowly emptied.

"I wonder if they wear uniforms at the restaurant in Seattle," said Ursa.

"Enough restaurant talk." I splashed water into a laying box, and resisted the urge to splash Ursa. "Go ask Caelum for soybeans so we can make the feed tomorrow. The recipe is three to one, corn to soybeans. We'll know more after we shell the corn, but I'm guessing he gave me ten pounds. So go ask him for the right amount of soybeans."

"Say it again, slower." Ursa opened our bag of diatomaceous earth and prepared to add it to the layer of pine shavings on the floor of the coop.

"Three parts corn to one part soybeans. We have ten pounds of corn," I repeated.

"I need . . . three and a third pounds of soybeans?"

"Good. I already put in our seed order with Adam for the co-op. We should be ready to mix by tomorrow afternoon." I had been working with Ursa on her math, since I had a knack for it. When Iron and I were expanding the coop, we spent long hours calculating the square footage needed for each hen, indoors and out, the number of laying boxes and watering containers. Not to mention the amount of lumber and building details for the construction. We spent as much time with pencil and paper as we did with hammers and saws. Fern Moon said I was as good with numbers as Douglas Fir. I think that was the reason EARTH made Doug his apprentice. EARTH was always working in numbers.

Ursa and I stayed in the coop until the dinner bell rang and then ate with the Family in the long room. Indus sat near Caelum and Iron at the end of the table, and I sat with Ursa and Fern near the middle. I caught him glancing at me a few times, but I tried to act like I hadn't noticed.

It was Wednesday and time for Story Night, so after cleaning up, we all gathered in the living room to share songs, poems, and memories. The living room was large enough for thirty people if folks sat on the floor as well as on the sofas and chairs. The fir floors were covered with a red rug, and there was a coffee table made from a tree slab in the center of the room. Our farm dog, Steven, a twelve-year-old yellow Lab, curled up on his bed in the corner near the fireplace.

Adam usually led the Story Night music on guitar, with Caelum playing the banjo and Bithiah on our un-tuned piano. Children on the Farm were encouraged to switch around on instruments until something resonated to their touch. Mine was a wood flute that made a lonely, mournful sound when played on the hill by the apple orchard, but managed to sound happy around the fire in the family room. Indus played an emotionally raw harmonica, his rough farmer's hands holding it like a tiny bird. Lately, Lyra had lately been smashing about with a tambourine, drowning out all the subtlety of the music with her clanging.

I sat on the worn velveteen couch, my feet tucked under me to make a ball. With fourteen people in the room, I saw no one but Indus. He sat on the floor with his back to the bay windows, his long legs stretching to the middle of the room, where his socked feet were crossed. If I reached out my foot, I could have touched his. I didn't know a foot could long to touch another foot. *Will he walk me home again? Will he kiss me against the spruce tree? Will he even look at me?*

"Thank you for coming together tonight, Family." Adam gave our traditional opening words and then strummed his guitar as other members joined in on a formless jam. After two songs, Adeona offered to tell the first story.

"My Outside parents were drug addicts in eastern Washington." She stood near the fireplace as people put down their instruments. Her voice was thin and she held on to the mantel like it was a walking stick. Adeona was probably thirty years old and didn't have any children herself. She was our primary teacher. She never used to tell stories or speak much in large groups, but her confidence had bloomed in recent years since she started spending most of her time with Gamma.

"They lost custody when I was seven, and I got put in the first foster home. It was a nightmare place, and the other kids there were vicious. The second one wasn't horrible, just sterile. I was actually happier on the streets. Street kids are decent, as long as they aren't addicts." Adeona's voice grew thicker as she spoke, but she still held the mantel. Gamma came in from the office and sat on the arm of the sofa next to me, putting a hand on my shoulder.

"We all panhandled and shared whatever food we could get, tried to make sure no one went hungry. Anyway, I was singing in front of the co-op in Spokane when he saw me. I was Jennifer then, and I had a dog and a sleeping bag and a sign that said, ANYTHING HELPS on one side and FREE HUGS on the other. I kept nodding off leaning against a brick wall, because it had rained the night before and I could never sleep when it rained.

"'Child of God, are you hungry?' said this man's voice. I opened my eyes and there he was, standing over me in gray robes and long hair outlined by a watery sun. No one ever talked to us. They tossed money at us if they were nice, but they never talked to us. I thought God had come to save me. He gave me an entire bag of groceries that he had just bought at the store, and he left. He didn't ask me for anything. All the street kids had a feast under the bridge that night, on hummus and bread and organic fruit. The next day, the Mission van drove by the co-op again and they asked me if I wanted to move to the Farm. They said I could bring my dog. They said all the kids could come, but I was the only one who got in the van. EARTH came to Spokane to save me. He said the Cosmos told him where to find me."

Family members nodded and sighed, some touching their hands together over their hearts. Gamma squeezed my shoulder.

"I don't know what happened to the rest of those kids, but I think about them all the time. It's hard having EARTH gone right now, but I know he's out there finding other Family members who need to be found," she finished, thumping a hand on the mantel for emphasis. More people nodded and murmured, "Yes." Every part of me smiled. Adeona was a true Believer and she was right about the importance of EARTH's Mission. I gave myself a harsh lecture about my day spent moping and complaining about the chicken coop. *How could I be so selfish?*

"Thanks, sister Adeona," said Adam. "Anyone else?"

Caelum propped himself up and squatted on his heels. "One time I saw EARTH hypnotize a chicken." Caelum loved to tell stories. He always volunteered. "It was a Feast day and I was out there helping Pluto collect eggs. This was before you worked in the coop, Starbird. Anyway, EARTH was out in the driveway talking to Mars and Jupiter, and I didn't latch the gate right, so a few chickens got out. I went to collect them and one walked right up to EARTH. So EARTH scooped up the chicken and held its wings down close to its body." Caelum imitated the action of holding the bird. "Then he bent down and laid the chicken on its back in the dirt. He took a stick and drew three straight lines in front of the chicken's face and the chicken froze. EARTH took his hands away and the chicken just lay there like it was paralyzed, staring at those lines in the dirt. Mars started laughing and the chicken stayed there for, like, a minute, until it finally jumped up and started walking around again like nothing had happened."

People in the room laughed and a few clapped their

hands. I wished I had been there to watch EARTH hypnotize a chicken. I made a mental note to ask him to do it again when he got home from his Mission.

"Let's take a tea break," said Adam.

Gamma disappeared back into the office as Family members went to the kitchen for tea and cookies. Indus got up, put down his harmonica, and then sat down next to me on the couch. My heart did fifty-seven jumping jacks. Then it did three back handsprings. I tightened my ponytail. I pulled my sweater sleeves down over my hands, and felt the splotches start appearing on my chest.

"So, what's the story with that girl Venus who did the café pickup today?" His broad shoulders seemed to take up half the small couch. I pulled my feet farther under me, making myself into a tighter ball.

"She lives at Beacon House, but she's been to the Farm before. She stays with Mercury in the tree house," I said. "Why?"

Indus shrugged. "She seemed cool. You know, like, really *Seattle.*" Indus gestured with his broad, coarse hand and I remembered how that hand had reached for mine in front of the fire pit at the mouth of the yurt village. How it had pulled me around to face him and then pushed me until my back was touching a spruce tree. And how he had pressed his body against mine and into the tree trunk until a tidal wave of blood flooded my every vein and artery. On the couch, with him so close, the sap was rising inside of me again.

That's why it was so wildly aggravating when Iron John emerged from the long room and tapped me on the shoulder. "Walk me to my cabin," he said gruffly.

"Story Night isn't over." My voice was a higher pitch than I wanted.

"It's important."

"I'll meet you there after."

"You should go." Indus put his hand on my arm. Indus respected Iron over anyone else in the Family.

I tried not to look as thoroughly pissed off as I felt when I dropped my flute back into the instrument chest and followed Iron out through the front door. I resisted the urge to look back.

We walked along the gravel drive from the main house toward the rest of the property. To our right, the corn was high enough for hiding in, and I could hear Pavo and Ursa chasing each other through the stalks, Ursa screaming Pavo's name. The sun had just gone down and the ground was covered in a red-orange glow; my favorite time of day, despite the relentless and bloodthirsty mosquitoes that also kept a community on the Farm. Gravel crunched under our feet as we passed the Sanctuary, a crack of light peering from under the door.

"The boys are moving in this week." Iron pointed to the structure that was once a barn and now our most sacred meeting space. "I said I'd help them weatherize. Gamma needs to keep those boys happy, because there's no way I can get the back field harvested without them."

"Eve doesn't approve," I said. "She wants to know what will happen when EARTH comes back and the Sanctuary has been turned into a residence."

"I'll worry about the harvest and let Eve worry about EARTH coming back," he said. It was a hard subject in my relationship with Iron. We had become very close while working on the coop together, but I hated the way he talked about EARTH. Of course Iron was a valuable part of the Family, but he didn't participate in Translations or Feasts, and it had always seemed as if he tolerated EARTH when he should have loved him.

There had always been people in the Family who weren't true Believers, kids whose parents were Believers but they themselves weren't, or people who once Believed but lost their faith. But it had gotten worse since EARTH went on his Mission. Some non-Believers left, but others just stuck around and murmured about how EARTH wasn't coming back. Even Indus had expressed doubts the night we kissed. I wanted the non-Believers to either regain their faith or leave. Iron was an exception, though; we wouldn't last very long without Iron.

We walked on, past the chicken coop and the entrance to the yurt village, toward the dark stand of woods beyond them. "Follow me through here," he said as we reached the edge of the fir trees. "The way can be tricky before the moon comes out."

The path to Iron's cabin was a small dirt one that was endlessly encroached on by ferns and fir needles. For several years, the Family had a business selling the young firs off as Christmas trees, allowing customers to wander into our woods and cut their own. But attracting customers who could manage chopping and hauling their own trees wasn't easy, and the advertising cost more than the money we made. Like most of our Family businesses, it had been abandoned within three years. The hand-painted sign advertising FREE FAMILY CHRISTMAS TREES still leaned against the old growth near the driveway.

"Mind the roots," Iron told me as we passed through a narrow spot on the path, but I was already stepping over them. I knew the way to Iron's well enough to walk it in the dark. I had been racing through these woods my whole life.

We made it to the front porch of Iron's cabin, a platform just large enough for two chairs, hand carved from cedar stumps, to sit side by side. As Iron opened the door, I wiped my feet on his mat and started unlacing my boots. Inside the house, we both took off our shoes.

Iron's house was the oldest building on the Farm. It's a log cabin made of western red cedar by homesteaders, the first white people who came onto the land. Iron says that the cabin is more than a hundred and twenty years old, and he should know since his ancestors built it.

Inside was one large room with exposed wood logs patched together by some sort of clay. The stone facade of a fireplace divided the north wall, but Iron used a wood-stove for heat instead. The floor was covered with a heavy rug, and smaller rugs masked its threadbare patches.

The furniture was limited to a wood table with one stool, two overstuffed chairs positioned on either side of the woodstove, and a bed in the south corner next to the only window. A teakettle and a pan sat on top of the woodstove, and a collection of ceramic mugs hung from hooks in the wall.

"Cider?" Iron asked, holding up a glass jug he had brought from the main house. "Last bottle from the fall press. A bit sour. I brought your mug." Iron loved the Family apple cider as much as I did. Every autumn we gathered in the orchard for apple picking and cider pressing, making almost two hundred gallons over the course of a weekend. It was one of the few celebrations that continued after EARTH left. Iron and I had our own ritual at the end of each pressing that involved drinking cider out of ceramic mugs we had made ourselves.

I nodded and sat down in one of the big chairs. Although we had logged a lot of time together working on the coop, I hadn't spent much time in Iron's cabin. He wasn't the easiest person to socialize with; Iron seemed more comfortable with a tractor than a person.

The back corner of the room by the bed served as a makeshift closet, with hooks drilled into the logs every few inches. The opposite corner contained Iron's extended tool collection, his favorite items that he kept inside to prevent moisture from bloating the wood or rusting the metal. Our lives in the Pacific Northwest could be boiled down to a daily struggle against the damp.

"Why did your ancestors decide to settle here?" I was already feeling the desire to light a fire in the woodstove, even though it was just September.

"Fraser Canyon gold rush. They came up from California and planned to go on into British Columbia, but they found enough land left for homesteading and decided to start farming. Two brothers built this cabin by themselves." He handed me my mug and sat down in the other chair. "They claimed a hundred and sixty acres after five years. Before them, this was all trees."

"Does it bother you that this was your land before the Family moved here?" I always thought if I could get to the bottom of Iron's reluctance to embrace the Family's beliefs, then I could change his mind.

"Ownership," said Iron, taking a sip of his cider, "is an interesting concept. Did my family own the land after taking it from the native people? Did the U.S. government own this land and have the right to give it to us? I don't think of land as something that belongs to us, but something that we have to take care of. Do you know who legally owns this property now?"

"We all do," I said. "We own everything together."

Iron laughed. "We say that, but it would be difficult to put the name of every Family member on a deed. When my mother gave the farm to the Family, they had to name a group of legal owners, so they formed a corporation. EARTH is the president, and the elders are, or were, the board of directors. Of course, we lost Venus Ocean, so EARTH put Ephraim on the board to replace her. Other members have left the Family, like Jupiter and Pluto, but never resigned from the board."

Jupiter Rock had famously left the Family after quarreling with EARTH during a Translation. He publicly called EARTH a "false prophet." After he left, most Family members referred to him as Judas rather than Jupiter.

"But were you angry when Callisto gave the property away?" I tried to imagine Iron as a nine-year-old boy when EARTH and the others came.

"What I thought then doesn't matter now," he said. "You're here and there are certain bonds." He looked down and touched a hole in his wool sock. "Now, let me ask you some questions." The deep wrinkles on Iron's face rippled out from his eyes. "What do you think about this Calling?"

The stupid Calling again. "Why do people keep asking me this?" I said. "Does everyone think a restaurant job is the best Calling I'm ever going to get?" I knew I sounded whiny. *I can't believe he called me away from Indus to talk about this.* "Even if I wanted to work there, I couldn't. I'm off-grid."

"Massive rivers start from tiny springs." Iron seemed unfazed by my harsh tone. He gripped his right ankle with his left hand. A tough, wiry man, Iron was especially agile for his age. "Starbird, what do you want to do with your life?"

"It doesn't matter what I want," I mumbled, feeling guilty for complaining again. "We each get our Calling and the Cosmos leads us to our life path." I thought Iron was reminding me of our Family Principles and gently chiding me for being willful.

He looked at me for a quiet second. Then he stood and walked to the wall of the cabin, beside the stone fireplace.

"I love this house," he said. He put one hand on an exposed cedar beam of the wall. "I plan to stay here until I die, working the farm and fixing things until I can't fix them anymore. While I can still use a shovel, I plan to dig a deep hole in the middle of the fir trees, and when my time comes, I will drag myself to that hole and lie down in

it. I would cover my own body over with dirt if I could."
Iron was half looking at me and half looking at the wall as
he spoke. He closed his eyes for a minute, as if the cedar
log was saying something back. Then he sat down again in
his chair.

"The Cosmos might have another idea. Maybe the fir
stand will be struck by lightning and my cabin will burn
to the ground. Maybe Mount Baker will erupt and ash will
cover the back lot. Maybe a new owner will show up with
a shotgun and point me toward the road. I don't know
about any of that, but I do know what I *want*. Starbird,
unless you have a plan for your life, how would you even
hear a Calling if it came?"

I twisted the cup around in my hands. "EARTH will
tell me."

Iron grunted. His dark eyes peered at me from under
heavy, white eyebrows. "I'm going to tell you something
that most of the Family doesn't know. Maybe I shouldn't
tell you, but I will. The Farm is not in a good financial position. That corporation EARTH set up has mismanaged
our businesses and property, and Gamma came to me for
help. Like I said, my plan is to stay here in this cabin, but
the rest of this"—Iron motioned toward the main house,
orchard, and back lot—"I don't know what will happen.
You're young. You should have the life you want."

I had to put my mug down on the floor because my
hand started trembling. Family members never talked

about finances; it wasn't exactly forbidden, just highly suspect. Plus, this was the longest conversation I'd ever had
with Iron that wasn't about the coop or the harvest.

"EARTH says that if we doubt the Cosmos will provide for us, we're inviting lack into our lives."

Iron cleared his throat. "Everyone has a right to her
own beliefs. I just want to make sure you have a choice."
He leaned over to the woodstove and grabbed a brown paper envelope that was leaning against the copper teapot. I
hadn't noticed it sitting there before. He handed it to me.

With a nervous twist in my stomach, I took it. The
seal was old and the glue that once held it together had
no stickiness left. Inside was a piece of heavy, embossed
paper.

State of Washington, Department of Health
Certificate of Live Birth
Date of Birth: 7/5/1996
Place: Whatcom County, Washington
Sex: Female
Given Name: Starbird
Last Name: Murphy

"Starbird Murphy?" My hand shook as it held the page.
"Certificate of Live Birth?" I had seen the name Murphy
before. There was a weathered wooden sign in the barn
with the words MURPHY'S FARM carved into it. I kept
reading the page.

Mother's Name: Elizabeth Stone
Father's Name: John Murphy

"John Murphy." I was unable to contain my surprise, or my sadness. "You're my father?"

"No." Iron held up a hand toward me. "Well, I honestly don't know." He dropped it again. "I might be. We were young and we didn't have traditional relationships. Lots of us had seen our parents' marriages turn into divorce. I had seen my mother widowed. We didn't want that; I didn't want that. We wanted to avoid the concept of ownership," he explained, even though I had heard it all before. I had grown up with my mother describing the early days of the Family, when there were few marriages or exclusive partnerships. Several married couples that had joined the Family, like EARTH and his wife, Uranus Peak, or Indus's father and his mother, Bithiah, had dissolved the marriages when they became part of the group.

Of course, sometimes it was obvious who someone's biological father was; like Badger, who looked so much like Adam, it was impossible to imagine they weren't related. My brown eyes looked like Fern's, but my strawberry-blonde hair at least could resemble EARTH's.

"Your mother came to me when she was nine months pregnant," Iron went on, "and she was scared. EARTH wanted all babies to be born here on the Farm, not in hospitals, not with birth certificates and not registered with the federal government. *Living off the grid*—that was the gift he said we were giving our children."

"I was born on the Farm."

"So you were." Iron smiled, showing his crooked teeth. "But a few days before, Fern knocked on my door late at night, her belly so big she couldn't sit or stand without help. She was terrified that she might die in childbirth like Venus Ocean, or that something else might happen to her when you were little. She wanted to make sure that you had a safety net and made me swear to take care of you if anything went wrong. Then she asked if I would go with her and get you a birth certificate once you were born. And I said yes.

"When you were a week old, we told everyone we were going foraging for chanterelles and took the truck to my old family doctor in Bellingham from when I was a boy. He got us that birth certificate and helped us apply for your Social Security card, too." Iron pointed to the brown envelope that was still sitting on my lap. I opened it and saw two small paper cards sitting inside. They both said the same name, *Starbird Murphy*.

"Of course, we had to go behind EARTH's back, and your mother asked me to hold on to it because she thought you would probably find it if she kept it hidden in the yurt. She made me promise not to tell you." He shrugged. "Some promises you have to break."

I wasn't surprised that Iron would disobey EARTH,

but Fern? It was like realizing that a tree I'd been climbing all my life was rotten in the middle and ready to crumble. When a Family member betrays EARTH, she betrays all of us. I wanted to open the door to the woodstove and throw the papers right in the fire. How could they?

"Why are you breaking your promise now?" I unclenched my teeth to ask.

"Fern doesn't want you to go to Seattle." He leaned forward in his chair again. "She's afraid of life out there. And after losing Doug, I don't think she would ever agree to it. But you're sixteen now. You need to decide. Is your future here or is it in the World Outside?"

6

A bright half-moon was up when I left Iron's cabin that night, giving me plenty of visibility as I stomped along the path through the fir trees.

First, I had said, "Thanks anyway, but I don't want this," and tossed the papers back on the woodstove.

Iron replied, "Do what you see fit, but you can't leave them here," and handed the papers back to me.

I got angry and yelled some things about how he never loved EARTH and nobody is supposed to know who her dad is, and then I stormed out with the envelope shoved in my pocket. I had never talked to Iron that way. I had never talked to any adult that way in my life. I didn't recognize myself. But then, until five minutes ago, I didn't even know my name.

Murphy. It rolled around in my mouth like a marble as I mumbled it aloud to the trees. I hated the sound of it. When people joined the Family, they came with names. We called them "old names" or "outside names." A person's true name was translated by EARTH. So if Murphy wasn't my true name, why did I have the sickly feeling that it was important, that maybe it meant something about my relationship with Iron? Did Fern go to him because she knew he was my father? She'd always told me she didn't know who my father was, but she had withheld my birth certificate, so maybe she'd withheld that, too. I didn't want Iron to be my father; I wanted EARTH to be my father. If I kept this birth certificate, would I be accepting Iron, a non-Believer, as my dad?

I didn't walk toward the yurt. Fern might still be awake and I wasn't ready to face her. True, she defied EARTH because she was concerned about my future. But she didn't tell me about it. Even when she saw that I might be getting my Calling and would need a birth certificate, she withheld. No one in the Free Family is allowed to interfere with someone else's Calling. She broke Family rules twice yet claimed to be a Believer. Was she lying about that, too?

My thoughts swam around like a school of fish, turning suddenly right and then left, threatening to swim for hours. I could still hear music coming from the main house, some sweet harmonies being sung along with the piano and guitar but no harmonica. Light was leaking from the door and gaps in the wooded planks of the Sanctuary. I needed someone I could talk to.

I walked to the back door of our Sanctuary, the one the Family used to enter through for Translations. I was going to our sacred room at night looking for Indus. I knocked and heard a muffled word inside that sounded like *yes*.

The door creaked on its rusty hinge and swung open. There, on top of one of the rugs that covered the floor of our Sanctuary, Indus was stretched out on his back beside a huddled group of candles. And on top of him was Lyra Hay, and she wasn't wearing a shirt.

Indus sat up with a jolt. Lyra giggled and didn't cover herself. "Hey, Starbird," she said.

"Sorry," I stammered, grabbing for the side of the wooden door and pulling it toward me, scraping the back of my hand painfully against the barn's wall as Indus attempted to move Lyra off him.

I turned and ran hard up the gravel drive, not looking back to see if the barn door opened after me. Flying past the main house, I could hear Adam's guitar and Caelum's banjo playing a cheery duet as I ran toward the apple orchard, which stood dark and cool beyond the patio and garden. I didn't slow down as I entered the neat rows of trees but kept going at the same speed until my foot found a grounded apple and tossed me down on my chest so hard, the wind was knocked out of me.

I gasped, unable to breathe, rolling left and right on my back, kicking my legs, beating my hand against the soppy ground that splattered mud on my face. When my diaphragm finally let air in again, I clutched my raw hand to my lips where the barn wood had scraped off the skin

and started to sob. I didn't hear footsteps of anyone running after me. No one was calling my name. I was alone
in the trees.

Indus, too? Is there anyone I can believe in? I beat my
good hand against the cold, damp ground again, sure my
back was a disaster of mud. I rolled onto my side thinking
I would throw up. I felt like I'd eaten a beehive whole.
Everything inside me was churning.

After a few minutes, the nausea subsided. I rolled onto
my back again and took several deep breaths. Dozens of
apples were hanging over my head, and everything in the
orchard smelled sickly sweet. Whatever this feeling was
inside of me, I wanted it out. *Jealousy?*

True Believers didn't indulge in jealousy, not like in
the World Outside. Sexual desire was considered natural
and healthy, and not intended to be locked up in a room
to which only one person was given the key. EARTH said
that shame about our bodies and our desires has no place
in our Eden on the Farm. *The animals are God's creatures
and they know no shame,* he said at my fifth Translation.

But seeing Lyra and Indus together made me feel en-
raged and weak at the same time. Was this the desperation
of ownership that the Elders were trying to avoid? Indus
said that he wanted to love one person, right before he
kissed me against the spruce tree. Was I a terrible kisser?
Maybe Lyra was better since she was from the Outside
and had probably already had sex. But I was the one who

had known him his whole life. Didn't love matter more than sex? Did he love her? He seemed so impressed by Venus Lake because she was from Seattle. Maybe I just wasn't exciting enough for Indus.

For the second time that night, questions and worries wandered around my head in dazed circles. I lay staring at the constellations that peeked through the gnarly arms of the trees overhead until an apple dislodged from its limb and fell to the ground beside my head with a *thonk*! *If this is what it feels like to get a Calling, I wish I had never heard my name.*

7

I stayed in the orchard for a long time, not ready to take my thoughts back into the crowded space of the yurt. But my fingers were freezing cold and the music had stopped in the house, so eventually I wandered back across the driveway. There were no more lights on in the Sanctuary as I passed, and I felt another pang wondering if Lyra was still in there with Indus.

The yurt village was impressive when I was little, with twelve dwellings surrounding a central fire pit, two out-houses, and a bathhouse a short hike away in the woods. But most families packed up their yurts and took them during the exodus after EARTH left. Now there were just three yurts besides the one I shared with Fern, where she was sleeping soundly when I entered.

Our yurt was one of the more modest on the com-pound, with just enough room for three cots and a wood-stove in the center, its exhaust pipe reaching through the canvas roof. A wooden platform held the round fabric structure off the ground and provided a deck area beyond the door. The building committee had constructed the yurt for Fern and Doug Fir before I was born. I left my boots on the platform and hung my coat on a hook by the door. I was asleep as soon as my head hit the pillow.

"Starbird." Two hands were gently rocking me side to side. They didn't belong to Fern. "Starbird," Gamma said again, pushing me on the shoulder. "I'm sorry to wake you." It was still dark in the yurt and Gamma was holding a flashlight, a wool shawl wrapped around her shoulders. "The restaurant called and they have to do another pickup. Cham and Ephraim are still sick and today is the only day Venus can make it. She's going to need all the eggs you can give her, so include the ones you were saving for the Farm. I know I asked you to run the math class today, but that can wait." Gamma was talking a mile a minute even though my eyes were barely open.

"Sure," I mumbled. I sat up in my cot and stretched.

"What happened to your hand?" Gamma took my right arm and shined the flashlight on it to inspect the red scrape where the barn wood had skinned me.

Memories of the night before came back, the image of Lyra and Indus, what Iron told me about the Farm's finances, my birth certificate.

"Just an accident," I said, cradling it in my other hand.

"Be sure to put some arnica on that," she said, and then shuffled out of the yurt.

I dressed in the dark and took a flashlight along to the bathhouse. When I came out, the orange sun was peeking one eye over the top of the Cascades. I heard Chocolate crow, followed by Bad Boy and the others. Pulling my jacket up around my ears, I went to the henhouse.

"Good morning, Chocolate. Any trouble last night?" I always inspected my roosters in the morning to make sure they hadn't had any scrapes with foxes or other predators. Bad Boy lost a toe fighting off something in April, but he had protected all the hens. Iron and I set a catch and release trap and nabbed two raccoons.

The roosters looked healthy, so I checked the feed containers for evidence of pests. "Okay, chickens, egg time," I announced morosely to the flock of rousting birds. Normally, I didn't do my first collection until mid-morning, so I knew I would get a smaller take, but I only had twelve dozen stored for the Farm, and the restaurant would need all I could gather.

There is a special calm I have only ever experienced while collecting eggs from the coop. The endless mystery inside those perfect brown and white ovals always managed to sooth my anxiety. After five minutes of stacking eggs into my coated wire container, I heard Ursa at the gate.

"It's so early," were her first words.

I reached into a box and withdrew three eggs. "Did Gamma wake you up, too?"

Ursa nodded and picked up another wire basket and started down the opposite row of boxes. "She said V is coming back."

As soon as my hand released the eggs I was holding into the basket, it strayed automatically to my pocket where the envelope containing my birth certificate was still folded.

By the time we finished gathering, Ursa and I carried a hundred and twenty eggs to the house for washing. Other Family members were already making breakfast or gathering what vegetables they could harvest for pickup. Eve and Fern were furiously baking cinnamon buns, and the rich smell filled the house.

Ursa prepared the egg bath in the kitchen sink while I got the carriers ready. We barely got the eggs washed by the time we heard the truck rumbling up the gravel drive.

V walked through the front door of the house in the same sandals and jean shorts, but with a bulky wool sweater on top. Ursa and I were still drying eggs and placing them in storage containers at the kitchen table.

"I'm super sorry about this." She dropped into a chair and pushed her sunglasses back on her head. "I couldn't leave the restaurant this weekend, so it was now or never."

"Ease your mind," said Eve, setting down her rolling pin and putting both hands on her lower back. "We all have to work together for the greater end." Even in the hard moments, Eve could be counted on to quote EARTH. I wondered how she would give birth on the Farm with no midwives left to help her.

"What a glorious morning," announced Lyra Hay, walking into the kitchen and tossing her thin arms over her head. "Ooh, cinnamon buns . . . I'm starving!"

All the little hairs on my arms stood straight up, and I bit my bottom lip hard enough to taste blood. The jealousy I'd felt in the apple orchard made its way to the kitchen.

"Lyra, you must wear shoes in here." Fern put her hands on her hips. "We're baking for commercial sale."

A flash of irritation passed over Lyra's face. "Sorry, Mother," she said sweetly, backing up over the threshold so that her feet were technically in the long room.

It was only because I treasured my eggs so highly that she wasn't scraping yolk from her forehead.

"Gamma said she looked for you to ask for your help baking," Fern said, stirring some orange icing with a wooden spoon.

"I wasn't in my room," said Lyra.

The egg I had been drying broke in my hand. I turned away quickly and started washing it off in the sink.

"One less omelet for the weekend," V said, laughing. "Hey, Starbird, are you going to come back with me and be our new waitress?"

"Yes," I said, over the running water of the faucet.

"What did you say?" asked V.

I turned off the water and grabbed a towel. "Yes," I said again, turning around to look at the room. All eyes were pinned on me. Fern had stopped stirring.

"Really? That's awesome," V was saying, at the same time Ursa was saying, "Yes, yes, yes!" and Fern was saying, "Wait a minute, what?" and Eve said, "I don't know how we will manage without you, but a Calling is wonderful news." Lyra Hay just stood under the doorframe, inspecting her fingernails.

"Okay, well, I'm going to go get my stuff. Ursa, will you finish packing the eggs?" I said awkwardly, putting down the towel and grabbing my jacket.

Fern took off her apron as I put on my coat. "Let's talk outside," she said, following me toward the front door and then onto the gravel driveway. It was still brisk out. Although the sun was fully risen, the fog hadn't burned off yet.

"There's no reason to rush this," Fern started as soon as the door was closed. "I'll ask Gamma if I can share her room and give you the yurt to yourself. That's better than what you would get at Beacon House."

"This isn't about space," I said, walking quickly through the gravel.

"You'll have to enroll in school if you go to Seattle. Ursa isn't old enough to manage the chickens. You don't have a birth certificate." Fern rattled off a battery of reasons.

I stopped in the middle of the driveway and turned my heels in the gravel. "Family members don't lie to each other."

Fern took a step back and almost lost her footing. She looked at me with eyes the size of eggs. My mother's hair was once strawberry blonde like mine, but streaks of gray gave it a silvery glow in the morning light.

I took the envelope out of my pocket. "Starbird Murphy," I said, slapping it against my thigh. Fern had kept the information from me before, but she hadn't flat-out lied about it until now. I squeezed the paperwork until it crumpled. Turning again in the gravel, I walked faster toward the yurt. I didn't bother taking off my boots before going inside.

"It was for your own good." Fern followed me through the door. "You don't know about the World Outside, about how cruel people can be. You haven't seen that here. You're not ready."

"Do they do things worse than lie out there?" I asked, stuffing two flannel shirts, a skirt, and two wool sweaters into the canvas bag I used for hauling wood.

"Yes, Starbird." Fern dropped down onto the cot. "They do much worse than lie."

"Well, you weren't worried about Doug Fir out there," I said. "You didn't try to get him back."

"That's not true. I went to the police," Fern said, her voice starting to break. "What more could I do?"

I froze. "You went to the police? On the Outside? How many other forbidden things have you done?" Tears starting to roll down Fern's cheeks. "Are you even a Believer, or is that a lie, too?"

"It's not safe out there," she said, clasping her hands together. "I just wanted him home."

I looked at the bag of clothes sitting on my cot and at Fern with her tear-stained cheeks, and I knew I couldn't turn back. I couldn't tell V to go without me or wait until next year or even next week.

"You can't interfere with my Calling, Fern." I picked up the canvas bag and walked back toward the driveway.

Iron was at the refrigerator truck talking to V when I got there. "I'll help Ursa with the chickens," he said before I could say anything.

I nodded without making eye contact. Maybe I shouldn't have felt angry at Iron, but I did.

Other Family members were emerging from the house and standing around in the driveway. Clearly, the news about my Calling had spread. V opened the passenger side door, and I stuffed my bag behind the seat. Ursa emerged from the house with a container of eggs, and I helped her pack them safely into the refrigerated rear section. If there was one thing the Free Family had perfected in the past three years, it was saying good-bye.

"Peace, Sister." "Go with God, Starbird." "We are Family." They hugged me one by one.

"You are a child of the Cosmos." Eve held the back of my head as she hugged me. "Stay on your path as a true Believer."

"I wouldn't go back out there for anything," said Lyra, but then Eve nudged her and Lyra added, "Peace, Sister."

Fern emerged from the direction of the yurt, her eyes red and swollen. She walked slowly across the gravel and didn't look in my eyes as she opened her arms to embrace me. "Be careful," was all she said.

I kept my composure, not allowing myself to break down until Ursa said, "I'll take care of our chickens." Then tears sprouted in my eyes like new feathers. I nodded and jumped into the passenger seat of the truck.

Gamma emerged from the house in time to catch us in the driveway. "Starbird, I know you will be a true asset for the café." She squeezed my hand through the open truck window. Then she looked at V. "Tell Ephraim to respond to my calls. I know he's been sick, but the situation is serious."

"Copy that," said V, putting on her purple sunglasses and starting the engine.

The music was turned up and V was singing along before we were halfway down the gravel drive. So when Caelum and Indus emerged from the back lot, and Indus started running toward the truck, she didn't even notice. I didn't tell her to stop. I didn't even wave.

8

"**H**ere's the plan!" V yelled over the music. "If we get pulled over, I'm going to act like it's no big deal. Then, I'm going to reach over like I'm grabbing my purse, slap my forehead, and say, 'Oh no, I must have left my purse at the Farm. I'm sorry, officer, I don't have my license on me.' Then, when he asks me my name, I'm going to say 'Felicia Hale,' who is a girl who works at the restaurant and looks like me. As long as he believes I'm her, it'll only be, like, a ten-dollar charge for forgetting my license."

"How hard would it be to get a real driver's license?" I asked, wishing V would look at the road more while she was driving.

"Well, first I'd have to get a birth certificate and Social Security number, and for that I'd need a lawyer. There's a lawyer in Seattle who has helped other Family members, but you know what you need to get a lawyer."

"What?"

V laughed. "I forgot, you really don't know. Money.

You need money. And that's one thing the Family has less and less of these days. Iron told me about your birth certificate. So I guess you're not really off the grid anymore."

I nodded, reaching again for the crumpled paper in my pocket.

"I'm sorry to tell you this, but that means you're going to have to go to school. At the Farm, they can still claim to be homeschooling because they got licensed once, but we don't have the resources at Beacon House. And since you'll show up on the radar as having a job at the café and living in Seattle, you have to show up at school, too. Don't worry, Cham goes to Roosevelt, and he'll show you how to get through it."

We were flying down the highway at an unimaginable speed. Still, vehicles passed us on both sides. They weren't like the trucks that drove onto the Farm, either. They were tiny cars, shiny red, blue, and tan, zipping by us on the right and left. Most of them had only one person inside. When cars showed up at the Farm, they were always packed with people.

"Where are these people going?" I asked, feeling queasy from the motion of the truck.

"I know, right?" she said. "Where do they all go?"

"This is really fast," I said, not sure if I meant V's driving or my decision to leave the Farm.

"Do you think I'm a bad driver?" V looked at me. *Please look at the road.* "Because Devin says I'm a bad driver, which I said is ridiculous. I've been driving since I was ten." She held up all ten fingers at me. That meant no hands on the wheel.

I decided to stop talking to V so she would stop gesturing. I closed my eyes and tried to control the motion sickness. *I'm leaving the Farm*, I thought. *I'm leaving the Farm*. My mind wandered back to the day three years ago when EARTH told us he was leaving.

It was days after Doug Fir had run off in the middle of the night. I was almost thirteen years old and walking around inside a dark cloud. I barely had the heart to come to the Translation at all and only went because Indus came to the yurt to get me. I was upset that my brother was gone, and missed him terribly, but I was also horrified to discover that he wasn't a true Believer, that he would abandon his Family. He was EARTH's apprentice. What kind of person would do something like that?

EARTH had called Fern Moon and me to an audience that morning. Mars Wolf brought us up the stairs of the main house and into EARTH's massive room with its thick, red curtains and heavy blue tapestries. We sat on pillows across from EARTH in front of the altar. EARTH's white hair was an uncombed mess, and his blue eyes wandered around the room as if he was looking for something. His hands seemed to flop thoughtlessly around his knees.

"Why would Doug leave us?" he asked Fern.

My mother broke into the same heaving sobs I had

been hearing every night since Doug disappeared. She collapsed into EARTH's lap, and he stroked her hair as she moaned. EARTH motioned for me with his other arm and wrapped me into his chest where I soaked his robe with tears. Mars Wolf finally asked us to leave, saying that it was time for EARTH to prepare for the Translation.

After everyone was seated in our orbits in the Sanctuary, EARTH entered through the north door and perched on the platform. One of the Planet Elders recited the Family history and then EARTH began to speak.

"Each member of the Free Family receives a Calling." EARTH's voice crowded the air in the barn. He wasn't the same person I had cried to just moments before. He was taller, younger, more focused. "I, however, receive many. The Cosmos spoke to me last night when I was alone in my rooms, deep in meditation. It told me to go on a Mission to California. There are Family members there who haven't been able to find us, wandering alone in the wilderness. I have been instructed to take two with me." EARTH paused. "Mars Wolf and Bathsheba Honey will accompany me."

The congregation was silent. EARTH had gone on Missions before, usually for a few weeks to a month, either south to California or east to Idaho, so it wasn't unheard of, but it still caused a certain amount of stress among Family members whenever he left. Mars Wolf always went with him, as did one of the women in the Family. I felt as if someone had punched me right on top of a bruise. How could I be losing EARTH the same week as losing Doug Fir?

"The Cosmos instructs that the party should leave on Sunday," EARTH said, raising his hands toward the sun coming through the window of the hayloft, a halo of light forming around each of his hands.

When Sunday came, they packed up one of the Family's VW buses and left in the late afternoon. Family members lined up in front of the house, old and young, over a hundred and fifty all together. EARTH said good-bye to each of us, one by one, hugging the women, touching the heads of the children, pressing his hands together and nodding at the men. Even though I was still twelve, he treated me as an adult and hugged me rather than patting my head. Then he looked into my eyes and smiled, one hand on each of my arms. His blue eyes were so piercing and his look so comforting, I nearly forgot to feel sad.

"I'll find him," he said, as if reading my mind.

I didn't ask EARTH about the upcoming apprenticeships, which included mine. We all assumed he would be back soon enough to assign them. When EARTH turned away, I broke into a moaning cry and had to prevent myself from running after him. That's when Indus Stone, sixteen and strong, put his arm around me and squeezed. It was a sweet gesture, something an older brother would do.

EARTH appointed Gamma to manage the office and

paperwork in his absence, which we thought would last a few weeks, four or five at the most. After the first month, we received a letter, which Eve read aloud after Sunday afternoon brunch in the long room. It was written on parchment paper and related EARTH's latest Translation. "Children of the Cosmos," Eve read, "continue as if I am there. The Cosmic Intelligence will provide for you. The Family is Free."

So we continued as if EARTH were there. Iron organized labor for the harvest, and we started making plans for the Winter Solstice. Children made drawings in school that they planned to show EARTH when he got back. Disputes were set aside until EARTH could settle them at the next ceremony, and a new letter came every month. "Children of the Cosmos, we are spreading news of the Family and finding many of our brothers and sisters. I am needed here, so you must have the Winter Solstice without me. Continue as if I am there. The Family is Free."

And so we continued, through the Winter Solstice and the long rains that followed, through the spring planting season, and into plans for the Summer Solstice. It wasn't until a year after EARTH left that things began to fall apart. Small disagreements over housing, the division of farmwork, and preparations for the Solstice Festivals started boiling over. Members began gossiping about one another—who was lazy, who was using too many resources, and who wasn't getting enough attention from the buyers. When Spring Meteor and Firmament Rise got into a fistfight in the middle of the yurt village that ended in Spring ripping the door off Firmament's house and tossing it into a fire pit, things everywhere seemed to explode.

Several groups left the next day, and many more over the next two years, taking everything they thought should be theirs with them. EARTH's letters became fewer and fewer, but I listened to each one expectantly, for news that EARTH had found Doug, or that EARTH had a job for me or that EARTH was coming home. We didn't have any way to write back or call him, so those of us who stayed had to exhibit great faith, to set an example as true Believers.

I was still tied up in memories when I saw the first sign for Seattle. The air in the truck suddenly felt stifling. I rolled down the window, and wind screamed into the truck like a tiny tornado, whipping hair across my face. It got even harder to breathe. There were still tall evergreens on both sides of the highway, but they were interrupted by colossal concrete structures and electronic signs. We passed an entire lot full of vehicles, each one four times the size of one of our vans. The only truly familiar thing in the landscape was the Cascade Range, still snowcapped and watching me from a distance. Cars continued to flood past us. *So many Outsiders. So much space. What if the Outside just swallows me up like it did Doug? What if I disappear, too?*

V took an exit off the highway, and our speed slowed to a reasonably mad thirty miles per hour. We crossed a bridge and wound through a few steep streets before passing a block with three brick buildings and a vacant lot full of weeds and grass. At the end of the block, we turned left and then pulled into an alley buttressed by chain-link fences. A dog started barking as we passed.

V parked the truck in a tiny two-car lot. We were a million miles from the Farm. We were in a city made of asphalt, brick, and rain clouds. V turned off the engine, looked at me, and said, "Well, here it is, Starbird. Your new home away from home."

9

A small sign on the building in front of us read, FREE FAMILY CAFÉ, PLEASE USE FRONT ENTRANCE.

"I'll get Devin to help us unload," V said as she got out of the truck. "I'm not technically on the schedule today, but I might have to do a few things before we can go back to the house."

I automatically put on my work gloves, which I had stuffed in my coat pocket.

"Love that farm girl attitude," said V, closing the driver's side door and going into the café.

I walked around to the refrigerated section, grabbed the first box of egg cartons, and waited for V at the door. She returned, followed by a tall skinny boy with black hair and a T-shirt that said SUB POP. He was younger than V, maybe twenty-three.

"Bird of the stars." He bowed to me. "The walk-in is on the right."

"We call Devin 'Skinny Cook,'" said V. He grabbed at her like he was about to tickle her side, but she lurched away.

Following Devin's directions, I carried my box of eggs through the back door and took a right down a hallway and into a substantial walk-in cooler. It was the size of a large bathroom and had wire shelving along each wall. We had some industrial refrigerators on the Farm, but nothing like this. I passed Devin and V in the hall as I got a second load and met them again in the walk-in.

"She's been here four minutes and she's already out-working me," said Devin, reaching over to squeeze one of my biceps. "Check out these pythons."

"I know," said V. "The Farm girls are workers. Maybe she can pull us out of our downward spiral."

"Save us, Starbird, we're drowning." Devin panto-mimed a desperate swimmer.

"Venus, I need to talk to you about the schedule," a girl's voice broke in.

"What a surprise," mumbled V, continuing to unload.

"I'm not working the double tomorrow, and I don't care who's sick, either. That would be twelve days straight. *Twelve*." An attractive, dark-haired girl had entered the cooler. She looked remarkably like Venus.

"Good news, Felicia," said V. "Starbird is our newest waitress."

The dark-haired girl turned toward me and then looked me up and down, folding her arms over her chest.

I put my hands together in prayer position over my heart and bowed my head to greet her.

She kept staring at me, her arms still folded. "Okay," she said to V, "I'll take the afternoon shift tomorrow. I'm sleeping in."

"Human resources meetings outside the refrigerator," said Devin, pushing Felicia and V out of the walk-in. "Also, there's only enough eggs here to keep us going until around two o'clock Saturday, unless you've got some hens riding shotgun."

"We're doing a polenta special this weekend," said V. "Everything that traditionally involves eggs is now made with cornmeal." She signaled for me to follow her down the hall to an office opposite a swinging door. The space was tiny, with barely enough room for an overloaded desk, a row of hooks holding coats and aprons, and the two of us to fit inside. I stood in the doorway while she grabbed a clipboard from the wall.

"Do they both live at Beacon House?" I asked.

"No." V looked down at the clipboard. "Felicia isn't Family. Devin used to be, but his mom moved out of Beacon House when EARTH left and they took their Outside names back. His brother, Paul, works here, too." She was talking to me, but she was concentrating on reading the papers in her hand. "Okay, here's the schedule. So, in a perfect world, each of us would work five days and get two days off."

"Only five days?"

"Oh right." V laughed. "There's no such thing as a weekend on the Farm. Don't worry, between school and work, you will feel like you're working eight days a week. Ideally, we each work five shifts, but I guess the world hasn't been perfect in forever, because we never seem to get there." She looked down at a chart on her clipboard. "We're closed Mondays and we have two shifts a day. Weekdays we have one waitress on, weekday evenings we have two. Saturday and Sunday breakfast is hustle time, so we need three members of waitstaff working full tilt, and weekend nights we fall back to two. With three waitresses, you can imagine how crazy that's been."

"Yeah, you've each been working seven and a third shifts," I said.

V looked up from the clipboard. "What?"

"Well, I guess you don't divide shifts into thirds, but you would each work seven or eight shifts," I said. I could feel the red blotches start on my chest because I felt stupid for saying someone would work a third of a shift.

"Did you just do that math in your head?"

I shrugged.

"Are you messing with me?"

"I just added the three weekday shifts a day to the five-per-day weekend shifts, and then divided those twenty-two by three. Someone must have to work both shifts on Saturday and Sunday, because there are five shifts that day."

V studied me. "We have four cooks," she said, resting the clipboard against her thigh. "There are always two cooks on a shift, except for weekend mornings when there are three."

"So they work six and a half shifts. But they probably don't do half shifts either."

V tapped her pencil against the clipboard. "All right then. Well, for now, I'm going to add you to tomorrow's Saturday morning shift and our Sunday morning shift. I won't lie, it's going to be insane having your first shift on a Saturday breakfast. But I'll help as much as I can. On Monday I'll take you to get enrolled in school."

"So soon?" The blotches spread from my chest to my neck.

"School started last week for Cham. Sorry, but the time is now. Okay, let's go home and find you something to wear that says 'waitress' instead of screaming 'farm-hand.'"

On the three-minute drive from the café to Beacon House, we passed fifty homes that were the size of our farmhouse, all sitting right next to one another. There were trees growing in tiny ribbons of grass between the road and the sidewalk. There were stoplights and wires running over our heads in a complicated spiderweb of black lines. It made me feel nervous, like I was allowing myself to be coaxed into a cage. *This is how Outsiders live*, I reminded myself. *They aren't like us. They don't love the natural world.*

V pulled up to a curb and backed the truck into a space between two cars. "Welcome to your home at home, Beacon House."

We were sitting on a narrow street lined with houses, mostly made of brick. But it wasn't hard to tell which one we belonged with. Beacon House was a collage of peeling purple paint, orange trim, and a mural of a cloud with sleepy eyes blowing wind in the eaves below the roof. I opened the passenger side door, grabbed my sack of clothes, took a deep breath, and followed V up a steep set of stairs toward a green door, rounded on the top.

"Where are the vegetables?" I was looking at all the gardens in front of the houses on the street. "These are all flower beds."

"Yeah, the next few days are going to be full of culture shock for you." And with that, she opened the door to a living room just as music started blaring out of a speaker inside the door.

"Are you kidding me?" V yelled, crossing the threshold and going straight for the volume knob. "You should be so sick that you can't move, not so sick you're rocking out!" She turned down the music, then grabbed a pillow and threw it at the boy holding the remote control.

"I was trying to turn it down." He protected his head from the pillow with his arm. "I *am* sick, but I can't just sleep for twenty-four hours straight."

"Starbird," V sighed, "this is your new little brother, Cham."

"How old are you?" the boy demanded, putting the pillow under his head.

"Sixteen," I said.

"Right. So, *big* brother." The boy smirked at V.

"We'll see," V said back.

I recognized Cham from his occasional pickups at the Farm and from Family gatherings. He had a head full of curly black hair that was hard to forget.

"Where's Ephraim?" V asked him.

Cham pointed toward the ceiling and settled back into the brown corduroy couch, pulling an afghan up to his chin.

"Way to take care of others," V said.

"I checked on him an hour ago." A woman walked into the living room with a small child resting on her hip. "He just needs soup and sleep. I'm Europa." She put her free hand in front of her heart and nodded toward me. She was older than V, maybe in her thirties, with tired bags under her eyes. Her blonde dreadlocks were tied in a tall knot on her head, and she had enough jewelry on her neck and fingers to fill a silverware drawer.

I put my hands together in front of my heart and bowed my head to her.

"This is Eris." She wiggled the child's foot. "He's two, and my daughter, Kale, is five. She's at Outside school right now, if you can call it that. I shudder to think what she might be *learning*."

"Europa works at the café, too," said Venus. "She moved here a few months ago from the Farm in B.C. and probably works harder than anyone."

"I just think that Beacon House should look somewhat presentable when EARTH gets back," said Europa. "Are you a Believer?"

"Yes," I said.

"Good, you can help tip the scales. Cham, do you need some more tea?"

"Yes," Cham groaned from the couch.

Europa went back into the kitchen and I followed V up the stairs. "My room." She pointed to a blue door to the right of the landing. "There's one of our two over-used, undersized bathrooms across the hall. This is Europa's room, which she shares with Kale and Eris, and, yes, two-year-olds *do* cry in the middle of the night, and it *will* wake you up. This is the way to Ephraim's." V touched a string hanging from the ceiling that was attached to a rectangular wooden door. "But you probably want to see your room." She walked to the door directly across the hall from hers, knocked twice, and opened it. A pretty girl with short, curly blonde hair, wearing a slim red slip, was holding a hairbrush in front of a full-length mirror. She looked at us, her glossy lips open and her eyes wide.

"I will share anything"—she held up her brush like it was a cross and I was a vampire—"bedroom, bathroom, toothbrush, diary—but I'm not giving up this closet. V, you know how long I had to wait for my own closet."

V took the ratty bag of clothes out of my hand. "Since these are all her worldly possessions, I don't think you need to worry." She dropped it in the middle of the rug.

I felt ashamed, looking at the bag I once used to carry wood, sitting there in the middle of the floor with everything I'd brought with me, the ragged flannel shirts and the pilled sweaters. I was a farm girl who was very far away from the farm.

"Those are *all* your clothes?" The girl clutched the hairbrush over her heart.

"This is your new roommate, and I'm going to offer you a deal, Io. You can keep all the closet space and give Starbird the small dresser, *if* you find this girl something to wear tomorrow that's acceptable for food service, and something for school this week." V reached into her pocket and pulled out a green bill and handed it to the blonde girl.

It shocked me for a minute, watching the two exchange cash like it was nothing.

"Twenty dollars will hardly buy a T-shirt." Io sighed, examining the paper money. "Luckily, I'm a miracle worker. Plus, she's my size."

"Great," said V. "I'm going to check on Ephraim. There are sheets in the linen closet for your bed, Starbird."

V pulled the string in the hall ceiling and a row of stairs connected to the wooden panel descended. When she disappeared up them, I turned back to Io.

"Shower first. I prefer to cut hair wet," she said, pulling on a T-shirt over her slip.

"Cut hair?" I reached for the ponytail that was snaking its way down my back toward my waist.

"Don't worry, I'm not thinking bob or pixie. It will still be long, it will just have some . . . shape."

She walked past me to a little closet in the hall and handed me a towel. "Hot water is a problem in the morning, but this time of day you'll have plenty."

I left my things on my new bed and took the towel into the bathroom, closing the door. The space was cramped, with enough room to turn around between the claw-foot tub and the sink, but nothing extra. I disrobed and stepped into the tub, pulling the makeshift shower curtain around the rim. It was not unlike the shower in the main house on the Farm. The thought of it made my stomach ache.

Did Ursa give the chickens their second feeding? What if she doesn't close up the coop properly and the coyotes get in? What are Fern and Eve making for dinner? Does Indus care that I'm gone?

I turned the knobs by the faucet. Hot water ran down my neck and shoulders and stung my scraped hand. I pulled it up to my face, looking at the red lines that ran from my thumb to my pinky. I closed my eyes and tipped my head back into the water. As it disappeared down the drain, I tried to let the Farm go with it. I was in a new life. I was in the World Outside.

10

Io's scissors sliced through my hair. "Your red highlights look amazing out here in the sun."

It was the first time in my life that someone other than Fern Moon had given me a haircut. When Fern did it, she used a piece of twine to make a straight line above the split ends, and cut right across my back. Io seemed to have a more artistic approach, studying and snipping and studying again. We were sitting in the backyard where the early evening light was still bright enough. Chunks of reddish-blonde hair lay around my feet in a ring.

"Do you work at the café?" I asked as Io pulled the comb. I was wearing a pair of sweatpants and a T-shirt she'd loaned me.

"Used to," she said, picking up her scissors again, "but the food industry is not my thing. I work at Red Light now. Mostly vintage, some new clothes. I'm a buyer."

"Did EARTH make you a Buyer?" I was thinking about

the Traders on the farm, the ones who were allowed to handle money and do business in town.

"EARTH?" She laughed. "My boss at Red Light made me a buyer when he noticed I had an eye for fashion. I'm not real big on the EARTH thing, with the Translations and all. I'm like V. I sort of outgrew it."

My breath caught in my throat. Io didn't believe in the Translations? She had "outgrown" EARTH and so had V? I already liked V and Io so much, and they weren't true Believers?

Io seemed to notice my discomfort. "You shouldn't listen to me," she added brightly. "I'm cynical and sometimes I upset people. How do you feel about bangs?"

"Bangs?"

"Believe me, with your gigantic eyes, you will break hearts with bangs." Io stood in front of me, comb balanced in her left fingers, scissors in her right.

I'm in the World Outside now. "Okay, bangs."

Io combed the wet hair over my face, dropping a curtain on my sight. "Speaking of broken hearts, did you leave any on the Farm?"

The image of Indus and Lyra in the Sanctuary played like a movie clip. "Maybe my own."

"Oh sorry." She cut three times through my hair, and I could see again. Io leaned in to me, her gaze darting critically at the hair around my face. She had delicate lines of black on her eyelids and gray powder above them. "Well, he would be kicking himself if he could see you with this hot new haircut." She handed me a mirror with a handle.

My hair was not in a ponytail, as I had worn it every day of my life at the Farm. Instead, it was hanging straight and silky around my face and shoulders, several inches shorter than it had been, especially the side-swept bangs that reached to my jaw. It looked healthier, somehow shinier, and Io was right about the red highlights that reached to the feathery ends of the cut.

"Stand up and turn around," she said. When we stood toe to toe, she looked me over. Io and I were roughly the same height and build, except that she was soft in all the places I was muscular. "Don't shave your legs," she said, "even if most of the girls at school do. It's cooler if you don't, but they might still make fun of you."

"They might make fun of me?"

Io took one of my hands. "You're really pretty, Starbird." She sounded almost sad when she said it. "Did they tell you that you need to be careful in the city? Don't walk alone at night. Don't talk to men you don't know. Watch out for the boys at school, too. It can be dangerous here."

I opened my mouth to ask exactly what I needed to watch out for when a voice came booming through the screen door from the kitchen. "Our newcomer has arrived!" A man in his midfifties was standing there, gray hair streaking through his brown beard and a warm smile on his face. "Welcome home, Starbird." He put his hands together in prayer position over his heart.

I did the same. I had known Ephraim for years from his Farm pickups and Family gatherings. I had loved him since I was little, but so had all the kids on the Farm. He was a giant teddy bear of a man.

"Come in and talk with me over a cup of tea." He held open the screen door.

I left Io to sweep up my hair and followed Ephraim through the kitchen where Europa and V were chopping vegetables for dinner. We went to an adjoining room and sat at a large wood table where a teapot was waiting. Ephraim sat down but then started coughing so hard, he had to stand again. After a minute, it passed.

"I remember when I got my Calling," he said, pouring us each a cup and fixing me with his hazel-colored eyes. Ephraim's eyes were such an unusual blend of green and brown, they always seemed to be dancing. He had this way of looking at you that made you feel like you were a rare bird that he was the first person to discover.

"My Calling came during the Summer Solstice twenty years ago. I had never been one for cooking, but that year they were shorthanded in the kitchen and EARTH put me in charge of fixing green beans for two hundred people, which meant several sauté pans working at once. I'll admit, the camaraderie of the kitchen was exhilarating. But it was really when I watched the Family members dish-ing my green beans onto their plates, adults feeding green beans to their children, children asking for more, that I knew. It felt just like waking up. *I'm Called to be a cook*, I thought, or discovered, or realized. EARTH agreed and he sent me to the café, and here I am still, the happiest man you ever met." Ephraim spread out his arms, and his eyes danced all around his face. Then he coughed again.

"And so, Starbird has gotten her Calling," he said when he had cleared his throat. "Tell me, how did it feel?"

"Well"—I pulled one foot up onto my chair and grabbed my ankle—"V said you needed help at the restaurant . . ."

Ephraim nodded.

"And then Ursa said it must be my Calling . . ." I continued, "and so I figured I should come here." It was a shaky dismount at best.

"And did you just *know* in your heart that you were being Called?"

"Not . . . exactly."

Ephraim looked at me, the wrinkles around his eyes contracted slightly. He took a sip from his teacup. "Starbird, have you experienced the wisdom of the Translations?"

"Yes," I said. "I've been to Translations every Sunday from the time I was ten until EARTH left. Fern taught me about the Translations before I was born, or when I was too young to hear them."

"And do you believe that EARTH is Translating the Cosmos?" Ephraim was still smiling.

"Yes," I said. "I'm a true Believer."

"And do you believe that EARTH is coming back to our Family?"

"Yes. I've read all of his letters," I answered, trying to sound fully assured. "What about you?"

Ephraim leaned back in his chair. "Yes, yes, and yes! I'm a Believer. Actually, you could call me a Knower. I know it's true because I've felt it. I've felt the Imagination of the Cosmos, and I know EARTH feels it, too, and deeply. EARTH's real gift is giving *voice* to the Cosmos." Ephraim touched his chest. He looked like he was about to laugh or cry, and I couldn't guess which.

"Do you know that EARTH saved my life?"

I shook my head.

"I used to be a drinker before I met EARTH. No, scratch that, the truth is I used to be a *drunk*. I lied to people, drank all day, couldn't keep a job. I had a wife and a kid, but I let them down so many times, they left me. The day I met EARTH, I was at rock bottom. It was a Wednesday, and I was half drunk by mid-afternoon. I had just lost my latest job working at the docks, which was the best job I had ever managed to get. I swore I wouldn't lose it, and then I did, because I tied one on and slept through my alarm. I was sure I was about to lose this house. Anyway, I was only half drunk, and I wanted to find some lunch so

I could keep on drinking, and I wandered right into the café, probably raving like a jerk, I don't know. I ordered something and EARTH delivered it. Can you imagine, EARTH playing waiter at the café?" Ephraim held up his hand like he was holding a tray.

"Well, he sat down with me at my table and started talking. You know what? We didn't stop talking for five hours. We ate lunch and then we ate dinner. He must have had other things to do, other people to worry about, but he didn't leave me. He just stayed with me for five hours pouring me tea and bringing me food, asking me about my life. Every time I tried to leave, he would say, 'Just stay for five more minutes, friend. You're safe here.' I don't know how he did it, but I didn't go for another drink that night. Can you imagine? I was a dedicated drunk and all I even thought about was my next drink but I didn't want to leave him. How do you explain that?" Ephraim paused and shook his head. "Anyway, EARTH talked me into going back to the Farm with him the next morning, and once I was there I couldn't get my hands on a drink without walking twenty miles to Bellingham. And that was it. I didn't have another drink ever again, Starbird. That's how I know it's true." Ephraim pointed a finger toward the ceiling. "I never got my wife back, but I do have my son."

I had never seen a member of the Free Family drink. EARTH Translated that the use of alcohol would corrupt us and lead us from our path.

"We both know something about losing people." Ephraim put his hand on top of mine. His knuckles were thick and wide, and his skin was covered in dark brown spots. "I've always listened for news of Doug. Whenever traveling Family passes through the café, I ask."

Ephraim had been really kind to me and Fern during his café pickups after Doug disappeared.

I nodded.

"But this is your time now, Starbird. Doug was very smart—I mean, Doug *is* very smart. He'll be fine." I thought Ephraim was trying to convince himself as much as me.

V walked into the room with a kettle and started to add hot water to the teapot.

"V, we have another Believer here." Ephraim motioned toward me. "Maybe she can join me and Cham and Europa in helping our stray lambs."

V didn't look at me; she just kept filling the teapot. "Dinner's ready," she said. "Come and get in line."

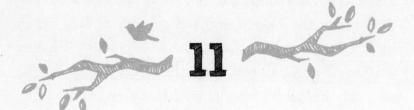

11

The next dawn brought a strange, new experience. Instead of a rooster crowing, I woke up to the sound of an alarm clock.

"Turn it off," Io muttered, before rolling over with a pillow on her head.

After some fumbling, I found the switch that made the horrible buzzing sound stop. It was five thirty in the morning and the sun had not yet popped its forehead over the mountains. In my sleepy daze, I reached for my old jeans and wool sweater, and then I remembered: I had new clothes, because I had a new life. I dressed in the dark and met V in the foyer. She was holding out a travel mug to me.

"Coffee," she said in a gravelly voice, handing off the cup. Then she added, "Look at you."

Io had prepped my wardrobe the night before. I was wearing black pants that were a little too big in the hips and waist, a white button-up shirt that was a little too small across my shoulders, and a blue cardigan that had tiny flower patches to hide spots where holes had been mended. Io didn't have any shoes that fit me, though, so on my feet were the same muddy farm boots I'd shown up wearing.

Europa came out of the kitchen holding her own mug and said, "Ephraim's watching the kids. Let's go."

It was a twenty-minute walk from Beacon House to the restaurant, and V talked for fifteen of them. "I'll give Starbird the two-tops in the windows after noon so she can practice on tables. Europa, you take the booths, and I'll take the four-top rounds, plus the two-tops in the morning. Starbird can bus so she gets used to carrying trays. I hope Felicia folded napkins before she left yesterday, because we're going to be in the weeds all morning."

"Wild guess says Felicia didn't fold napkins," said Europa.

"She serves a necessary purpose," said V.

"You get a stolen identity and we get a non-Believer serving our food," said Europa.

I tracked their conversation for a while, but there was so much I didn't understand, I finally tuned out and focused on the scenery, passing the travel mug of coffee back and forth with V.

I had seen suburban neighborhoods on trips to Bellingham, but I was caught off guard by the amount of pavement in Seattle. The roads with their dark asphalt were one thing, and the sidewalks the color of cream were another, but the parking lots were expansive. How many trees were cut down to make all this emptiness?

I couldn't stop staring at the web of wires crosshatching the sky above us. Near the intersection there was a bare, sanded tree trunk planted in the concrete, and attached to it near the top was a cross arm, making a giant letter *T*. About thirty thick, rubber-coated wires met there going in all directions, north–south and east–west. Those wires continued as far down the street as I could see, periodically dotted with black birds. Smaller wires connected the larger ones to the houses and businesses on the street. One of them ran right above a sign that said FREE FAMILY CAFÉ. It hung from a brick building next to a large vacant lot where grasses fought weeds for control.

"And so it begins," said V, turning the handle and opening the door.

"Does Felicia know how to use a rag?" were the first words we heard in the café.

"Good morning, Paul," said V.

Immediately to our left was an *L*-shaped counter lined with stools that surrounded the open kitchen. A tall boy with dark hair who looked like an older, meatier version of Devin, and turned out to be Devin's older brother, Paul, was wiping the surface. Devin, aka Skinny Cook, had his back to us, scraping the surface of the grill with a metal tool. He was moving back and forth in a jerky dance move. A third guy, muscular with short blond hair, came through the swinging door holding a box full of apples. "Behind you," he said to Devin, who didn't move but continued his jerky dance until he bumped into the blond boy.

"Sorry, Sun." Devin yanked a cord from his ear, and I could hear faraway music.

"Watch it," the blond guy said.

"Half hour till open!" V yelled as I followed her across the floor, through a beaded curtain and into the tiny office. "Let's start your crash course in carrying a tray."

Much of the morning was a frantic blur. I learned that a four-top is a table where four people can sit, and "Behind you" is something you say in a restaurant when you're carrying dishes or hot coffee behind someone's back. "Busing a table" means picking up plates coated in syrup and empty jam containers and dirty knives, and carrying the tray through a busy restaurant to the dishwasher without dumping it into a pile of ceramic shards on the floor. The restaurant opened at six thirty, and by ten, I must have walked twenty miles in tiny circles.

"Starbird, could you water table two?" "Starbird, can you bus table six?" "Starbird, a clean fork to table one, and rye bread to table seven." So much noise. I took coffee to the table that wanted sour cream, spilled juice on a child who thumped his head against my drink tray, and gave someone a hot tea who asked for an iced tea. At least I didn't drop a tray.

"Could you bus table eight?" Europa asked around noon, breezing by with a pot of coffee in each hand.

I grabbed my busing tray from the wait station and headed to a booth. The check was still on the table in a black plastic tray, along with three bills. The top bill said *Five Dollars* along the bottom edge and had a number 5 in each of its corners. There was a picture of a stern-looking bearded man in the center and the words *The United States of America*, along with seals, stamps, and numbers. I recognized money, but I had never seen it so close before.

I cleared the table all around the check, but I couldn't take my eyes off the bill. Using a napkin so I didn't touch it with my bare hand, I slid the top bill aside and looked at the one underneath it. The second was distinctly green with a massive building in the middle and the number 10 in each corner. The words *In God We Trust* hovered over the building like it was floating in the sky.

"Could you drop that by the register for me, Starbird?" Europa rushed past with four plates. "I'm weeded."

My tray was sitting on the table, now full of all the dishes and glassware. The rest of the table was cleared and wiped down, except for the check and the three bills. I hesitated. EARTH taught us that money was the root of corruption. But Europa had been touching money all morning, tucking it in her apron, putting it in the register, and she was a Believer. I scooped the money and the check into my hand in one movement. Nothing changed. The noise of the restaurant was all around me as I walked toward the register by the front door. I put the check and the money beneath a paperweight and took my tray to the dish sink.

When our morning shift ended, I had touched money seven more times, cleared fifty tables, and eaten one slice of bread with butter standing up in the dish room. It was a miracle I never broke a plate.

When Felicia showed up at one thirty, V told me to grab an empty stool at the counter and order whatever I wanted. The morning rush had eased enough to leave an open spot near the register.

"I recommend the polenta. I highly suggest you steer away from the eggs," Devin said, leaning on the counter with a pen in his hand and an order pad in the other. "Nice hustle today."

"I'll have the veggie scramble with tofu and rye bread."

"Tofu scramble rye," Devin yelled to Paul, who was at the grill behind him. "Tofu scramble rye," Paul chimed back.

By the time I finished eating my heavenly, hot, life-affirming meal, several spaces had freed up at the counter, and there was no longer a line of people waiting at the door.

"What's this?" Felicia was at the register. "Why aren't these in the till?" She held up the checks and cash I had been piling under the paperweight all morning.

"I put them there," I said. "Europa was weeded."

"I hope no one wanted change," she said, waving them around toward me. "Well, I'm not ringing them up. You put them there, you can do it."

"I haven't learned the register yet."

"Of course," she said. "Fine, I'll do it."

From my stool, I watched Felicia ring up the first check. She typed the cost with the decimal point and then hit a button saying FOOD or BEVERAGE and a large plus sign. She did this for each item and hit SUBTOTAL. After that, she keyed in the amount the customer left and hit CASH, causing the register to ring and the drawer to fly open. The screen told her how much change to take out.

"Order up, table ten," Paul called, sliding two plates into our pickup window at the other end of the counter.

Felicia slammed the cash drawer, put the change in the tip jar, and speared the check on a metal spike. Then she went to the pickup window and took the plates to a booth in the corner.

I got up and went to the register, reminding myself of the steps. I was delighted when the register rang and the cash drawer slid open, confirming the amount of change I had already figured in my head for the first bill. I dropped the change in the tip jar and skewered the check. I did the rest of them quickly, punching the numbers into the register just the way I punched them into the calculator back on the Farm when Iron and I figured measurements for the new chicken coop. I felt a pang of sadness. I missed my roosters. But I felt a rush of anger, too, thinking about Iron. A few splotches sprang up on my chest.

All the checks lay impaled on the metal spike when Felicia found me at the register.

"I guess you want me to train you." She sighed, moving me away from the machine. "Where are the rest of the checks?"

"I did them."

"You said you weren't trained on the register."

"I watched you."

"Did you put the change in the tip jar?"

I nodded.

"And the check here?" She pointed to the spear.

I nodded again.

"Well, I guess we'll know how bad you screwed up when we run the Z report." She shook her head. "Not like it isn't always wrong," she added before she walked away through the beaded curtain.

12

All I wanted to do when V and I got back to Beacon House was sleep for fourteen hours. I hadn't felt so tired since the last apple-pressing day on the Farm. But a nap was not in my future because the minute V opened the front door of Beacon House, Ephraim said, "Great, babysitters! I've got to go to the café and call Gamma. If I don't talk to her today, she's going to convene a war council and the Farm is going to attack Beacon House." Ephraim was lying on the couch with a picture book spread out below him on the floor. Kale was sitting on the rug holding a plastic horse, and Eris was in his playpen banging a rattle across the bars like a prisoner in a cell.

"You didn't call her back yet?" V took off her shoes and hung her purse on the coat rack.

"Had to watch the kids. People before profits. Don't worry, it's all good." Ephraim sat up with some effort and then stood from the couch only to lose his balance and sit right back down again.

"Yeah, all good," V muttered, going to him. "Don't go in today." She touched him on the forehead and cheek.

"You're a little young to be mothering me, aren't you? It was just tunnel vision."

V insisted on driving Ephraim to the café, leaving me to watch the kids. I spent the next thirty minutes lying on the couch, watching a three-inch-tall horse weave in and out of chair legs, climb onto the arms of couches, and perform death-defying dismounts from end tables, while using all of my effort to stay awake. At one point, Kale's horse galloped up my leg, across my back, and took a leap from my head onto the rug. I thought about Indus, the way he ran after the truck when he saw me leaving. I didn't stop to talk to him. I didn't even wave. The back of my hand was still red and raw from where I scraped it against the barn wood the night I saw him with Lyra. It felt dry and inflamed from all the times I washed my hands at the café.

"Makes you wonder how Europa does it," V said, coming in the front door and finding me comatose on the couch. She folded her arms over her chest and stared at Kale. Fern Moon folded her arms that way sometimes when she looked at me. Fern would have the yurt to herself now. It must get quiet at night.

"What's a Z report?" I asked.

"When each shift ends, you run a report of sales from the register. Then you compare it to the money in the till. Why?"

I sat up. "I want to go back to the Farm. I think I was wrong about my Calling. I should probably go back with Ephraim on the next pickup."

"Wait, hold up." V made the sign for time-out. "You did great today. It's just new job jitters. You can do this."

"What if I don't want to do this?"

"Well, you need to get off the Farm sometime."

"Why would I have to get off the Farm? EARTH probably wanted me to stay on the Farm. He never said I should leave."

V bit her lip and stared at me. "The next Farm pickup isn't until Tuesday. If you still want to go back, then no big deal, okay?"

Tuesday sounded as far away as spring. *What if Indus forgot what he wanted to say to me?*

I was about to answer when the front door opened and Io walked in, holding a cloth bag in each hand. "You won't be as amazed as you should be by what I have in my hands, but you should be truly amazed. Hi, Kale." The little girl ran over and circled Io's leg with her horse. "Behold your new wardrobe, purchased for $19.57."

Io dropped the two bags and her purse in the middle of the living room rug. Kale's horse jumped over each of them.

"I started at the five-dollar box at Crossroads, shopped the half-price tags at Value Village, and then the free box in the staff room at Red Light. I want you to know that I seriously considered keeping the yellow dress for myself." Io dumped the contents of both bags on the rug, revealing three T-shirts that were worn but had cute patterns; two skirts, one orange and cotton, the other plaid and wool; and a yellow dress with elastic at the waist and a rainbow across one shoulder.

"Won't I be cold?" I asked touching the fabric of the thin dress.

"I'm not going to get mad because I know you're just off the Farm, but seriously, I did just spend two hours shopping for you with pennies in my pocket." She collapsed the dress she had been holding up onto her lap. "And these are insanely cute."

"I'm sorry." I stood up from the couch. "I do really appreciate it."

"No shoes?" V got Eris out of his playpen and bounced him on her hip.

"Tall order, but give me time."

Io and V played with the kids while I halfheartedly modeled my new clothes for them. Then we started making dinner. I was starting to like V and Io. It was too bad we could never be *truly* close, since they weren't Believers.

"Hidy ho," called Ephraim as he opened the front door an hour later.

"We're in here," yelled V. "How bright is our future?" she asked him after he had taken off his shoes and joined us.

I was toasting bread to go with the garlic soup.

"Smooth seas. There's no better business than the restaurant business. In every economy, people have to eat." He took a small piece off my bread plate and popped it in his mouth.

I flashed back—was it really only two nights ago?—to when Iron told me the Farm was failing financially. At least the café was doing well. *What if I did go back to the Farm and then it failed?*

V looked at Ephraim for a moment with her hands on her hips. Then she turned around and dished up a bowl of soup from the pot. "Yeah, people have to eat," she said with a sigh, handing him the bowl. "Including us."

"Three dollars and seventy-six cents," Felicia said before we even took off our sweaters. She was already behind the register, wearing her apron and drinking a glass of orange juice when we walked into the café the next morning.

"Huh?" V said, partly because the music was turned up on the café speakers. Paul, Devin, and Sun were behind the counter, prepping food. Europa wasn't with us because she had the afternoon shift.

"Z report." Felicia puckered her lips together into a smirk.

"Not bad!" V shouted. "That's better than we usually do."

"It's not *better*. It's *wrong*. These are supposed to be equal." She waved a register slip at us. "Maybe people should be trained on the register before they start ringing people up."

"Mine were correct," I said. I had double-checked all the numbers in my head against the register totals. Even though I had been tired, I was sure I hadn't made a mistake.

"Right, because it's always somebody else's fault," Felicia snapped at me, her eyes blazing.

"Whoa, Felicia, go easy," said V. "The sun's barely up. Come on, Starbird, let's put our stuff down."

I followed V toward the office. I was shocked, and hurt, by Felicia's reaction. No one had ever spoken to me that way on the Farm, even if I had made a mistake. The red blotches started to spread over my chest, and I reminded myself it was only a few days until I could go home. As I walked past the counter, Devin looked at me, pulled his shirt collar away from his neck, and made a choking sound.

"She's just like that." V parted the beaded curtain. "I know it isn't what you're used to, but we need her. Well, I need her."

V trained me on the register for real before we opened. When the rush started, I did better at busing tables, but I still mixed up regular and decaf, and one woman was manic and angry after her third cup of caffeinated drip. I screwed up three drink orders before V said, "Why don't you ring up my checks and I'll handle beverages? Don't forget to eat something during your shift. I'm surprised you didn't stab anyone with a fork yesterday."

On her advice, I went to the dish room to eat some bread while Sun washed bowls. With his blond hair and bronzed skin, Sun didn't seem to belong in the cloudy world of the Pacific Northwest. He was older than the other cooks, probably in his forties, and handsome with a strong jaw. His back was to me as he rinsed dishes with the industrial nozzle on the faucet hose.

"It's even busier than yesterday." I tore off a bite of my roll.

Sun nodded and washed.

"Do you like working in the kitchen?"

"Sure. Whatever."

"What's your second name, Sun?"

"Just Sun."

"EARTH didn't give you a second name?"

He stopped rinsing and sighed. Then he started rinsing again without answering. I ate the rest of my bread in silence. *Even Family members on the Outside are more isolated and sad. It must be their exposure to Outsiders. I need to get back to the Farm. I can't let that happen to me.*

Ephraim came in around eleven and worked in the office. When my shift ended, he asked for me and V. She squeezed into the tiny space by the aprons, and I stood in the doorway.

"Let's start Starbird with four shifts a week." His voice sounded raspy and thin like a wooden flute with a crack in it. "She'll need some nights off for schoolwork. I'm thinking Thursday to Sunday.

"I'll work with her the first weekday so she isn't the only waitress." V adjusted Ephraim's scarf to fit more tightly around his neck. "Are you warm enough?"

Ephraim patted her hand. "Did you tell her about paychecks and tips?"

V spoke softer. "You'll get a paycheck every two weeks because we need to show that we're paying documented workers, but you will deposit your check and then give the money back to Ephraim for living expenses at Beacon House. You get to keep five dollars in tips every shift you work."

"Didn't you tell him I want to go home?"

"Home?" said Ephraim, looking up from his papers, his reading glasses making his eyes seem magnified on his face. "You are home. You're with Family here."

"I know, but—"

"Homesickness," said V.

"You just need to adjust is all," said Ephraim.

"I just don't think it's right—"

"Well, we definitely need you here. I think that if EARTH were here, he would say—"

"But he's not here!"

They both stared at me.

"Okay." Ephraim took off his glasses and rubbed his eyes. "If you want to go back to the Farm, you can go with Cham when he does the pickup on Wednesday."

"Wednesday? I thought it was Tuesday."

"Had to change it. Oh, here, I made a copy of your birth certificate," said Ephraim, returning the brown envelope I had given him earlier. "I didn't know you were Iron's child. Iron's a wondrous soul. One of my favorite non-Believers."

"He's not my father. I mean, he probably isn't. He just helped my mom with the paperwork," I said, shoving the envelope into the pocket of my wool sweater on its hook.

"Sure," said Ephraim, not looking up from the papers in front of him.

"He might be. No one can say," I said.

"All right," said Ephraim.

"What do I do with the five dollars?"

V and Ephraim both laughed, causing Ephraim to start coughing. "Take the bus, buy a candy bar, whatever sixteen-year-olds do," said V. "Just don't mention it to Felicia. Her tips work differently."

If it was possible, I was even more tired when we got home from the café the second day. Cham was watching Eris and Kale, so no one stopped me as I climbed the stairs to my room. I thought I would fall asleep instantly, but I didn't. I lay in bed teetering on sleep. I was thinking about Indus, and then about Kale running her plastic horse around the house, and then the two images blended together and Indus was a pale horse running through the apple orchard on the Farm, and I was trying to run after him on the thin, tired legs of a girl. My thoughts mixed into a dream, and Indus the horse was moving briskly and gracefully through the trees while I was running after him through quicksand. Even in the dream I knew: I had to catch him.

13

I woke just before sunrise and expected to hear Chocolate crow before I remembered that Chocolate was two hundred miles away. I rolled over toward the window and saw Io sleeping on her back, her hands clutching the blanket. I wanted to go back to sleep, too. It would be hours until the alarm rang for me to get up and go enroll in public school, but my internal clock was still set to Farm time, and my body was ready to start working.

I rolled over and faced the door, closed my eyes, and tried to go back to sleep. I couldn't stop thinking. *Why bother enrolling in school if I'm just going to go back to the Farm on Wednesday? Do I really want to go back?* My mind drifted back to another morning just before sunrise, when I was eleven and Doug Fir woke me up before the rooster.

"Starbird." He jostled my shoulder. "Wake up. EARTH is calling a sunrise Translation."

Fern was already moving around the yurt, putting

on a sweater and rubbing her eyes. "Why this morning?" she asked Doug. "He hasn't done one in years."

"He just told me to gather everyone."

"Were you up all night with him again?" she asked.

"I've got to wake the others." Doug pulled off the shirt he was wearing and tossed it onto his cot before grabbing a fresh one and leaving the yurt. He left the door open, and I could see other Family members moving around in the dusky light outside. It was July and the air was cool but sweet. I put on a sweater over my pajamas and went out with Fern.

There was a line at the outhouse. Firmament Rise was in front of us.

"Haven't had a sunrise Translation in years," he said, stretching his arms overhead. "Feels like the old days." Firmament pulled his wiry gray hair back into a long ponytail and then bent down into a yogic chair pose.

The first bit of actual sunlight popped into view above the mountains and Fern said, "We'd better hurry." Our old rooster, Ringer, crowed from the coop.

Ten minutes later, we found our seats in one of the outer orbits of the Sanctuary. Adeona was still laying out cushions, and there was a sleepy, rumbling murmur throughout the barn. Doug was onstage pouring water into a glass on the table next to EARTH's pillows. Hazy yellow light fell through the hayloft window and pooled on the platform.

Finally, Mars Wolf entered through the north door. That was the summer he let his beard get long, and it looked like a wire horse brush was growing on his chin. Family members were still arranging their seats and getting comfortable as he started our customary words.

"Our Family was summoned together in 1970 by the Cosmic Imagination that Called the eight principal elders to witness the first Translation by our interpreter, EARTH . . ."

While Mars spoke, Family members were still arriving with their mugs of tea and coffee. None of the Farm visitors who came to Sunday Translations was there. It was only those of us who lived on the Farm, maybe a hundred people.

". . . We live by these Principles because We are the Family and We are Free."

"The Family is Free," we chanted together.

When he finished, Mars sat down on some pillows on the edge of the platform, and the north door opened. EARTH walked in.

EARTH wasn't wearing his usual robes. He was wearing a thin pair of cotton pants that he often wore during Family yoga sessions and a loose brown shirt. He didn't walk contemplatively across the platform, but quickly, rubbing his hands together. He didn't take a seat on the cushions laid out for him, but instead he walked to the center of the stage, held his arms out straight at this sides, and said, "I am not your messiah."

Any rustling in the room stopped. No one took a sip of coffee. Next to me, Fern froze in place.

EARTH grinned his sweetest smile. Sunlight poured through the window above him. His eyes looked red and squinty.

"I'm not your savior." EARTH still had both arms raised. His bare feet gripped the plywood below him. "Don't worship me. Don't *believe* in me. Don't place me above you in any way." EARTH turned a slow circle all the way around on the platform, as if to show us every side of himself. "Am I anything other than a man?"

No one in the congregation answered him, but I noticed a few people shaking their heads. Ringer crowed out by the chicken coop and EARTH threw back his head and took a deep breath. I started to feel anxious. This was nothing like a Sunday morning Translation.

"If you came here," said EARTH, his head still tipped back, looking at the ceiling, "looking for someone to follow, you should leave." He pointed toward the Sanctuary door at the south end of the room. "If you want a mystic to tell you how to live your life"—now EARTH lowered his head and looked around at all of us gathered—"then *leave this Sanctuary right now!*"

I gripped my cushion, then inched closer to Fern, lacing my arm through hers. Fern gave my arm a reassuring pat, but I could tell by her expression that she was worried, too. I glanced over at Doug, who was seated on the platform to the right of EARTH. His hands were clasped together in his lap and his back was straight as a board. He was looking down at his knees.

No one moved or spoke. Hay particles and dust danced in the light of dawn. EARTH smiled again.

"What is the greatest human need?" He looked around the room, his hands now lowered to his sides. "What is it? Is it money?"

A few heads shook. One woman muttered, "No."

"No, it isn't money. It could be food. We all need food to live, right? Is it our *greatest* need?"

Heads shook again, tentatively, but no one spoke.

"What about shelter? What about love? What about sex? Is sex our greatest need as humans?"

"No," said a few people in the crowd. I glanced at Fern Moon. Her hair was hanging long and loose because she hadn't bothered to braid it. She chewed her thumbnail.

"What human beings long for"—EARTH raised his arms again, as if he were holding a large, invisible moon over his head—"what we all need more than we need money or food or sex or recognition or accomplishment or any of the other stuff that the Outsiders tell us we need, our strongest desire and deepest goal, is *belonging*. BE-LONG-ING. We *long* to *belong*."

A woman behind me whispered, "Yes, yes."

"It's what all the Outsiders are after, they just don't *get it* yet," he said. "What we get here"—EARTH gestured to the floor—"what they don't get out there, with their separation into countries and religions and ethnic groups and identities and households and cubicles and *selves*, is that separation is what's making them so miserable." EARTH started to pace slowly along the front edge of the stage, holding his hands to his chest now. "The division of individual ownership is killing them inside.

"And when you really open your eyes, when you see what is true underneath all of the borders and the false walls that we think we're building to protect ourselves, it's all bullshit. Because we're all the same. You can't worship me, because my self isn't different from your self. We're the same person."

EARTH stepped off the front of the platform and started walking through the rows of pillows. As he passed each Family member, he touched them in some way, on the shoulder, arm, or head. But he kept his eyes moving around the crowd.

"All our human fates are linked. The Outsiders need only one great epidemic to learn that lesson. We call ourselves the Family and we call them the Outsiders not because we aren't them and they aren't us, but just because they don't *get it* yet. They haven't seen the truth. They're bent on building walls and we're bent on belonging. What they don't know yet is that belonging is the easiest thing in the world. Everyone is eventually going to *get it* and then we're all, all of the human race, going to be part of the Family." EARTH started talking faster and moving more quickly through the room, touching each Family member as he went. Some touched him back or sighed. Adeona burst into tears as EARTH touched her shoulder. She crumpled onto her cushion.

"You can't worship me, because you are me," EARTH said, nearly running through the room, hopping between the orbits, touching people like he was tagging them in a game of chase.

"Say it. I don't worship EARTH! I don't worship EARTH!" he said.

"I don't worship EARTH." We chanted. "I don't worship EARTH."

He circled closer to our row, touching members, now only a few steps from me. I braced myself for the touch I knew was coming while I chanted, "I don't worship EARTH. I don't worship EARTH."

And then he touched me. He reached out a hand and placed it down on my shoulder, and it felt like the sunrise was happening in my soul, like a spirit entered through my arm and spread its wings in my heart. I was one with everyone in the room, and the sun came in through the hayloft window and backlit everyone's hair so everyone appeared to have a halo, and the chanting shook the barn and I pounded my fists on my legs to keep rhythm with the chant, and others started pounding on the walls or the floors. And when EARTH had made it to the back of the room and touched the very last person in the last orbit, he kept going and he ran right out the door. But we kept chanting without him after he left. The door of the barn stood open and we chanted to the sunrise. *I don't worship EARTH. I don't worship EARTH.*

14

I must have fallen asleep again, remembering that sunrise Translation, because I woke up to the alarm clock buzzing. It was time to go enroll in public school.

When I was little, we had school every day but Sunday. The school—which was actually a glassed-in porch on the side of the main house—had up to forty students. We were divided into three or four groups according to age and ability until we were seventeen.

Our subjects included: history, math, writing, creative brainstorming, music, visual art, Mother Nature, community responsibility, and science. Teachers tried to link our lessons to things happening on the Farm; like the year aphids attacked our tomato crop, we did a science lesson on insects and a history lesson on pesticides. When Bithiah's father, a Vietnam vet, came to stay at the Farm one summer, we focused during history time on the 1960s. He visited our class for a week, and so did Firmament Rise, who was an antiwar activist.

Like Doug Fir, my best subject was math, which Gamma Lion taught before she had to take over the office. After EARTH left, our little school slowly deteriorated. Two years later, there were fewer than ten kids.

As I turned off the alarm and got dressed, I thought about the coop. Were the roosters confused when I didn't come in the morning? Would Ursa remember to check the wire fencing for holes? *Are they safe? Do they need me?*

When you have spent your life dressing according to the weather, it's a strange thing to decide which T-shirt will look good with an orange skirt. On the Farm, we would dress up for special occasions like Feasts and naming ceremonies, but a normal day usually involved the choice between rain jacket or wool sweater, thermal long johns or jeans.

I dressed in the outfit Io suggested, awkwardly pulling on the stretchy gray tights under the orange cotton skirt and a navy-blue T-shirt with white stripes. *This is vanity,* I thought, putting on the T-shirt. *This is the consumer culture. I shouldn't have to dress up just to learn.* I looked in Io's full-length mirror. I didn't look like a farm girl. Is this what Indus meant when he said "really Seattle"? *Just two more days*, I reminded myself. *Then I can go back.*

V and Cham were waiting at the bottom of the stairs, V holding her travel mug. "To the bus stop," she said, dropping a pair of sunglasses over her eyes even though it was barely light out.

We walked half a block and waited five minutes for a bus. V handed me a dollar, which barely made me blink after two days of making change at the restaurant. I fed it into a machine beside the driver.

After a fifteen-minute ride, we pulled up near an enormous brick building. Except for the columns, it wasn't unlike the building on the back of the ten-dollar bill. I couldn't imagine how much firewood it would take to heat a building that big, but I would hate to chop it all.

As we stepped off the bus, Cham muttered, "I can't be late," and slung his backpack over one shoulder.

"Take it easy, you're still recovering," said V.

"Thanks, Mom." Cham jogged off as if we were walking too slowly for him.

"Sometimes I get the feeling he's ashamed of us." V adjusted her clothes to conceal the red bra strap that managed to peek out even from under her blazer. She had worn a slim-fitting black dress under a jacket and shoes with heels. She didn't look like any Family member I had ever seen. "I went to high school here, too. Just pray they don't remember me."

People streamed past us up the stairs. Tall and short, fat and thin, people with all different colors of hair and skin and jackets and sneakers were threading around us. It was the widest variety of individuals I had ever seen, with one major exception: They were all my age.

After the exodus, Indus was the person closest to my

age on the Farm, even though he was three years older. If Indus was helping Iron harvest the back lot today, he would have been up for hours already. It would have been cold when they started up the tractors, and torture getting out of bed. *Was he sleeping alone?* There was a bee still trapped inside my stomach, trying to sting its way out.

V and I walked past a row of locked bicycles as more students darted around us. That's when he walked past me, dangling his bike key at the end of a string, his green army surplus jacket torn just above the elbow, his reddish-brown hair in lazy curls above his ears, his walk as confident as always. My legs turned into dry sticks. "Doug?" I sputtered with a thick tongue. *"Doug?"* I lurched toward his jacket, just managing to grab his sleeve.

He wrenched around and snatched his arm back, the boy who wasn't my brother. He looked at me like I was a spider in the woodpile.

"What did you say?"

"Sorry," I said, "sorry."

He turned and darted up the concrete steps to the school. Of course he wasn't Doug. Doug wasn't sixteen anymore. *Somewhere my brother is nineteen, if he's even—*

"Did you know that guy?" V asked, taking my arm in hers to climb the stairs.

"No," I said, not crying. Somehow.

✳   ✳   ✳

"Star. Bird?" The woman seated behind the desk in the main office pronounced my name like it was a country she had never heard of. Her hands were paused over her keyboard.

"Hippie parents," said V with a wink.

"You're not the parent?" The woman didn't wink back.

"Legal guardian." V unfolded a paper and handed it across the desk. The lady glanced at it and went back to typing.

"And your name is"—she looked back to the paper and read aloud—"Felicia Hale."

I glanced at V, who refused to make eye contact with me.

"Yes," V answered. "And Starbird is all one word, no hyphen. Her last name is Murphy."

The woman tapped away on her keys. Something about her wasn't right. She looked to be the same age as Gamma Lion, whose gray hair sprouted from her temples and cowlick. This woman's hair was vibrant red.

"She went to an accredited home school?" the red-haired woman asked, staring at her screen.

"She did. The Family Farm School."

"We're going to need transfer documents, or else she'll have to take placement tests."

"I think the tests would be best."

After more questions, the woman led me down a hall to a room with a clock, desk, and chair.

"You don't have a cell phone, do you?" She motioned me toward the chair. "Can't have you looking up answers."

"I don't have that," I said.

"Thirty minutes per test." She handed me a pencil. "Math, history, and writing. Have you ever filled in a multiple-choice test before? Nice, dark mark inside the oval."

For an hour and a half, I sat in a windowless room turning tiny white ovals into tiny black ovals. *I could have collected and washed the eggs in this time. I could have weeded the herb garden.* Besides the clock ticking on the wall, it was impossible to feel the time passing. I had never been in a windowless room before. Even the root cellar at the farm had a window.

Periodically, the red-haired woman would poke her head in to check on me. Math was a breeze. I tripped on a few terms, but the problems were basic. The writing section wasn't bad, but history was a baffling slog through unintelligible muck. The test must have been written by a military general, because almost every question involved war. What event started this war? What event ended that one? If it wasn't Vietnam, I was lost. I ended up just filling in the ovals to make the shape of a wave.

The secretary came when my time was up and returned me to V, who was hiding her face in a book.

"I'll get the results, and then you can meet with our

eleventh grade counselor." She walked into an adjoining room, leaving us alone.

"Legal guardian?" I whispered. I had been thinking about it the whole time I was in the testing room.

"The Family should start a business forging documents, we're so good at it. I had to use Felicia's name for her Social Security number, and another Family member's address, because we're not in this school district. Beacon Hill is districted for Cleveland, but Roosevelt has a lower dropout rate," she whispered back. "Do not tell Felicia."

"Why is her hair red?"

V looked confused for a second, then collapsed the book onto her chest and laughed. "Oh. She thinks it makes her look younger."

"Why would she want to look younger? Being an Elder commands respect."

"Yeah, you're going to learn a lot here."

The woman appeared again. "I'll take you to Ms. Harper, the junior guidance counselor."

"Welcome to Roosevelt, Starbird." Ms. Harper motioned us to two chairs across from her desk. She was pretty, about the same age as V, with brown hair piled on her head in a high bun. "You're joining us from homeschooling, right?"

Suddenly the room was full of frogs, like it was dusk at the pond near the road. I looked around in shock.

"Oops, excuse me." Ms. Harper went to a metal cabinet and took out a leather bag. "I thought I silenced that." She fished through it and pulled out a device the size of her palm, then pushed a few buttons before placing it on her desk. "So, Starbird, what's the reason for your transition?"

"I got my Calling." I sat down.

Ms. Harper cocked her head. "Your calling?"

V cleared her throat.

"I, um, mean I just felt like it was time to go to a, um, bigger school."

"Well, Roosevelt has over fifteen hundred students. What now?" That same device was making a soft buzzing noise and lighting up. "I'm super sorry. My dog is at the vet today." She took the device and started tapping on it with her thumbs. "I'm just going to ask my husband to pick him up." We sat waiting for her to finish.

"Okay." Ms. Harper swiveled around in her chair and looked at the computer screen to her left. "Roosevelt. We're a diverse population, so there are lots of ways to fit in. It looks like you're sixteen at the start of the school year, so you should be a junior." She swiveled back to the stack of papers with my name on them just as her computer started making a noise like a phone ringing. "No you don't, Skype meeting! They're trying to call me early. You can't call me now. I'm not answering," she said to her computer screen, clicking her mouse until the ringing stopped.

I stole a look at V, who rolled her eyes. What was wrong with this woman?

"English comprehension score is solid, writing needs improvement. Math score exceptional, we'll try you in precalculus over geometry." She was typing things into her computer as she talked, and she wasn't looking at us. "No test on science, but math scores show chemistry could work. Hmm. History's a problem. You don't like history?"

Another wall clock was ticking audibly.

"I . . . like it . . . sure."

"This score barely puts you into ninth grade." She tapped her nails on her desk and studied the screen. "One of our social studies teachers, Mr. Bell, runs an after-school history club two days a week. It's cool, not like another class, and it's helped a lot of kids improve their grades. I'll make you a deal: I will start you in junior social studies if you go to the club twice a week after school."

"I have a job," I said.

"It's Mondays and Wednesdays. Maybe you can work your schedule around it."

"No problem," said V. "I'm her manager, too." She winked at Ms. Harper.

"Starbird, I don't want to scare you." Ms. Harper finally made eye contact with me. "But sometimes homeschooled students have adjustment challenges joining a large public high school. This is a crisis pass." She opened a drawer and withdrew a red laminated card. "It will let you leave class and come talk to me if you need to. Now, don't use it every time you have a challenge, but if you really need it, it's there."

Ms. Harper's computer started ringing again. "I'm going to email your schedule right now before I forget." She turned back around and started typing again. "Okay, Skype, yes, I hear you."

The red-haired woman gave me a student handbook and locker assignment, as well as instructions for getting a bus pass. She said they had to finish my enrollment paperwork before I could attend classes, so she suggested I start the next morning. Then we went to the transit office and finally back home, where V could explain to me what email was and how a person could "check it."

"Our connection is molasses-speed." V held down a button on the computer in the basement of Beacon House. I had used a computer in our school on the Farm, but it was much older than this one and not connected to the Internet.

A second later, the screen lit up and boxes full of pictures and text opened one after another faster than I could see what was on them.

"Cham didn't log out again." V ran the mouse over

the tabletop. "Your attention deficit guidance counselor emailed it to me, but we need to set you up with your own account. Just click on this, save it to the desktop, and print."

She might as well have said, "Buzz here, rescue the ax to the counter, and then high dive."

Within two minutes, she handed me my schedule for school in Seattle, and we learned that there had just been an earthquake in Turkey.

"Isn't it kind of pointless to start school tomorrow if I'm just going to leave on Wednesday?" I said.

"If you leave, we'll just withdraw you and it's no big deal. But if you decide to stay, you will have started already and it will be easier to adjust."

"Are you trying to trick me into staying?"

V took my hand. "I swear, I'm not trying to trick you into anything. I just want you to know your . . . options."

"But you promise to let me leave on Wednesday if I want to?"

V kept hold of my hand. "I promise."

"How was registration?" Europa came down the creaky basement stairs holding Eris. "Did they start the brainwashing today or is that tomorrow?"

"Europa grew up on the Outside," V explained. "She went to public school."

"So I know what kind of snakes slither the halls," Europa said. "The only purpose of public school is to make you a good consumer."

"That reminds me." V stood. "Don't tell anyone at school about the Family—friends, teachers, especially guidance counselors. If the school finds out, it won't take them long to realize I'm not Felicia Hale, your legal guardian, and that would lead back to Beacon House and then to the café, to our undocumented workers, maybe even to the home school on the Farm. Fly under the radar. Nothing is more important than that."

"And don't make friends with any Outsiders," Europa added. "They'll only contaminate you. The only people you need live here."

15

"Who will come to Story Night?" I asked Ephraim over dinner. It was almost seven o'clock, so V had already turned on the porch light and straightened up the living room for our guests. Europa was upstairs trying to put Eris to bed. We barely got Kale to sit still long enough to eat her carrots, and now she was in the kitchen supposedly helping Cham make tea for our guests. I popped the last bite of asparagus in my mouth and started gathering dishes.

"Let's see." Ephraim pushed back from the table. "Adlai and Penniah almost always bring their kids, Dathan and Sapphira. Devin and Paul come, and sometimes their mother, Seta. Sometimes others."

"What about Sun?" I was curious about the quiet, brooding cook.

"Oh no, Sun would never come to a Story Night. He has . . ." Ephraim tapped two fingers on the table, "unprocessed feelings about the Family."

"Make sure you talk to Penniah about your cough, Ephraim." V walked through the dining room toward the living room. From the window she yelled, "They're here! Would someone let them in?" before she disappeared upstairs without answering the door.

Adlai and Penniah turned out to be the sweet but tired parents of ten-year-old Dathan and eight-year-old Sapphira, who immediately turned the living room into a gymnastics exhibition full of headstands and cartwheels. Devin and Paul showed up a few minutes later, and Devin jumped into the show, holding Sapphira in the air by her ankles while she wriggled around telling everyone she was doing a levitating headstand. Paul grabbed a guitar and started making up a song with the chorus "Levitating headstand," and Story Night was under way.

People filed into the room, selecting instruments from the music box and joining in on the jam session. After a medical consultation with Penniah, who turned out to be a nurse, Ephraim brought his ukulele out and played beautifully along with Paul. Cham joined in on harmonica, while Devin played a hand drum. I found a wood flute, a poorer version of the one on the Farm. Europa, V, and Io were the last to join in, all coming down the stairs together.

V was now wearing a loose-fitting black dress that fell to her knees, with thin straps over her shoulders. Her hair was no longer in a ponytail, but swinging down her back in gentle curls. I wasn't the only one who noticed. I caught Devin absentmindedly beating his hand drum while his eyes followed her.

Our little jam continued for five minutes, with family members periodically returning to the chorus, "Levitating headstand, oh sweet levitating headstand." It was the first time since leaving the Farm that I felt the anxiety and sadness, expectation and disappointment, drain away. For a few minutes, I was taken away by the music. Indus never galloped through my thoughts.

Ephraim raised his hands to welcome a crescendo, and everyone started playing harder and singing louder until he swept his hand to the side, and we finished our song with a flourish, laughing and complimenting one another. The same magic seemed to work on us all. Cham looked the happiest I had seen him, and the little kids could hardly calm down. Kale continued dancing long after the music ended.

"Thank you for coming together tonight, Family," Ephraim said when we were quiet.

"We'll have some songs and stories and poems, but first, I want to honor the newest member of Beacon House. She spent her whole life on the Farm and got her Calling to come join us. Welcome, Starbird."

A bunch of voices said, "Yes" and "Welcome, Starbird." I wasn't expecting it. Hot tears jumped into my eyes, and

I realized how good it felt to be welcomed and safe in this strange place.

"Starbird, will you start us off with a story?" Ephraim strummed a few times on his ukulele.

I had been telling stories my whole life, practically from the time I could talk. On Story Night, anything could be a story—something that had just happened, something that happened years ago, something significant or mundane. There were no rules, and yet I drew a blank. I must have seemed lost because eight-year-old Sapphira stood up and said, "Tell it about EARTH."

Penniah hugged her daughter around the middle. "She's been very curious about him lately. She was five when he left for the Mission, so she doesn't remember much about him."

"Great idea." Ephraim strummed again. "Tell a story about EARTH."

The living room got quiet. Even Kale stopped dancing and sat down on the rug to face me. I looked at Sapphira, enthusiastic at eight years old. My mind wandered back through time and settled on a day when I was a few years older than her.

"One time EARTH let me sit next to him during a Translation," I said.

Sapphira's eye doubled in size. She sank down on the floor and crossed her legs.

"We were all in the Sanctuary waiting for the Translation to begin. We had been seated for twenty minutes, but EARTH still hadn't appeared. I was next to my mother, and my brother was seated on the platform, looking fidgety. He was EARTH's apprentice," I explained. Sapphira gasped and put a hand over her mouth.

"I suddenly realized that I hadn't gone to the outhouse after brunch, and I knew I wouldn't be able to hold it all the way through. So Fern told me to run to the main house since it was closer than the yurt village.

"I ran up the gravel drive and tried to get into the bathroom on the first floor, but the door was locked. So I used the one upstairs. When I came out, the door to EARTH's bedroom was open, and EARTH was sitting there on the floor, staring out an open window.

"When EARTH noticed me standing at his door, he nearly jumped. 'You startled me,' he said, then he snapped his fingers. 'Seeing you just reminded me that I'm expected at the Translation. Did they send you to get me? I was just watching the storm clouds move in from the west. The Cosmos is sending us rain.' Looking out over the back lot, I could see a bank of slate-colored clouds rolling in.

"EARTH stood and adjusted his robes. 'Mars Wolf is feeling ill,' he said. 'Could you be my Mars Wolf today, Starbird?' My joy could have scared away the clouds.

"EARTH and I walked to the Sanctuary together, and he let me enter before him through the north door. My brother's mouth fell open when he saw me walk onto the platform. I sat on the right side of EARTH, while Doug sat on the left, all the way through the Translation."

"Wow," said Sapphira, looking up at her mom again.

"Lovely story," said Penniah.

"Big honor for a girl who couldn't remember to use the bathroom before Translation," said Europa.

"EARTH recognized something great in you," said Ephraim.

"I don't get it," said Dathan. "How could he just forget that everyone was waiting for him? That doesn't make any sense."

Everyone looked at me and I looked down. I had purposely left out part of the story because it was private, a secret between me and EARTH. EARTH's door wasn't really standing open when I came out of the bathroom that day. It was just cracked a bit and there was a skunky smoke drifting out into the hall. I had walked to EARTH's door, pushed it open, and said, "Is something on fire?"

EARTH had turned his head to me suddenly, a short, thin cigarette burning in his hand. He exhaled a cloud of smoke through the window.

"Starbird," EARTH had said. "Come in here a minute. Seeing you just reminded me that I'm expected at the Translation. Did they send you to get me?"

I shook my head. "Bathroom," I said.

EARTH motioned me in to sit on the cushion in front

of him. "Do you know what this is?" He held up the cigarette.

I shook my head again.

"It's called marijuana. It can get you high, so you feel"—he paused and looked out the window—"clear. Sometimes I smoke it when I need to get some clarity. Do you understand?"

I nodded, but I didn't understand.

"The Family in Canada introduced me to it. They use it together as part of the Translations. It's good for them, they need it. But it isn't right for the Seattle Farm. We have too many people here who drank or did other things on the Outside, before they knew how to use it properly, and they had problems with it. Does that make sense?"

I nodded again. EARTH's eyes were bluer than the tapestries hanging on his walls. They were the color of icebergs, but the whites of his eyes were bloodshot.

"So I need for you to keep this"—he held up the cigarette again—"a secret between us, okay?"

I nodded.

He stood and adjusted his robes. "Mars Wolf is feeling ill," he said. "Could you be my Mars Wolf today?"

Then we walked downstairs and I heard the sound of Mars Wolf getting sick in the bathroom. I couldn't tell that part on Story Night.

I cleared my throat and looked at Dathan. "He didn't

exactly forget. He was watching the storm clouds come in, and the Cosmos started speaking to him," I said.

Dathan nodded but he didn't look convinced.

"I want to meet your brother," said Sapphira. "Can I meet him?"

"No," I said, my throat suddenly dry. "I don't know where he is."

"Hey. I've been working on a Woody Guthrie song," said Ephraim from his reclining chair. "I need you to let me know what you think."

"From my window, sad and lonely . . ." Ephraim started crooning along to his ukulele, and soon we were all absorbed in the song.

The rest of our Story Night contained more songs and stories. Io read a poem she had written, and Devin and Paul sang a perfect duet. Venus didn't stay at Beacon House that night but went home with Devin. I climbed the stairs to bed, wishing it was a moonlit night and that I was walking to the yurt village, wishing Indus were holding my hand.

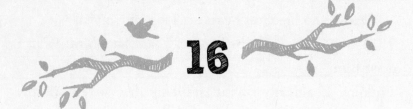

16

The schedule that Ms. Harper emailed looked like this:

Period 1	Social Studies	room 218
Period 2	Precalculus	room 312
	Lunch	cafeteria
Period 3	Chemistry	room 112
Period 4	American Literature	room 324
Period 5	Spanish	room 204
Period 6	Horticulture	greenhouse

Every junior gets one elective per semester, so I chose horticulture for period six. Apparently, there was a greenhouse on the top of the building, and it seemed like a great opportunity to be around growing things again.

I trailed Cham to the bus stop. For my real first day at school, Io had suggested the plaid wool shirt, a white T-shirt with a lamb on it, gray tights, and my boots. Over it all, I wore one of my bulky wool sweaters from the Farm.

I was willing to wear some nicer clothes for school, but I didn't want to just look like an Outsider.

Still, I was on the Outside and, so far, it didn't seem that great to me. This was what Doug ran away to? As we passed houses and apartment buildings, I found myself thinking, *Could Doug be in one of those houses?* I tried to peer through the glass, looking for people inside. *Would I recognize him? Would he recognize me? Should I even be trying to look?*

"Bus is here." Cham jogged the last few feet to the stop.

We swiped our cards and grabbed seats near the back. Cham slouched down and put his knees on the back of the seat in front of us.

"Do you like Roosevelt?" I asked.

"Sure." Cham didn't look at me much when we were together. This time he stared out the window.

"Did you grow up in Beacon House?"

"Born there, left for a while. Ephraim's my dad."

Usually only younger kids on the Farm would have said something like that. Ursa knows Adam is her father, and Pavo knows Firmament is his dad. After Adam and Eve had Badger, the Planet Elders realized that people in the second and third generations might become parents and would need to know if they were closely related. Fatherhood became a big issue when people started leaving the farm, too. Birth mothers wanted to keep their children with them, which was horrible for fathers if the birth mother wanted to leave the Farm, or if the father did. Some non-Believers stayed in the Family because of their kids, which I thought was wrong. Having non-Believers in our Family stole harmony from the collective.

"Dad joined. Mom didn't." Cham pulled his right hand out of his pocket and chewed the edge of his fingernail as he talked.

I felt a bizarre jolt of jealousy. Even though Cham's mother wasn't around, Cham knew who his father was. I thought about Iron and my chest got red. "Ephraim says you're a true Believer."

"I don't advertise it." He shoved his hand back in his pocket. "You going to let them call you Starbird at school?"

"That's my name."

"Up to you," Cham said as the bus pulled up to our stop. Then he added, "Just don't tell them where you're from," before climbing out through the rear door.

My first full day at Roosevelt, I felt like part of a strange school of fish, all darting into the massive building and down the halls in flashes of dazzling color. Even on our biggest Summer Solstice Festival before EARTH left, I hadn't been around so many people at once. V had given me a few notebooks and binders that she found in the basement at Beacon House and an old army bag to hold my books. I clutched a binder to my chest and made my way into the school.

Cham pointed me in the general direction of my first class. I held the plastic binder so hard my hands were sweating as I walked up the stairs and down the giant hallway, looking at the number above every door. My legs felt weak from being in such a large, noisy place, and I was tempted to run back outside just for the comfort of seeing grass. I had located the right corridor when a horrible buzzing sound, worse than my alarm clock, filled the air. I looked around and saw that the halls were suddenly empty, where a minute ago they were frantic with youth. With a little more searching, I found my classroom number and opened the heavy door.

Every person in every chair turned to stare at me. I smiled. No one smiled back. They wore the blankest expressions I had ever seen. I would have gotten more response from the chickens. I could feel the red splotches start to blossom on my neck where no T-shirt could hide them. I held the plastic binder higher on my chest so it nearly reached my chin.

A voice filled the room. It said, "Please rise." I looked behind and around me. I looked at the teacher standing in front of the class who put one hand on his chest. The students got out of their chairs and mimicked his gesture. Following along with the amplified voice, they began a strange, emotionless chanting. "I pledge allegiance," they said together, "to the flag. Of the United. States. Of America."

I stepped back against the door. This is what Europa was talking about. This is how they are indoctrinated and brainwashed. The students looked forward with dead eyes, mumbling the words as if they were sleepwalking or hypnotized. *I can't let this happen to me.* I felt around behind me for the knob on the door and turned until it opened, releasing me back into the hall. The amplified voice was there too. "And to the Republic. For which it stands."

I had taken three steps toward the stairs when a man's voice said, "Wait."

It was the teacher, standing at the door to the class. The loudspeaker continued, "With liberty and justice for all."

"You found the right classroom," he said. "We're expecting you."

I didn't move, but stood there gripping my binder.

"Come on," he motioned, "come join us." The man had a thick brown beard that needed trimming. He was wearing a wrinkled brown shirt with khaki pants. His smile was warm. Something about him reminded me of a Family member. He motioned to me again.

I walked back reluctantly. *I'm not staying here*, I told myself. *I'm going home soon.*

"Welcome," said the teacher once we were back inside the classroom. He motioned to an empty chair. "It's okay that you're late. I know you're a new student."

As I slid into the chair, he shuffled through his papers on a podium.

"I'm Mr. Bell, but you can call me Teacher Ted, everyone else does. And you are . . ." He ran his finger down a paper. "Murphy. Star . . . Star Bird?"

A boy sitting behind me laughed. Two girls leaned together and whispered.

"Yeah, Starbird." I felt annoyed to hear the name Murphy attached to mine. It was like the Outsiders were forcing a dad on me.

"Well." Teacher Ted looked up from his podium. "What a . . . refreshing name." He stared at me for a moment. "I like it, Starbird. Welcome. You're a transfer student, so where are you joining us from?"

I thought about what Cham had said at the bus stop. "Bellingham."

Teacher Ted turned back to the class. "Okay, everybody, today we're talking about the French and Indian War."

Of course my first history class starts with a war.

The same "Let's welcome our new student" scene played out in my next class, precalculus, except there was no creepy group chanting, and the teacher did not invite me to call her by her first name and did not call mine refreshing. Also, I was there for roll call, so I heard the other students' names. They were things like Kevin, John, Julia, and Allison. They weren't named after animals or comets. Their names didn't represent anything other than names. I was starting to understand why Cham asked me if I would use Starbird. Maybe there was a good reason Cham didn't go by Chameleon and V didn't go by Venus.

The clock said nine thirty, and a smell came to my mind. You know how every hour of the day has its own smell? If it's a sunny day, especially after several days of rain, nine thirty smells like a tree waking up and like wet moss. Eleven smells like cucumber and mushrooms. Six in the morning just smells like chickens. This nine thirty smelled stale, like chalk-coated rulers. I got a surge of panic. It reminded me of the feeling you get when you're far from home at dusk, and you realize you didn't bring a flashlight. Why was I sitting in a math class? I was supposed to be on the Farm. I reached into my backpack and found the laminated edge of the crisis pass. I held on to it, debating with myself about taking it out. Then I remembered Lyra with Indus that night in the barn. I let go of the pass again. *I can go back tomorrow if I want.*

We did a worksheet and had to exchange them with our neighbor for correcting. I gave mine to a boy sitting next to me name whose name was Ben. I tried to associate it with something so I could remember it. It sounded like *den*, a home for a cougar or wolf. He was tall and painfully skinny with dark hair and glasses, and he had large hands that seemed too big for his body.

When he gave me my paper back, he had drawn a picture in the margin. It was a dark bird with a wingspan wide enough to flap into my math work, and behind it, graphite stars were winking against a loose-leaf sky. He stole a sideways glance at me as I looked at it, and then bent over his desk farther so his hair fell over his glasses.

By lunchtime, I had a list of questions in my head to ask Cham.

1. Why do people raise their right hands to say something?
2. What is a nerd?
3. How many other schools like this one are there?
4. How can a person possibly do this much homework?

After stopping by my locker, I followed the thickest group of fish toward the noisy, tiled box called the cafeteria, foolishly thinking Cham would be easy to spot. All around me were people. Standing bored or running, hitting one another or making out, whispering together in a cluster or sitting alone looking sad. It reminded me of the way the chickens acted when there were too many crowded into the tiny coop.

And I couldn't believe the stuff they had. People

walked by with bright white sneakers and leather back-packs. They wore sparkly earrings and space-age watches and had teeny, tiny phones. At the edges of the room kids were grouped around electrical outlets, each connected to the wall with their own wire like an umbilical cord. What were they all looking at on those bright screens?

"Come here, you bitch. I am gonna stab you!"

From behind me, a girl ran into the lunchroom. She grabbed another girl by the wrist and spun her around before drawing back her hand with a plastic fork in it. "I cannot believe you bought that jacket before me!"

"I know you're jealous," the other girl said, grabbing her lapels and pouting her lips.

"I'm gonna kill you, you nasty whore!"

Then the girl with the fork put her arm around the other girl's shoulder, and they walked toward the soda ma-chines together.

"Over here." Cham was suddenly in front of me, mo-tioning to a table.

"Peter and Jeff," Cham said, pointing to the boys sit-ting there. He didn't tell them my name, so I said, "Star-bird," and caught myself before putting my hands together in prayer position.

"Cham, did you see that kid Fred in first period? That guy's such a loser," Jeff said.

"Everything that guy says makes me want to punch him in the face," said Peter.

I thought I saw Cham steal a lightning glance at me before saying, "Yeah. Totally."

The rest of the day went like this. "Yes, Starbird. Like star [point to the sky] and bird [flap hands like wings]. Starbird." At least sixth period was held at the top of a spiral staircase above the science wing in the greenhouse. The warm, wet air and the smell of dirt brought me back to myself, to thoughts of the Farm, thoughts of Indus. I was thinking about him when the final bell of the day rang, releasing me back into the ocean full of fish.

17

The next morning, I packed my canvas wood-carrying bag in dark and silence so I wouldn't wake Io. I considered taking the clothes she bought me back to the Farm, but it just didn't seem right. I left them folded on the bed with a piece of paper that said, *Thanks.*

I figured I would catch Ephraim downstairs having breakfast before his pickup, and I could just have him say good-bye to everyone for me. I hadn't mentioned it at dinner the night before because I didn't want anyone to try and talk me out of it. I tiptoed down the stairs and found the kitchen dark and Cham standing in the foyer.

"I'm not going to school with you," Cham said, putting his shoes on by the door. "I'm doing the Farm run."

"Why not Ephraim?"

"Too sick."

"I'm going with you."

"No, you're not."

"Yes, I am."

"There's no room." .

"V said I could go back with you, and so did Ephraim." I gripped my canvas bag.

"There is literally no room. I have to return machinery that we borrowed during the café remodel. It's already packed."

"I'll sit in the refrigerated section."

"I'm saying it's all full. You should have told someone you wanted to go."

"I did tell someone I wanted to go!"

"Sorry." Cham shrugged and grabbed the keys off the hook in the hall. "Ephraim's going again Saturday. You can bail on your new life then."

"I'm not bailing! This stupid job isn't my Calling."

"Tell me about it," said Cham, closing the front door behind him as he left.

Venus came down the stairs holding Eris. "Was that Cham leaving?" she said. "I wanted to remind him to get the check from Ephraim."

"You said I could go." I dropped my bag on the floor. "You promised. There wasn't any room."

"When you didn't mention it last night, I thought you changed your mind." V adjusted Eris on her hip.

"I didn't. I didn't change my mind."

"I'm so sorry." V started bouncing Eris. "There is too

much to keep track of. Ephraim's going again on Saturday." Eris started chewing his hand and whining. "He's going to melt down if I don't feed him," she said, walking toward the kitchen.

"Well, I don't want to go to school today," I said.

"You really have to. You just enrolled, and if you don't attend, then your counselor is going to call me and start asking questions and get curious about you. I'm sorry, Star, but as long as you are here, you have to go to school."

"Cham's not going."

"Cham's a senior."

"I hate that place," I said. "The Outsiders are just trying to get me to be like them, and I didn't do my homework."

Eris started kicking and let out an angry squeal. "EARTH would want you to go," said V, before disappearing through the swinging door.

A miserable rain fell on my head as I stomped all the way to the bus. I couldn't believe I had followed some crazy fake Calling because I was mad at Iron and Fern and jealous about Indus. I screwed up. I screwed everything up. What if Indus was in love with Lyra by the time I got back? What if I was too late? Right then, I would have given anything to be in the henhouse collecting eggs.

I had made a hasty change after talking to V and dressed for school in a green sweater and the orange skirt.

It might not have been the most attractive color combination. Going to Roosevelt without Cham wasn't a mortifying loss, since he hadn't been a stellar guide through my first day. But at least he was someone familiar. Everything else was so painfully foreign.

In first period, Teacher Ted had us discuss the homework reading I hadn't done on the French and Indian War, and then we looked at color-coded maps of North America to see where the British and French were fighting over land.

In second period, I sat next to Ben-rhymes-with-den, and when we were instructed to exchange and check each other's homework, I switched with him again. I had spent my morning bus ride on a sloppy version of the worksheet and was pleasantly surprised when he handed it back with nine correct answers out of ten. I was also pleased to see another drawing. This time it was a cardinal sitting in the branch of a tree with its beak open and a line of tiny, five-point stars sprouting from its mouth like a song. The tree's branches extended all the way up the page to cradle my name, and the roots stretched to the bottom.

I looked at him again. His skin was pale, and his glasses sat too far down on his nose. He looked like an under-ripe tomato that had grown in too much shade. From his skinny arms, I could tell he had never lifted a hay bale or pushed a wheelbarrow. He wouldn't last an hour working the harvest. I might have stared too long, because he had to reach over to my desk to get his own homework back with ten out of ten marked correct.

After morning classes, I got my lunch from my locker and started toward the cafeteria. That's when I felt a hand on my shoulder.

"Hold up. You don't even know me and you can't keep my name out of your mouth? I didn't sleep with him, and if I did, you wouldn't need to be talking about it because it's my business, not your business!" A girl with hot-pink lipstick and a deep tan poked a nail into my shoulder.

"Not that one," another girl with long black hair said, grabbing the tan one. "It was her!" She pointed to a girl standing by her locker with her thumbs on her phone.

"Oh," the first girl said, looking me up and down. Then she swung around toward the girl at her locker and said, "*You're* the bitch who needs to stop gossiping."

The two girls who had just surrounded me now closed in on the girl using her phone. She looked up at them like a cornered barn cat. I couldn't handle it anymore.

Instead of going to the cafeteria, I took a left and exited toward the back of the school where the oval football field and the tennis courts were planted in a large, otherwise empty field. A man on a riding mower was working his way in wide, sloping rectangles through the grass. The rain had let up, but a thick fog was clinging to the evergreens edging the field, and my boots were wet within a minute. I pulled my scarf up around my neck and closed my eyes, heading out toward the center of the grounds.

I inhaled the wet air, the pine from the trees, tried to pretend I was at the Farm again. But the Farm never smelled like cut grass, and even out here I could still hear those awful buzzing signals in the building. I started to eat the veggie sandwich V had packed for me as I walked. Back home I would have been eating a hot lunch that Fern made and sitting around the farm table. A sudden tear rolled down my cheek and all the strength left my body. I collapsed into the grass, ignoring the wet as it seeped through my tights and skirt, all the way to my skin. I lay in the grass and cried.

My tears managed to make me late for third period, where I got a verbal warning from Ms. Weaver and a headache from crying. *Go ahead, give me detention. I won't be here to serve it.* I could sense kids staring at my wet back. What did Outsiders know about lying in the wet grass when you're sad? What's weird about that?

At the final bell, I dragged myself back to the heavy door of Teacher Ted's room for my first history club meeting. I was only going because V said I had to do it for the Family, that EARTH would have wanted me to. When I got back to the Farm, this would be a bizarre and distant memory.

The atmosphere was a real change from first period.

"Who wants popcorn?" Teacher Ted asked as I entered. He was plugging in an air popper next to an electric tea-kettle. "Starbird, pick out a flavor of tea."

There were five other students in the room, two sitting on top of their desks instead of in the chairs, and one perched on the windowsill with headphones on. I chose peppermint and Teacher Ted got me a mug. Then he had us put our desks in a circle.

"Let's start with names since we have a new club member today."

"Rory," said a girl with long brown hair, black makeup around her eyes, and two hands covered in silver rings. She was slumped over in her chair to my right in the circle. I recognized her from my horticulture class. Next was Kevin, who took out his earbuds to say his name. Then Jake and Danny, who had been sitting on the desks and seemed to be friends already, and finally Alex, who didn't make eye contact with anyone in the room and hit himself in the arm several times before telling us his name.

"Are you okay?" I asked him, but Teacher Ted caught my eye and subtly shook his head, so I didn't press the question.

Ted reiterated his name and then it was my turn. "Starbird," I mumbled.

"Your name is Starbird?" Rory watched me through thick eyeliner.

"Hippie parents," I said.

"I'll review the club setup for Starbird." Ted saved me from further questions. "We use the inquiry method of learning, meaning you guys are more likely to learn if you are curious. Everyone writes a question for the day, anything you want to know some history about. It can be something that's been on your mind for a while, or something you cook up right now, for a class or for yourself. Your only job is to be curious."

Ted handed a stack of index cards to Alex, who took one and passed the rest. Rory, Jake, and Danny started writing immediately. Kevin and Alex sat staring into space until Teacher Ted said, "Any question will do." The popcorn was passed.

I had no shortage of questions. If I could really ask anything, like Ted said, I would ask, *Did I do the wrong thing by coming to Seattle? How will Indus act when I get back to the Farm? When is EARTH coming home?* If it could be anything, I would ask, *Where is Doug Fir?* None of my real questions seemed appropriate. I scratched something down and handed Ted my card.

"'How many witches were burned in Salem?'" Ted read from the first card. "I'm guessing that's from Rory, our expert on the occult." Rory was chewing her pinkie nail. She took it out of her mouth and waved at Ted. "Great for research. Let's avoid some sensationalism and say, 'How many people were *accused* of witchcraft in Salem and burned?' The answer might be surprising."

Rory nodded and wrote something in her notebook.

"Next question: 'What is trench foot?'" Ted read. "That's got to be one of my war guys, Danny or Jake. I'm guessing Danny. Soldiers in most wars of record have suffered from trench foot. Great topic."

"How was LSD invented?" Teacher Ted raised an eyebrow at the next card. "I'm guessing that was Kevin. An interesting answer, I'm sure."

"Who killed JFK? Well, Jake, this might take a year of research instead of a day, but let us know what you find. Alex, I'll work with you on your question later because this one isn't school appropriate, so last question from Starbird. . . . What is homesteading?" Ted looked up and studied me. "Great question.

"Grab a computer. You have fifteen minutes to research and report back. Write down the facts so you don't forget them. Curiosity may have killed the cat, but it also made her life more interesting."

Everyone headed toward the bank of computers located at the back of the room, so I followed, with no idea what to do with one once I got there. I had used the Internet for the first time two days before. Luckily, Ted said, "Mind if I join your research team today?"

By the end of history club, I had done a Web search, visited four sites, and learned that homesteading was a program of the U.S. federal government that gave away land in the western states to white settlers regardless of what tribes were living there. Individuals could claim, or "prove up," a certain number of acres as long as they lived on the property and had a working farm or cattle ranch. *Ownership is an interesting concept.*

Rory learned that no suspected witches were burned at the stake during the witch hunts in Salem. Instead, most of them were hanged.

18

When I finally got home from school, I was starving and didn't hear anyone in the house. *Ephraim's probably asleep in the attic,* I thought, *and Cham is probably finishing his run.* Europa had the café shift, so Eris and Kale had to be with someone. I looked through the first floor and then climbed the stairs to the second. V's door stood open, and I could hear Kale's little voice babbling happily away inside. I looked through the doorway to see Eris sleeping on a mat on the floor, Kale sitting in front of a pile of perilously stacked blocks, and V on the bed collapsed onto Io's lap with tears streaming down her face.

"What's wrong?"

V gasped and sat up. "Hey." She said, wiping the tears on her palms.

"We didn't hear you come in," said Io.

"How was history club?" V stood up and sifted through a drawer until she found a cloth handkerchief.

"Why are you crying?" I asked. Kale ran over to me, so I picked her up.

"I have this issue with worrying. I get started and I can't stop, but I'll be fine. How are you?" V sat back down on her bed, and Io put an arm over her shoulder. As V wiped the handkerchief across her eyes, her eyeliner came with it, smearing black marks along her cheeks.

I put Kale back down in front of her blocks and started playing with them, too, helping her build the tower a little higher. "What are you worried about?"

"Nothing that you need to be upset about," said V, sniffing.

"I disagree," said Io. "She's part of the Family, too. Why do you act like you have to take all this onto yourself?"

"She wants to go back to the Farm, and she's only sixteen," V said back. "She should just be a kid."

"I'm not a kid," I said.

"Well, you should be," said V.

"I'm not even sure we're talking about Starbird anymore," said Io.

"Ugh." V dropped her hands into her lap and fell back onto the bed. "Okay, my mother's dead and my father's crazy. Can we psychoanalyze me some other time, please?"

"I'm not trying to be mean." Io grabbed one of V's hands. "You know that."

They exchanged a few whispered words too quiet for

me to hear, and then V sat up again. Kale kept handing me a block and then taking it away from me.

"The restaurant is failing," Io said.

"Don't be dramatic." V sniffed and rubbed her temples. "We just have bill trouble. I opened the café mail for Ephraim today, because he refuses to rest and I thought I could stop him from coming into work if I took care of it, and most of the bills were final notices. We barely have enough money to cover payroll. I had a feeling things were bad, but Ephraim was hiding it." V flopped down on her bed again and threw up her hands. "Gamma's no help. I called her and she said that it isn't my job to open mail."

Just then, Kale's tower collapsed, sending blocks across the floor and waking up Eris, who immediately started crying.

"Damn it," said V, standing up and getting the baby to bounce him on her hip.

"But the café's so busy," I said, collecting Kale's blocks, "especially weekends."

"I know. I have no idea what's happening with the books. Ephraim is the only person who touches them." V walked over to the window and kept bouncing Eris. "I'm going to go see if he needs his diaper changed. Please forget I said anything. It will just get me in deeper shit with Ephraim."

When V left the room, Io scooted off the bed to sit with Kale and me. "She's only twenty-seven." Io shook her

head. "She shouldn't have all of this on her." Io placed another block on Kale's fledgling tower. "Anyway, happier
topics. How's school? Any boys?" Io lay down on her side,
resting her head on one palm.

I wanted to tell Io that school was noisy, crowded,
confusing, cruel, and hard. But I felt selfish saying that
with everything V was going through. "There's a guy who
draws pictures on my paper in math class," I said instead.

"Ooh, an artist." Io sighed. "I have a weakness for art-
ists. You should flirt with him."

"Flirt with him?" I wasn't sure I knew the definition
of the phrase. I also wasn't sure I had the stomach to flirt
with anyone. I looked down at the block in my hand and
didn't build with it.

"Still thinking about Farm guy?"

I nodded. "I might go back. I think I'm going to . . . go
back."

Io sat up. "You just got here."

"Maybe I belong there. I'm really a farm girl." I heard
Fern Moon's words in my mouth.

"How can you know who you are yet?" Io grabbed my
arm a bit too forcefully. Kale stared at us. "It's always hard
starting something new."

"I'm just thinking." I tried to pull my arm free.

Io looked down at her hand and let go. "Sorry. I just got
super intense on you." She lay back down on her side and
added another block to the tower.

"Maybe you can figure out a way to see Farm guy without going back to the Farm. Maybe if he saw you in this environment, with your new hair and clothes . . . We need to create a reason for him to come here."

I remembered the way Indus had described V as "really Seattle." Maybe I was "Seattle" now, more worldly like Lyra Hay.

"But in the meantime, you should still flirt with the boy who draws you pictures. You've got to practice, right?"

Io, Kale, and I built the block tower three more times, knowing each time we built it that it was going to fall.

Cham got home from his delivery around six. V's mood had lightened, and V, Io, and I were in all in the kitchen with the kids making burritos for dinner. Ephraim was still in bed and had been sleeping all day, so Io was making him soup, while Kale stood on a chair helping Venus scrub vegetables. I chopped onion and garlic.

"Iron said to tell you that the holes are patched in the ceiling of the coop," Cham announced as soon as he walked in from the foyer.

I clutched the knife like a weapon. "What?"

"And Fern Moon says that she wants you to come home for the apple pressing next weekend, and that little chicken coop girl said she wants to come visit you in Seattle." Cham opened the door to the refrigerator.

Suddenly, I missed the Farm enough to cry. "Did anyone else say anything?"

"A bunch of people said to say hi."

"Who specifically?"

"I don't know, like . . . everyone." Cham waved an arm that wasn't holding a carton of orange juice.

"Could you try to remember names of your own Family members, Cham?" Io snapped.

"Why do I have to do everything?" Cham half yelled, causing V to throw the vegetable brush she was holding hard into the sink.

"Yeah, you really have to do *everything* around here, don't you Cham? I'm so sorry you're the one who has to work so hard!" she yelled back.

And then everyone seemed to be talking at once. Cham was yelling at V and Io was trying to get Cham and V to stop yelling at each other by yelling herself, and then Kale fell off the stool she was standing on and started howling until V picked her up and took her upstairs.

I never did find out if Indus asked about me, or if he even told Cham to tell me hello.

Something was wrong with the plant. It was sitting on a stand to my left, next to the door of my precalculus classroom, and as far away from the bank of windows as it could get. Why would someone put a plant that far from the window? It didn't look yellow or dry, it just looked wrong.

The buzzer hadn't sounded yet, so I slipped out of my chair and walked over to it, snaking a finger into the pot to see if the soil was damp. Here's the thing—the soil wasn't damp, because there wasn't any *soil*! The plant wasn't a plant. It was some waxy, brittle imitation made to look like a pothos. Pothos is the easiest plant to grow. I turned to look at my math teacher, standing at her podium and scanning papers. What kind of maniac would have a fake plant?

I was still there next to the door staring at my teacher, holding a plastic leaf in my hand, when dark-haired Ben walked in. I let the leaf go.

Ben. Hen. Glen. The name had no other meaning than the sound it made starting in my mouth and moving down into my throat. *Ben. Pen. Margin.*

He sat next to me in the same spot as before. After the buzzer, we exchanged homework. I only got seven right out of ten because the homework included word problems instead of just numbers. For me, working with numbers is like making art. For a while, the Family had a pottery kiln and we sold ceramic tableware at a stand on the side of the road. Like most of our businesses, it failed, but it was interesting to see which Family members took to the craft. At first, clay feels foreign and unwieldy, especially when you use the wheel for the first time and watch bowl after bowl flop into a sloppy lump. But after a while, you gain an understanding of the medium, and the clay starts to speak to you, telling you how to manipulate it. That's how numbers feel for me. I can shape them and bend them and sometimes make them into something beautiful.

Ben got ten correct out of ten. He drew a flock of geese flying in front of a harvest moon with a tiny star beside it, and this time the drawing included a note. It said, *I know the secret to word problems.*

A tiny electric jolt rippled up my arm. I considered Io's advice. Unfortunately, I didn't have much practice at flirting, so I just awkwardly smiled with half of my face.

During class, I stole glances at him. Ben was definitely skinny. His arms sprouted from his T-shirt like stalks that had grown too quickly, plenty of water but not enough sun. The fingers that gripped his pencil were bony and ungraceful. There was even something strange about the way his back leaned against his chair, as if it was twisted to the right, instead of straight up and down. If there were a math equation comparing Ben to Indus, it would be an easy answer. Indus was the greater sum.

The buzzer signaled my heart to pound. Time to flirt. "So, what's your secret?" I said, sliding out of my chair and grabbing my army book bag.

When Ben stood up, he was taller than I was by several inches, but still shorter than Indus.

"You have to get the words out of the way first." He started walking toward the door, so I followed. He wasn't looking at me when he walked, as if the floor had asked the question instead of me. "Think of it as a translation. Put all the words into numbers first, make an equation out of the problem, and then solve the equation. The mistake most people make is getting caught up in the words."

"You're good at this," I said, so very stupidly.

"My dad's an accountant." He shrugged. "I work in his business every summer. It's not what I'm into."

"What are you into?"

If our math class had been in probability, I might have known the actual chances that Cham would choose that moment to show the slightest interest in my well-being.

"Lunch?" he said to me blankly, suddenly appearing in front of me in the hall.

"Later." Ben gave a half wave and walked off.

"Yeah, lunch," I mumbled back to Cham.

The lunchtime conversation with Cham and his friends included some online video game that is *rad*, a new skate park in West Seattle that is *dope*, and a song that just came out and is *filthy*. I wanted to participate in the conversation, but I didn't know about any of the things they were talking about, and I didn't know any of their words. I just ate my leftover burrito and listened, but found myself looking around the cafeteria for Ben.

I wasn't sure why I was so interested. Ben wasn't what you would call my type. Plus, Ben was an Outsider. It's not like I was going to invite him over for a Story Night. *Ben, meet my Family of one hundred people. Any one of these men might be my father.*

Plus, he had to be corrupted by the Outside, its capitalism and greed. He was born into it. It's like Europa said: Outsiders would only contaminate me. *I'm just practicing flirting*, I reminded myself, and kept looking for Ben.

The rest of the day went well until horticulture, when two girls approached me in the greenhouse. A northwest rain was drizzling itself all over the glass with a quiet tapping, and the room was moist enough to soak the instructions for growing a new plant from a start. I could have forced a start twenty times before the sun came up on the Farm. In the class, we sat on stools along worktables that lined the walls, listening to long-winded instructions before we could put on our gloves. I was bent over my own nepenthe flower, preparing to cut.

"Why's your name Starbird?" one of the girls asked, leaning onto my worktable with a pair of open shears in her hands. She had perfectly curled hair and careful makeup, the same as the girl who stood behind her listening.

Rory with the silver rings from history club was sitting on a stool nearby. She looked up from her flower.

"Um, I don't know," I lied. My name is Starbird because EARTH Translated it for me during my solstice naming ceremony. It calls upon my cosmic guide and my earthly guide to watch over me during my life in a body.

"But, I mean, like, are your parents hippies, or did you, like, grow up in a cult?"

My shoulders tensed and my lips pressed together. The red splotches on my chest came suddenly and hot, creeping up toward my neck and jaw. *Cult* is a familiar insult to the Family. The Bellingham newspaper had referred to us as a cult. People in the town where we traded said it. Even people driving by the Farm had been known to yell the word at our roadside stands. EARTH said that it's language used by Outsiders as a method of testing our spiritual faith and devaluing our commitment as a family.

Insulting us is one of the ways Outside society tries to hammer us into the shape of them.

"I don't want to talk to you," I said.

"She doesn't want to talk to us," the second girl mimicked.

"Whatever." The first girl's shears snapped together. "Everyone's saying it. You should be glad I asked you to your face." They both walked away.

When the final bell rang, I couldn't wait to go to work at the café, where no one would inspect me like a precious stone, or avoid me like a poisonous plant. I took the bus there with my work clothes in a bag. Sun and Devin were behind the counter when I walked in.

"Winged creature of a tiny sun," Devin greeted me, raising a spatula. Sun had both hands in a mixing bowl. He nodded.

I waved and walked through the beaded curtain to the office, where I found Felicia sitting at Ephraim's desk. She didn't look at me but held up one manicured pointer finger in my direction. "Seventeen, eighteen, nineteen, twenty. V can't make it tonight, so I have to show you how to start your shift."

"Um, okay." Would this day ever stop getting worse?

"I counted the drawer for you, and now you need to recount it while I check on my tables. It should be two hundred."

By the time she came back, I had counted it twice. "There was an extra dime."

Her red lipstick exaggerated her frown. She took a brown bag with a zipper from the safe behind her. "Change the paperwork," she said before leaving again.

The form inside the bag looked pretty clear. At the end of a shift, you count everything in the register by amount: pennies, nickels, dimes, etc., and add it together. Then you subtract the $200 you started with and the leftover amount should equal the Z report. Felicia's number was off by $6.37.

I changed Felicia's paperwork to account for the extra dime, and then put it back into the brown bag that also held the money from her shift and put both in the safe. When I went into the café, Felicia was leaning over the counter talking to Devin and laughing.

"I'm finished," I said. She didn't look at me.

"Have fun tonight," she said to Devin, and then turned to me and handed me her apron.

The evening shift at the restaurant was nothing like weekend brunch. A smattering of tables came, with no more than three filled at the same time. I tried to study in between taking and delivering orders, but it didn't go well. I had to keep returning to tables to ask things like, "Did you want lemon tahini dressing or tomato tamari?"

or, "I'm sorry, did you say you wanted tempeh tacos or tofu tacos?"

"You'll be fine," Devin said after remaking the second order I screwed up. "One more weekend and you'll be Venus." I didn't tell him that I wasn't planning to be around one more weekend.

I barely squeezed my homework in by closing time when I went into the back to count out my register. Perfect to the cent. I put the money in the safe and let Devin drop me off at Beacon House.

20

The drawing I got back on my math homework from Ben on Friday morning was the most elaborate yet, and my score was the worst, six right out of ten. I had been so distracted trying to do math and take orders at the café, I made some dumb mistakes.

The top half of the margin had a sun, with rays poking through ominous clouds. The bottom was a night sky, shaded in with pencil with spots of white paper showing through to make the stars. A dove flew straight down between the scenes, from day into night with a banner held in its mouth. Written on the banner were ten numbers and two hyphens. It was a phone number. It was *Ben's* phone number. Also on the banner were the words, *If you need help with homework.*

Did Ben want to go out with me? Did Ben want to push me up against a tree and kiss me until my hair was sticky? I couldn't imagine anyone but Indus doing that. Still, this was a good sign. Maybe I wasn't too bad at flirting. Maybe my cool Seattle girl thing was working for me.

Ben didn't look at me much when the bell rang. He grabbed his backpack and hurried out the door.

I ate lunch with Cham and had a pretty good day until horticulture, when the same two girls from before stood whispering behind their hands and pointing at me as raindrops ran in lazy zigzags down the glass. I was trying to concentrate on germinating my seeds but kept noticing them poking around other students' chairs, talking. Our teacher, Ms. Frame, was at the far end of the greenhouse, working with a boy who never seemed to understand the lab work.

This is really the last day, I thought. *Tomorrow I can go home.*

"Can I have your spot?" Rory was standing behind the girl seated next to me. She was holding her bin full of tools, her seeds, and germinating containers.

"I'm sitting here," the girl said.

Rory cocked her head to the side and smiled, showing all her teeth. It was creepy.

"What?" the girl said.

Rory smiled wider.

"Fine." The girl next to me threw her bag of seeds into her own plastic bin and stood up.

"They're telling people your dad is Charles Manson." Rory scooted her new stool closer to mine and stole a look at Ms. Frame, who was still in the corner of the room.

"Who?"

"Bethany and Rose."

"I mean, who did they say was my dad?"

Rory leaned in and stared at me. "Charles Manson."

I shook my head.

"Are you shitting me?"

"I don't think so."

"Helter skelter, blood on the walls, swastika forehead?"

None of this was English.

"Are you from another country?" Rory asked.

"Bellingham," I said.

"Summary: He's not a guy you want for your dad."
Rory peeled her eyes off me and started taking items out
of her bin. "Flower seeds are boring," she said. "I want to
do herb lore."

"Me, too," I said, happy to finally hear something that
made sense. I loved helping Adeona with the medicinal
garden.

"You know about herb lore?" Rory started taking off
her silver rings one by one and stacking them around her
workstation.

"I've made salves and tinctures," I said, "but I'm no
healer."

"My mom's got cancer, so I've been learning about
herbalism. Have you heard of plant attunement?"

"No," I said. "Sorry about your mom." Neptune Fox's

mother had come to live with us at the Farm after she got cancer. She got progressively thinner and weaker for three years, until she couldn't get out of bed and eventually went back Outside to a hospital. We all helped take care of her, especially once she was bedridden.

"Do you really have hippie parents?" Rory asked. Now that she had her rings off, she started spreading the soilless mixture into her germinating container.

"Yeah," I said. *Don't tell her anything about the Family.*

"Did they really name you that, or did you make it up?"

"I wouldn't just make up my own name." I thought about Lyra-Joan. My neck got warm.

"I did," said Rory. "You want to know my real name?"

Not really.

"Ashley." She made a choking sound.

"All right." Ms. Frame clapped twice from her corner of the room. "Less talk, more germination."

After school, I took the bus to the café and found Devin behind the counter again, with Sun working the grill. When I went into the office, V had her head in her hands, sitting behind a stack of papers.

"I hate this!" She threw a pen down on the desk so hard it skidded across the surface and fell on the floor. "Of course the pen falls," she said into her hands. It would have been comical if she wasn't so upset.

"What are you doing?" I asked, putting down my things.

"I hate numbers. Numbers aren't life." She crumpled a pile of papers together in her fist.

Devin appeared at the door to the cramped office behind me and leaned against the frame. "She's trying to do the deposit."

"I could help," I said. "I like numbers."

V turned to face me. "Really? Could you?"

"I can try." I thought about my six out of ten on math homework.

"We need the totals for each shift entered here"—V pointed to the crumpled page as she got out of the chair to make room for me—"and the grand total here. But you have to count all the cash together to make sure it equals the total of all our deposit sheets. Then, fill out this slip for the bank and enter the amount in the ledger book here." V pointed to a book almost lost under papers. "I'll do all your tables. Thank you!" She kissed my cheek.

"I'll keep the chai comin'," said Devin.

It took under an hour for me to complete the paperwork, which really wasn't as big of a deal as V made it seem. The hardest part was reconciling the money with the amount written on our deposit forms because they didn't always match. Still, I had only just finished my first chai by the time I was writing the deposit amount in the large book where all the income and payments from the restaurant were recorded. It was lovely to see, all those pages of numbers in columns of red and black. It was like opening a watch and looking at the gears inside, or seeing the metal wheel that turns a music box. The numbers had a mechanical beauty.

V came back when I was finished.

"You brilliant little light," she said, hugging me. "Certainly a star."

"Why isn't Ephraim doing this?" It had been bothering me the whole time I worked.

"Still sick," she said, slipping out of her apron and grabbing her coat from its hook.

"So who will do the Farm run tomorrow?" I felt the red splotches start on my neck.

"Oh, yeah," she said, tying on a scarf. "I meant to talk to you about that."

"Are you lying to keep me here?" I said, pushing my chair away from the desk, suddenly furious. "Am I a prisoner?"

V slumped onto the edge of the desk. "Starbird, no. I swear. We are canceling the Farm run this weekend, but I swear it has nothing to do with you."

"I don't want to be here anymore, V. I want to go home."

V reached over and stroked my hair. It was something Fern Moon would have done. The thought made me tense up. My lip began to tremble.

"Is the Outside too much?" she asked gently.

I nodded. "Too much" was a good way to say it.

"We canceled the run because Cham and I both have to work the weekend shift and Ephraim's too sick. Plus, the week was so slow that we already have enough food. I could really use you on the floor for the brunch shifts if you can do it. I honestly don't know if we can make it without you," she said, dropping her hands against her lap. "One more weekend?"

I wiped my eye with the back of my hand.

"I've got to run to the bank. You're a lifesaver, Starbird," she said, and she left.

Starbird, table three needs syrup. Excuse me, you gave me milk when I asked for orange juice. Hey, can I get some butter? By ten a.m. Saturday, I wished I had said no to Venus and hitchhiked back to the Farm. At least chickens don't talk back. I broke three dishes and two mugs before V said, "Why don't you run the register and let me and Europa serve?"

I spent the rest of the shift picking up checks, making change, and running credit cards, leaving V and Europa to handle food. When I counted out the drawer, we had our first perfect brunch Z report since I had started.

"If EARTH was here, he would rename you Moneybird," said V.

Everyone laughed but Europa, who said that humor about EARTH was inappropriate.

✻   ✻   ✻

I walked home from the café alone since V and Europa had the evening shift, and ran into Io a few blocks from Beacon House. She was walking from the bus stop, wearing a pink-and-white striped dress, which peeked out from under her raincoat, and rain boots with blue polka dots.

She threaded her arm through mine and walked in step with me along the sidewalk. "I remember when I first moved to Beacon House," she said, as we passed under a madrona tree. It was drizzly out again and the sky was as gray as Spanish moss.

"Where did you move from?"

"B.C. The farm up there."

"You're from Canada?" Planet Elder Saturn Salt had started the Family farm in British Columbia. I knew it was at least as large as our Farm, but I didn't realize Io was from there.

"Yeah. I'm sure you heard a lot about us," she said.

"EARTH told me you smoke marijuana there."

Io laughed. "Tons of it. We call it 'tea.' But I don't any-more."

"Why not?"

"I was in a fog all the time. I quit and I'm so much . . . clearer now."

EARTH told me he smoked marijuana to get "clear," but I couldn't ask Io about that. "So you knew Europa growing up?"

"Yeah. I've known Eris and Kale since they were born. I knew their dad, too. Before he was excommunicated."

"Before he was what?"

"He met an Outside woman and started seeing her in secret. Europa was a ball of fire when she found out. That's why she came here. She's a U.S. citizen, so she could come back with her kids. He's Canadian, and off the grid, so he can't follow her."

"But doesn't that mean she's trying to own him? Isn't he allowed to be with whoever he wants?"

"Europa would say she left because the other woman was an Outsider, and that he wasn't a true Believer. I think it's garden variety jealousy."

"Why did you leave?"

"It got so toxic up there. When I was a kid, it was okay. Actually, it was amazing. But new people like Europa started joining ten years ago and things changed. People got fanatical and paranoid, didn't want anyone leaving, or any Outsiders visiting. I faked a Calling to come to the States, and my mum had to let me go. I managed to talk my way across the border with a birth certificate but no green card. Red Light pays me under the table."

"What do you mean fanatical? Did they become non-Believers?"

"Non-Believers? More like über-Believers. They propped up a photo of EARTH in front of the fireplace and meditated in front of it every night. But I don't want to talk about that." Io hugged my arm close to her side. "Let's talk about boys. What's going on with your artist?"

"He gave me his phone number, but I don't know if I want it."

"Intrigue," she said. "You *have* to use it! What about Farm boy?"

"I've been gone too long. V's keeping me prisoner here. He's going to forget me." I didn't expect the tears that came suddenly rushing down my cheeks.

Io wrapped her arm around my shoulder. "I'm sorry. Truthfully, I was the one who wanted to convince you to stay. I just wanted you to experience the Outside, so you know what's out here, beyond the Farm. V's not keeping you prisoner, she's just overextended."

Io stopped me on the sidewalk. I wiped the tears from my cheeks. "You should go back to the Farm. Take your new clothes. Let him know you were doing great without him."

We started walking again and approached a building that appeared to be abandoned, with a boarded-up storefront on the first floor. There was something in the alcove that looked like a pile of dirty blankets. As we got closer, I realized it was a man. I dropped Io's arm and ran over.

"Sir, are you okay?"

He looked up at me, his face so dirty it looked like he had been cleaning a fireplace. The hand he held out to me had long black fingernails.

"He's coming back. His judgment is coming for you," he said, his eyes jumping wildly around. He grabbed the sleeve of my sweater and started to pull.

"Starbird!" Io yelled, grabbing my other arm. "What are you doing?"

"He looks hungry. Child of God," I said to the man, "are you hungry?"

"God. God!" the man yelled, grabbing my sweater with his other hand. "He's coming back. He's coming."

Io yanked my sweater out of the man's grasp and started pulling me down the street toward Beacon House. "Starbird, you can't do that! You have to be careful in the Outside. You can't just talk to anyone." I had never seen her so upset, stuck somewhere between yelling and crying.

"But he needs our help." I tried to pull away from her, but she had a tight grip on my sleeve. She didn't stop dragging me until we were at the front steps of Beacon House.

"What money do you have to drop in his cup?" Io asked. "You're a girl in the city. You're not EARTH."

Just as I was about to protest, the green door swung open and Cham was standing in the foyer inside the threshold. "Ephraim's in the hospital," he said.

21

Felicia was about to throw a tantrum when V told her that I would work the register on the Sunday shift. But as she began to unbuckle her fury, V held out a hand and said, "I don't have the capacity for it this morning, so just deal with it or quit." Felicia glowered back but didn't say anything else.

Ephraim had been having chest pains on Saturday afternoon, so Cham called an ambulance and then called the café, and V went straight to Harborview while Cham stayed with Kale and Eris. The hospital concluded that it hadn't been a heart attack, but they decided to keep him overnight for tests. The situation was exacerbated by the fact that Ephraim, like most Family members, didn't have any health insurance.

"They couldn't turn him away from the emergency room," V said as we sat on the couch that night. "But we're still going to get bills for this. Plus, we have bills due at the café, and someone has to handle payroll." Her voice was hoarse from crying, and she was twisting a water glass around in her palm.

"I'll help," I said. "I'll stay after my shift."

"I don't want you to feel like I'm trapping you here."

"The Family's needs should come before mine," I said, ashamed of all the fits I had been throwing for the past week. I took V's hand. "I'll stay in Seattle until he gets better."

So after working the register all morning, helping bus tables as the Sunday brunch crowd cleared, and running the Z report, I ordered a tofu scramble and retreated to the tiny café office to start sorting through the mounting pile of paperwork. V gave me a slipshod tour of the desk.

"Bills here, receipts there, and the ledger book. Ephraim never made the transition to computer accounting, so everything you need is probably on a piece of paper somewhere on this desk. But use the computer if you want; it should be more than a paperweight." While talking, she had been drawing up a handwritten sign:

Mandatory Meeting
All Café Staff
Tuesday night, closing time.

"I decided not to have it on Monday," V said as she taped the sign on the wall above our apron hooks, "because I don't want to cancel Story Night. But Tuesday, we have to figure out how to cover Ephraim's shifts, and maybe make some shifts to care for Ephraim depending on what the hospital says. By the way"—she said over her shoulder—"if you have any questions for Gamma, let me call her. She wouldn't be happy if she knew you were helping with the books."

For the next few hours, Devin brought me chai while I formed papers into various stacks. The office had a radio with a hand crank, a tiny disco ball that hung from the desk lamp and cascaded specks of light over the papers, and a framed photo of Ephraim, EARTH, and Mars, all years younger, with shorter beards and fewer wrinkles around their eyes.

This is what he would want me to do, I thought, looking at the photo of EARTH. Gamma might think I was too young to work on the finances, but EARTH believed in me. *Maybe that's why I was brought to the café while Ephraim is sick. Maybe this is getting me ready to do an important job for the Family.*

I made piles of all the café's current unpaid bills, many of which had red bars across the top with the unsettling words *Final Notice*, or letters attached threatening something called *collections*. The amount due was straightforward at least. It was much harder deciphering the payroll, since some workers were paid as Family members and others weren't. I needed to know the number of hours each employee worked and their pay rate. Then somehow I had to figure out how much money we currently had and how much we needed to buy food and other supplies, so I would know how much money was left to pay our bills. The books were no help. Usually, when I looked at numbers, there was a pleasant simplicity. It was like looking at a flock of black birds flying across a white sky. But these birds were black and red and were flying in chaotic circles, fighting with one another.

Over dinner, I tried calling the bank to find our account balance, but it was Sunday evening and I didn't know any of our passwords. By six o'clock, the only real progress I had made was organizing Ephraim's paper clips and rubber bands into orderly piles. I was feeling in over my head and starting to panic. Who did I think I was, Doug Fir? Did I really think I was smart enough to do this?

I pushed back from the desk and let my head rest on the back of the chair. I couldn't call Gamma. I couldn't reach Iron without going through Gamma. *Maybe I should just tell V I can't do it.* But who else was there to do it?

That's when I noticed that someone had put glow-in-the-dark stars on the office ceiling, the kind that look dull yellow in the day but glow like bioluminescence when the room is dark. I closed the office door and turned off the light. All over the ceiling and walls, pale green stars emerged from the paint. They weren't in the shape of any constellations I was aware of, but they did have a harmonious way of leading the eye from one horizon to the other, the secret constellations of Ephraim's own invented sky. Somewhere in those stars, I got an idea.

"Yeah, I can be there at nine," Ben said over the phone. "I live right down the street."

It wasn't exactly math homework, but he did offer to help.

I had to reassure V three times that I wanted to be left alone, that I wouldn't open the door to anyone, that I would take a bus home and not walk, before she agreed to leave me there. By 8:59 I was practically pushing her and Devin out the front door, taking the aprons out of their hands, insisting I would remember all the locks. I opened the back door at a few minutes after nine and peered into the alley. Ben was leaning against the chain-link fence at the back of the vacant lot and doing a pathetic job of looking inconspicuous. V would split a lip if she knew I was asking an Outsider to look at our finances.

I waved Ben inside, reaching back to release my hair from its ponytail right before he walked through the door. He stood in the hall by the walk-in and stared first in one direction, then another. He was like a cat being teased with a feather; everything in the place caught his attention.

"I've walked by this place," he said, touching the beaded curtain as we passed. "We just moved to the neighborhood from Roosevelt. I'm not switching schools, though. My house has the red door, two blocks up. This reminds

me of my uncle's basement. He had a wet bar and a tan-
ning bed. Have you ever been to Phoenix?" He pushed the
mirror ball in the office so it sent a thousand little lights
spirographing the walls and ceiling.

"Um, no, I haven't. Do you want some chai?"

"You have energy drinks?"

"No."

"I'll have what you said."

"Chai."

"Yeah, chai."

I sat Ben at the desk while I got another chair from the
café and crammed it in beside him, clearing a space in the
clutter for our tea. In that time, he sketched a picture of the
alley behind the café, and our back door with the sign on
it. He was talented. He could draw a lot more than birds.

"I have to do bills and payroll." I opened the ledger book
and put it in front of him. "And I only have two hours."

"Why are you the one doing payroll?" Ben was still
shading in his drawing.

"It's a family business and my, um, uncle is in the hospital, and my . . . sister is really overwhelmed. I'm the only
one in the family who's good with numbers."

"These bills are overdue." He said as he fanned out
the notices on the desk with one finger. "That's a big pile
and I don't see any sorting system. My dad would lose his
mind. Did you do the math homework already? I thought
of you because it's word problems again, and I thought

about calling you, but you have my phone number. I don't have yours, so I was glad and really surprised when you called me. Cheez Whiz, this is a lot of bills. I'm talking a lot." Ben took a deep inhale and seemed to be fighting to keep his lips pressed together. "I had, like, three Red Bulls today."

"Is that some kind of burger?"

"Burger. That's funny. You're funny. I kind of knew you would be because of the things you wear. You remind me of the girl who plays bass in that band Tragic, the way she always wears complementary colors together like purple and yellow. Oh spit. I can't shut up. Can energy drinks make your heart explode?" Ben grabbed his drawing again and started coloring in the letters for the café sign.

"Is an energy drink some kind of alcohol?" *This guy is crazy or drunk. I was so stupid to invite him here. I barely know him. V's going to kill me. So much for impressing the Family.* I eyed the phone on the desk in case I needed to call Beacon House.

"Oh no." He stopped shading. "They're just full of caffeine, and it's probably really bad for you to drink more than one. Well, it's probably bad to drink any at all, probably. Are those glow-in-the-dark stars on the ceiling?"

"Here." I handed Ben the chai I brought him. "We make it herbal without black tea. And it's got cow milk in it."

Ben took the mug with a shaky hand and smelled it before taking a sip. Then he took another.

After a few more drinks of chai, and once he had the ledger open and a calculator in his hand, Ben seemed to relax, although he was almost working faster than I could watch him. "I do this stuff for my dad all the time," he told me. For the next half hour, he taught me about payroll checks and tax withholdings, and he discovered the café's version of a timesheet, where Ephraim recorded the actual hours worked on the schedule he had posted. It was in the file cabinet along with the hourly wage for each worker. There was a pretty simple program Ben downloaded that calculated taxes and printed pay stubs.

"Your uncle is still going to have to sign the checks, but he can do that from the hospital." Ben took the last pay stub off the printer. "You've got a lot of under-the-table workers. You could get in big trouble for that."

"We've got it under control." *V wouldn't be happy about this.* "Please don't tell anyone, okay?"

Ben looked at me. His eyes behind his glasses were a milky shade of brown. They reminded me of the thick pools of mud we would get on the Farm by November, which lasted all winter and could easily pull off a rain boot or suck your leg in up to the calf. I felt the red splotches start to sprout on my chest and radiate up toward my face.

"What happened to your hand?" he said.

I looked down at the scrapes on my skin, still red but starting to heal. It had been a week since I got them. "I was closing the barn door. It was an accident. Can you explain the ledger book to me?" The office was so small, our chairs were touching and neither of us could stand up without forcing the other one to move. His long legs barely fit under the desk.

Ben yawned. Whatever nervous energy he had been burning was turning to smoke. "Black and red, income and expenses. The income is listed as food and beverage sales. In this column, you record business costs: payroll, food, supplies, maintenance. It looks like the overdue bills are mostly big-ticket items, maybe from a remodel. Your problem is that the café's expenses are more than the income." Ben paged through the ledger and tapped a series of numbers into the calculator. "I don't want to say this, but your café is in the red."

"Yeah, I know. We just need to attract more customers," I said, shifting in my seat and accidentally brushing my leg against Ben's.

"Yeah, like a thousand more customers a week." Ben shook his head and yawned again. "What's this payment to Arnold Muller for? It isn't logged."

"I've never heard that name." I looked over Ben's shoulder at the ledger, my loose hair spilling onto his arm.

Ben flipped backward through the book. "Here it is again last month on the same day, but it doesn't say what the payment is for. Is he the landlord?"

"No. We own the property."

"It's the same amount every month in this ledger. None

of the payments have a memo, but they were all made on the twenty-eighth. Today is the twenty-fifth, and there's no bill from Arnold Muller in this stack." Ben pushed back from the table and flipped through the piles of bills again. "Wait a minute, what the pluck." He picked up the pile of pay stubs. "I thought the name sounded familiar. One of your employees is named Sun Muller."

"Sun's last name is Muller? Maybe his dad did some work for the café," I said. I was starting to think we were going too far. Whatever Ben was seeing, he shouldn't see it. Maybe I shouldn't see it. "Anyway, V asked for help with bills and payroll, so I'll let Ephraim worry about the rest when he's back." I started to put things away.

Ben watched me. "You definitely shouldn't pay anything to Arnold Muller without an invoice. It's sketchy. Plus, it's part of the reason your expenses are so high."

I glanced at Ben. His skin didn't seem so pale in the light of the office, and his bony fingers were graceful when they punched numbers into the calculator. His spine still seemed oddly twisted, but he smelled good, for a boy. Not like sweat and earth and plants, but like a T-shirt fresh from the wash that had been hung on a line to dry.

I was still smelling that smell when Ben said, "Starbird, are you in a cult?"

22

"I'm supposed to be home by eleven." I stood up and banged my knee on the desk, sending me back down into my chair.

"I'm sorry. I didn't mean it in a mean way," Ben was saying as I stood up again, pushing my knees against his to make space for my legs.

"How could you say that to me, when I invited you here?" I snatched a paper out of his hand.

"I was double-checking the address online and I found stuff about the Free Family. I was just curious." He tried to help me gather the papers, but I put my hands on his to make him stop.

"My Family is on the Internet?"

"There's . . . stuff. I have a freaky religious family, too. I didn't mean to insult you."

"We're not freaky religious." I turned around and hit my head on the low-hanging ceiling light. "I need to go home."

"I'll drive you." Ben stood up, too, and then we were both trapped in the cage of our chairs. "Sorry," he said, bumping into me, and then, "Sorry," again, without touching me.

"It's fine," I lied. *I can't believe I was starting to like you. Your graceful fingers and your stupid puddle eyes. Indus understands about EARTH and the Family. Indus is my Family. You're just some guy.*

I wanted to walk home for the fresh air, but I promised V I wouldn't, so I relented and let Ben drop me off, even though he wouldn't stop apologizing the whole way.

He let me out down the street from Beacon House to keep V from seeing us. Before I got out of the car, he said, "I was so sheeping stupid tonight. I couldn't shut up and then I said that cult thing. Will you just please let me tell you about my family sometime?"

"I don't think that sounds very relevant, but thanks for your help with the payroll." I slammed the car door.

V and Io were still up, sitting in the living room when I walked in. Ephraim wasn't home from the hospital, but he did talk to V on the phone to assure her that "It's all good," in between coughs. One thing was good: Ephraim didn't appear to be at risk for a heart attack. But his doctors were going to run tests on his lungs. There was a crease between V's eyebrows that wouldn't soften. I did a loose, sloppy job on my homework before crawling exhausted into bed.

✳   ✳   ✳

I faked my way through history Monday morning, but I hadn't done the reading. Things didn't become horrifying until second period, when I had to hand my math over to Ben. He had glanced up when I walked into class and then looked back down at his paper. "Hey," he said as I slid into my seat, giving me a casual half wave.

My body turned into a thing that didn't belong to me. My rogue left arm knocked my math book on the floor, and my right elbow bumped into Ben's head as he bent to pick it up. I was a marionette in a windstorm, and red splotches covered my chest like clouds.

But the worst part was when Ben had to hand me back my homework with only five marked right out of ten, and a drawing on the margin. It looked like a rock show poster, the kind people hang on our bulletin board at the café. A giant caveman was stepping over the Space Needle with a club in his hand, about to smash into it. In block letters, it said, *Free Math Tutoring*, and then in smaller letters at the bottom, it said, *Ben's lunch table. Cafeteria.*

It was a fantastic drawing that made me sick. I didn't want to be mean to Ben, but I also didn't want to have lunch with him. I forced myself to smile and whispered, "Thanks, but I can't," and got an F on the homework.

I sleepwalked through the rest of the day, zoned out while Cham and his friends talked at lunch, and ignored the mean girls in horticulture, where we took a quiz on soil testing. Rory sat next to me again, and then we walked together to history club.

She was right in the middle of telling me about how she moved to Seattle from Kansas at the start of the year and her parents couldn't pick her up until five, so they gave her the choice of either school clubs or taking the bus to the YMCA, except that she hated swimming. "Do you have the app called Smash? You can follow my blog on your phone." She pulled a small black device out of her bag and started tapping it with both thumbs while she walked.

"I don't have a phone," I said.

"My parents wouldn't get me one until we moved here," Rory said. "Just say you don't feel safe being out of contact, and yours will get you one."

"I don't think so," I said.

"Wait, have you heard this song by Blue Scholars?"

Rory stopped walking and held out a slender white cord that split in two pieces and had squishy nubs dangling from each end. I heard something coming from inside the nubs. Leaning my head down toward them, I held them an inch or two from my ears.

"You are such a space alien," Rory said, watching me. She grabbed the nubs and stuck one in each of my ears.

The music. The strange, swelling melody and the hard beat. It wasn't coming from a stereo somewhere or from instruments being played in the room. The sound was inside my head, inside my body, filling up the whole world. What instruments even made these sounds? There were voices too that could have been next to me, not singing but talking to me intimately, right in my ear. The sound was somehow wild, something strange, something new and miraculous.

I looked at Rory, who was smiling and mouthing, "Isn't it awesome?" just as a boy with bad skin wearing a leather jacket swept her off her feet, yanking the music from my head and down the hall with Rory and her phone.

"Jerk!" Rory yelled, dropping her phone with a clatter.

"Sorry." The guy waved his free arm out toward me, the one that wasn't wrapped around Rory.

Struggling away from him, Rory picked her phone up off the floor. "You're lucky it's not broken, idiot," she sniffed, winding the white music cord around it and stuffing it in her pocket. Then she turned toward the guy, grabbed him by the back of the neck, and kissed him for a solid two minutes.

Rory dropped her book bag on the floor as she stood on her tiptoes making out. I started inspecting the lockers, wondering if I was supposed to keep walking or wait for her to finish.

Finally, they unsmacked their lips and Rory pointed to him and said, "That's Sergeant."

"Whusup," he said.

"You need to stop kissing me because I need to go to

history club. Call me later," Rory said, waving him off.

"Keep your phone on," he said, walking the other way.

When he was halfway down the hall, she said, "We have nothing to talk about, but he is such a hot kisser." Then we walked on to Teacher Ted's room.

Alex, Danny, and Jake were all there, chairs already in a circle. Teacher Ted walked in right after us and said, "Cake!" He was holding a plate over his head with a third of a chocolate cake on top. "Leftover from one of the secretaries' birthday parties in the staff room." He put it on his desk with a stack of napkins. "Kevin is absent today. Let's get going on questions." Ted handed index cards to Jake to pass out, and Rory and I sat down.

This time I came armed with my inquiry. In fact, I knew exactly what Internet research I wanted to do.

Ted collected the questions. There were two war questions from Danny and Jake, and Alex's question was about the origin of the universe, which Teacher Ted said belonged more in a science club, but that Alex argued was natural history.

Then Ted read, "'What defines a cult?' That one must belong to Rory."

Rory shook her head and held out her ring-covered hands. "Area 51."

"The cult one's mine."

Teacher Ted's gaze was so penetrating, I felt like a window. "Good question, Starbird. I suggest you refine it to be less provocative and allow for a more nuanced answer. Maybe, 'What is the origin of the word *cult?*'"

So far, it had been a truly crappy day. Between worrying about Ephraim and what Ben said, I was wracked with anxiety. But as I walked to a computer, I felt a little thrill. I couldn't even mention the word *cult* around the Family. Here, I could not only ask about it, I could also research it. Still, I had to wonder if I could trust what I found out. Could I believe the *answers* I got on the Outside?

When we came back to the group to share, we learned that Area 51 was a huge military base in Nevada that the government lied about and blocked out on maps, flamethrowers were used in World War II, and the word *cult* is a critical term used against a group whose beliefs are considered abnormal or bizarre by mainstream Christians. The anti-cult movement started using it in the 1970s after some new religious groups did crazy, violent things like murder people and commit mass suicide. I found out who Charles Manson was. No wonder our Family was so wounded by the word.

One article quoted a social scientist saying the word demonstrates prejudice, and that labeling a group a "cult" makes people feel safe, because "it creates an imagined barrier between conventional religions and violence, insinuating that only abnormal religious groups take part in violence." But others said that cults generally involve "charismatic leaders who attract marginalized people into membership and then maintain control over them with brainwashing techniques."

When I shared my results, Rory said, "What about killing cats? Didn't a lot of cults kill cats?"

"Maybe you could research that question for us next week, Rory, because it's time to pack up," said Ted. "Starbird, could you stick around for a minute?"

"Dad, chill, I'll be right there. It just ended," Rory said into her phone as she left, turning to wave at me.

Everyone else filed out and Ted offered me the last piece of chocolate cake. Then he sat back in his chair, put his hands on the back of his head, and said, "So, has the Family heard anything lately from EARTH?"

23

The henhouse door was open, and I was facing down a coyote. "Why are you asking me that?" I said. *Did Ben tell him?* I was stupid to invite Ben to the café. This would lead back to Beacon House, the café, my legal guardianship, our off-the-grid workers, our school on the Farm. My feet were backing away without me telling them to move.

Ted stood. "I didn't mean to scare you." He motioned toward two of the classroom chairs.

I kept backing up, almost to the door. I would run down the hall to the closest exit, fire myself like a cannonball toward the bus stop, go home, and confess everything to V. How could I have done this? I was just starting to like history club, to feel like the research was a gift. I had let my guard down. It was so stupid.

"Wait, please. I'm sorry. I was so excited to meet a Family member, I didn't think about how that might sound," Ted said. "Of course I freaked you out."

"I don't know what Family you're talking about," I said.

"I need to get home." I reached behind me for the door-knob, wishing I hadn't let everyone else leave, wishing I had never enrolled in an Outside school. I was like a bug hiding under the safe, wet side of a rock that had just gotten picked up. I turned toward the door and twisted the knob. Almost free.

"Wait, Starbird." Ted followed me to the door. I stopped but didn't turn around.

"I must have been wrong. I'm sorry. I went to grad school at the University of Washington for sociology and studied a utopian community called the Free Family. Ever since I heard your name, I thought you might be . . . and then your question today. I'm sorry, I shouldn't have assumed."

"That's okay," I said, only half turning back to him. "No big deal."

"My wife says that one of my faults is treating people like history projects." Ted put his hands in his pockets.

I just stood there.

"Hey, hold on." Ted went back to his desk. "Since you asked that question about cults today, I have this book you might like." He ran his finger along the book spines on the shelf behind his desk and pulled one out. He came back to the door and handed me a book titled *Looking for Utopia: Intentional Communities in the United States.* "There's a rich history of utopian societies and alternative family structures in the U.S., with both positive and negative qualities. There's an interesting chapter on the anti-cult movement. It's a great read. I'm sorry again about the question." Ted frowned. "Every history teacher in Washington probably wants to know more about the Free Family, and I just jumped to a wild conclusion. I was way off base."

When I made it back to Beacon House, it was already getting dark outside. Any remaining sightings of our Northwest summer were being blocked out by the curtain of gray that would last until spring. My boots were wet to the laces when I took them off in the foyer. I could hear V and Europa in the kitchen, but I wasn't looking forward to seeing them.

I was ready to confess. I didn't want to be deceitful or keep secrets from my Family. Wouldn't that make me just like Fern Moon? I had showed Ben the café's books and now one of my teachers was asking questions about the Family. I'd let an Outsider in too far, and now there was no telling what could happen. I left my book bag in the hall and plucked up my courage to talk to V. I was just going to have to take the heat.

"The doctors think it's severe pneumonia," V said as soon as she saw me. She was chopping up beets on our kitchen island, and Europa was stirring something in a metal pan on the stove. "They're keeping him longer because he may have problems with his liver. The alcoholism left a scar." V cut through a beet that leaked a red stain all over the cutting board.

"We're not canceling Story Night," Europa said, as Kale ran into the kitchen from the living room with her horse in hand. "Ephraim insisted."

V wiped the beet juice from her hands onto a towel and walked over to me. "Thank you so much for getting those paychecks out." She put a hand on each of my arms. "I don't know how I would be doing this without you." Her eyes blossomed with tears. She put her arms around me and let three choked sobs release into my hair.

I held her and rubbed her back while she cried. I decided it wasn't the best time to mention Ben or Teacher Ted.

Cham was out with his friends, but Io made it home from Red Light in time for dinner. There was a missing note in our conversation where Ephraim's booming tenor should have been. V started crying again halfway through her corn soup and had to leave the table. No one was finding it easy to make conversation. I was relieved when the doorbell rang and Paul and Devin showed up with instruments in hand. They had brought their mother, Seta, who walked spritely with a cane to the nearest chair. Penniah and Adlai arrived soon after, with Dathan and Sapphira.

V came back downstairs and Penniah started asking her questions about Ephraim's condition, leading V to a third round of tears.

Europa leaned over to me and whispered, "Ephraim was practically V's father after Mercury went to live in the tree house."

"He was?"

"She told me that EARTH brought her here as a baby and Ephraim raised her. Mercury was out of his mind with grief over V's mother. Apparently, EARTH had to convince Mercury that he couldn't raise a baby living in a tree."

I looked at V again. She seemed so strong to me, even when she was sobbing. Devin put his arms around her and whispered in her ear.

Sapphira and Kale linked arms and danced around me, telling me I was in jail. Dathan ran a circle from the living room through the dining room to the kitchen and back, until Paul ambushed him and hung him upside down from his ankles as he squirmed and giggled.

The madness was finally interrupted by Adlai, who said, "Since Ephraim's not here, someone from Beacon House should probably announce Story Night."

The traditional words spoken at the start of Story Night were, *Thank you for coming together tonight, Family*. It generally fell on one of the older members of the hosting household to say them. Even though Europa was technically older, all eyes seemed to gravitate toward V, who was still wiping black eyeliner from the ridges of her cheekbones.

She gazed back at all of us, and that's when her leaky dam broke. "It's not enough that I'm trying to keep the café running and visit Ephraim and . . . and be a phony guardian to teenagers and make sure we don't go bankrupt? I'm twenty-seven! Run your own damn Story Night. Do something for yourselves!" She spun around, her long, dark hair swinging behind her as she took the stairs two at a time. Devin was right behind her.

Sensitive Kale started crying, so Europa took her into the kitchen. Sapphira crawled between Penniah's legs. The rest of us were quiet as a graveyard, shifting uncomfortably. I heard Adlai lean over to Penniah and whisper, "Maybe we should go."

That's when I cleared my throat and said, "Thank you for coming together tonight, Family." I thought of my best memory, my happiest time on the Farm, and told all of them this story.

Every fall for as long as I can remember, the Family held an apple pressing, which started on Friday and lasted until Sunday night, during which we made the cider we drank all year. Fern Moon said it started as a Family business, that they used to sell the cider at a roadside stand with pumpkins and corn. But to no one's surprise, it failed, so it turned into a Family tradition instead.

On the Farm, we had the old cider press and apple grinder that Iron's ancestors built long before he was born.

He said it was probably even older than the main house.

We worked all week in the orchard leading up to the pressing. Iron started by pulling the press out of the barn and cleaning it with boiling water to make sure no bacteria would harm the cider. Older kids got out of afternoon school to pick apples with ladders and bushel baskets and wheelbarrows until sunset.

Apple picking is a careful process. You have to steady your ladder in the tree so you can pick and load your basket without falling. And you don't just yank off an apple. That can make other apples fall, or damage the fruit. You cradle the apple in your palm and put a finger on the stem, then you rotate the apple until the eye goes up toward the sky and it breaks free.

By Friday, when other Family members started showing up, we had hundreds of pounds of apples picked and cleaned.

Together we worked all day, feeding the apples into the mill and then arranging the mashed apples in the wooden press. Iron and I would always sneak away to his porch and drink our first cup together in the quiet of the trees from ceramic mugs we made ourselves. We made apple cider, applesauce, apple cider vinegar, and hard apple cider. In the kitchen, women baked apple bread and made apple granola. The smell of apples snuck into the cracks in everything. Even the gravel smelled like apples by the time we were done. And at night, we had a big meal and then gathered into the Sanctuary for one huge Story Night, with all the visiting Family members sleeping in the barn afterward. Fern Moon let me bring my blankets to the Sanctuary so I could sleep there, too. I loved hearing the quiet sounds of all of us sleeping in the same room, sharing our dreams, all of us dreaming of apples.

I was so lost in my own story, I hadn't noticed that Europa had walked back in with Kale in her arms, the little girl's head resting sleepily against her mother's neck. And V came back, too, and was standing at the bottom of the stairs with Devin. After I stopped talking, she cleared her throat.

"I'm sorry for flipping out." V wrapped herself in Devin's arms like they were a blanket.

"No need," voices said. "You work so hard," and, "we love you," were muttered around.

"Hey, Starbird," said Adlai, "when is the apple pressing this year? It's coming up, right?"

"It's this coming weekend," I answered. "They're probably already picking apples." Which made me think of being in the orchard, which made me think of the night I got my birth certificate, which made me think of Indus, which made me want to join V in crying.

Fern wanted me to go to the Farm for the apple pressing. Maybe Ephraim would be well by then. Maybe I could still make it home.

24

"**G**et a chance to look at the book I gave you yet?" Teacher Ted asked before class started. I had arrived this time before the bell.

"Um, no." I was aware of a few students listening as others shuffled into the room. Honestly, I hadn't even finished my homework after Story Night, much less done any extra reading.

"Well, I'll be interested to hear what you think, when you get a chance."

Ben was already in his chair when I walked into second period. He sat up straighter when he saw me and then slouched again.

This time, when he handed back my homework (six right out of ten), there was no drawing. The margin was as clean as a brand-new T-shirt. Devastatingly blank.

I looked over at Ben, but he didn't make eye contact with me, bent over his own homework, drawing a picture there.

I found myself with a horrible itch on my back, right in the middle where it's impossible to reach. I turned my head and stared at the fake plant by the door while my eyes got wet. *I'm the one who pushed him away. It's better like this. He's an Outsider. He would only get in the way of me being with Indus. And he already knows too much about us. This is how it has to be.*

I turned back toward the teacher, hearing her voice but not understanding a word she said.

"Are you going to the café meeting tonight?" I tried to make conversation with Cham at the lunch table.

"It's mandatory."

"What do you think will happen with Ephraim's shifts?" The stress of the night before was clinging to me like socks from the dryer.

"Not my main concern right now," said Cham, taking a swig of the soda he had surprised me by buying from the vending machine.

I was such a jerk. Ephraim was Cham's dad. Of course he had bigger worries. "Sorry."

I felt a tap on my shoulder. *Ben?* It was Rory.

"Can I cram?" She stood there with a tray, looking at the bench beside me.

Cham scooted away to make room for her and started talking to his friends. I moved my leftover corn soup.

"I keep thinking about your history club thing on cults." She plopped down.

Cham cocked his head to one side. He didn't turn to look at us, but I knew he had heard.

"What did Teacher Ted want to talk to you about? Did he get creeped out like you're going to join a cult and he's a mandatory reporter so he has to tell on you to the school counselor?" She started taking off her silver rings and stacking them along her lunch tray.

"He just wanted to see if I was . . . learning . . . stuff."

Rory raised an eyebrow at me. "Okay. So, are you learning stuff?"

"Totally." I took a sip of soup.

"I convinced my history teacher to let me do my oral presentation on tarot, so I'm going to research it at club. I can read your cards if you want. I do horoscopes, too." Now that Rory's hands were ringless, she picked up the slice of greasy, orange pizza from her paper plate and started eating it. "Wait." She dropped her pizza and wiped orange grease from her hands onto a napkin. "Let me read your palm right now! I just got an app."

"No," I said, pulling my hand from the table into my lap.

"Please!" She said. "It's totally real. Seriously. It's amazing."

I glanced at Cham. It's not like Rory could find out anything about the Family by looking at my hand. It seemed harmless enough.

Rory pulled her phone out of her pocket and swiped her right thumb in a zigzag motion over the screen. Then, without looking up, she held her left hand out to me. I settled the back of my right hand into her palm, glancing around to see if anyone was watching.

She turned my hand over to look at the back. "What happened?"

My red scrapes were healing, leaving lines of soft, pink new skin. I had the sudden impulse to tell her about Indus, but I fought it. "Just a scrape."

Holding her phone in one hand and my palm in the other, Rory looked back and forth between the two in silence. It wasn't anything like the first time I got my palm read. The Family had a short-lived fortune-telling business run by Saturn Salt.

"Your life line is long. I think you're going to live to be, like, eighty." She put her phone on the table and trailed her pointer finger along my palm. "Okay, crazy, twisty love line. Do you see how it's interrupted right here?"

"Oh, that's a scar from when I was putting new barbed wire on the chicken coop," I said without thinking.

"There should be laws against making kids do farm-work," Rory said.

"Are you crazy? Do you even know where your food comes from? If you want to eat eggs, you should have to know how to raise chickens." I yanked my hand back from her. Outsiders were so selfish and lazy, with their noses in their cell phones, afraid of doing any real work.

Cham glanced over at us, then turned back to his friends.

"Wait, I'm sorry," Rory whined. "You're right. I'm super spoiled. Please let me finish your reading."

I twisted my hands together in irritation. "Chickens are very intelligent creatures," I said.

"I think it's really cool that you know about chickens." Rory held out her left hand and smiled.

I reluctantly put my palm out again.

"This part of your thumb is your logic, and this part is your willpower." She held the end of my thumb between her fingers and gave it a squeeze. "You have amazing willpower." She leaned over closer to my hand, her warm breath exhaling onto my wrist. "Your fate line is crazy. I think you're going to do something really, really important, like invent something."

"I wish I could invent something to help my Family pay the bills." I don't know why I said that. I didn't even bother looking over at Cham.

"Yeah, us too." Rory dropped my hand and picked up her pizza. "My mom quit her job when she got skin cancer, and she does weird things to make money now. Her latest insane idea is making crafts like corn-husk dolls. She's at home shellacking gourds right now."

"People here buy things like that?"

"Oh yeah. They go to pumpkin patches, corn maz-es, harvest festivals and buy it all. My mom has an event booked every weekend of October," said Rory.

"In Seattle?"

"No. Mostly on farms a couple of hours away. It's all city people who want to see how a tractor works."

"And people pay for that?"

"Mom says they do."

"Do they sell food too?"

"I guess."

An idea started to form in my mind. It was hazy at first, more of a pale watercolor than an oil painting. It was an idea about how we might pay the café bills. And if it worked, it could do more than just help the Family. It could get Indus Stone to come to Seattle.

When I got home from school, Io surprised me by giving me a jean jacket with a gold eagle patch sewn onto one pocket. "Covers a bleach stain," she said, having me turn around to check out the fit. "It was from the free box at work."

I wore it when Europa and I walked to the café that evening for the mandatory staff meeting. Io stayed home with Kale and Eris, who were both asleep before we left. Cham and V had worked the evening shift, so they were already there.

"How's school?" Europa asked as we walked. "Are they turning you away from us yet?" The damp air was being forced around by a north wind, a warning that winter was coming. You have to wear a lot of wool to live in the Northwest; otherwise the chill can make it all the way to your bones.

"No. I mean, it's fine," I said. "I guess."

"Down here in the states, you act casual about Outsiders, but it's not casual. EARTH doesn't want us being friends with them." She pulled her scarf down away from her mouth so it wouldn't muffle her voice. "I hope you aren't making friends."

I touched my hand where Rory had held it at lunch, thought about Ben being in the café office. "No," I said. "I just hang out with Cham."

"Like Cham's much better. Have you seen him do anything to make you think that public school is corrupting him?"

"No," I said, "nothing." What was it about being on the Outside that made it easier to lie?

"Well, even if it wasn't school, it could be happening at home. Io is a bad influence, and V isn't a true Believer. I don't think non-Believers should be living in Family houses, do you?"

I had always thought that non-Believers shouldn't stay in the Family. But when I said, "I agree," it felt like another lie.

"Good. At least we can count on you to do the right thing." Europa put an arm around me as we reached the café, where the CLOSED sign had already been flipped.

While the people on shift finished their closing duties, the rest of us arranged chairs into a few rows for the meeting. Family members are good at pitching in without being asked or directed, and soon all eight of us were seated for the meeting with tea and coffee cups. V stood up.

"Here's the update on Ephraim. His doctors confirmed that he has pneumonia and he's probably had it for a while. They would release him if it was just that, but they're investigating problems with his liver and possibly kidneys. I posted his visiting hours in the office."

"What about the medical bills?" Sun's voice was deep. He sat at the back of the group, closest to the windows, while V stood in front of the counter. His muscular arms were folded across his chest and he was leaning back in his chair.

"We're not sure, to tell you the truth." V seemed to carry the weight of the world for a second. "I called this meeting so we could change the schedule to cover Ephraim's shifts and some of mine, so I can work in the office." V ran a hand through her long, dark hair. "We need to hire another waitress, too, so if you know anyone who could be cool with the Family, we need them."

Devin said, "I know someone."

"I don't want another non-Family member," Europa said.

"That's hiring discrimination," said Felicia.

"You're allowed to run a family business," Europa shot back, "and I don't care about your Outside laws."

"Hold on, Europa, we do care about laws," said V.

"Well, I'm not taking any more shifts." Felicia turned sideways and propped her feet on the spindle of Cham's chair. "I can't make tips on weeknights if it's dead in here."

"We should close more hours," Cham said.

"We need more money, not less," Sun replied.

"There are whole hours when no one comes in." Cham turned to face Sun. "We're wasting money just having the lights on."

"So we advertise more, not close up more." Sun's voice rose.

The talking speed picked up. It was hard to keep following who said what.

"Are we ignoring the elephant in the room? Is the café going under?" (Paul.)

"Yeah, aren't we already broke?" (Sun.)

"Where did you hear that?" (V, hands in her hair.)

"Ephraim would only say, 'It's all good.'" (Devin.)

"Maybe that's all he would say to you." (Sun.)

"Is the café seriously going under? Because I need to find another job." (Felicia.)

"No one said the café is going under—" (V, interrupted.)

"But we do need to figure out how to get more business, or it will." (Sun, interrupting.)

"What did Ephraim tell you?" (Paul to Sun.)

"I can work more shifts, but I would need more child care." (Europa.)

"Then someone at Beacon House has to do the child care, which is like having another shift." (V, visibly frustrated.)

"I know it's work. I'm doing child care along with laundry, cooking, and cleaning." (Europa, also frustrated.)

"Work out your freaky commune business at home." (Felicia, throwing up hands.)

"Why are you even here?" (Europa to Felicia.)

"Europa, please don't." (V.)

"There aren't going to be *any* shifts if this place goes under." (Sun again.)

"How bad is it, V?" (Paul, concerned.)

"We do need to make more money." (V, reluctant.)

"How much do we need?" (Sun.)

V locked eyes with me. I was the person who had seen the books. I actually knew how much we needed. I knew it was my turn to talk.

"I would like to make a suggestion." (Me, standing up.)

Maybe there was an uncomfortable silence that

stretched across the room like a piece of string, or maybe I was just terrified of what I was about to say next. I had been working on it since lunch.

"What if we have the apple pressing here instead of on the Farm? We could sell the cider and pumpkins and baked goods all weekend. What if we use it to attract more customers to the café?"

I could almost see that silence pulled tight across the room. It vibrated for a minute like a guitar string being plucked. Felicia's laughter made it snap.

"Can we dress up like scarecrows and play banjos for tips?" she sniped.

"I like your optimism, Starbird, but there's a reason Family businesses usually fail," Paul said.

"The last thing we need is more Family hippies here." Sun shook his head. "You're talking about bringing the whole Farm to the city."

"People are already afraid to eat here because they think we're a cult," Cham added.

"Cham, don't you ever use that word again!" said Europa.

"I'm just saying what people think."

"It's not what I think," said Europa.

"It's what I do," said Felicia.

I could feel my cheeks turning red. I was the farm girl again, most of my experience in a chicken coop. But I didn't let myself give up. "A gallon of organic apple cider sells for fourteen dollars at the co-op. But ours would be made fresh that day, so people would pay more, especially when they'd get to help make it. Last year, we made 175 gallons in one weekend. We would also sell cider by the cup, plus vinegar and farm produce, not to mention the additional café business. Even after expenses, I think we could make a lot of money."

Devin spoke up. "It's true, it is hard to get organic apple cider. Most orchards were treated with arsenic in the pesticides, so it's difficult to get them certified. Our neighbor works at the co-op."

"We could set up the press in the vacant lot, along with a farm stand," said Europa. "It would be like a Family reunion."

"We have to do *something* to make additional money for the café, and it's really not a bad idea." V took a deep breath. "Lots of people do come here because we're organic."

The silence string came back, thick as a ship's rope this time.

"We'll take a vote," V announced. "All those in favor of throwing a cider pressing, raise your hands."

Four hands went up: V, Devin, Europa, and me. That left four down: Sun, Paul, Felicia, and Cham.

"Stalemate," said Sun.

My cheeks were still hot as a campfire. "What if I take care of all the work? I'll call the Farm and get Gamma and

Iron to agree to it. I'll call Family members in Seattle and Bellingham and get volunteers."

"I'm not doing any extra work." Felicia unfolded her arms just so she could fold them again.

"Isn't the pressing already planned for this weekend? They've probably been picking apples and inviting Family members. We can't possibly get this thing together in three days," said Sun.

"That's the good part," I said. "They've already made the plans—all we're doing is changing the location. I'll put flyers up. It won't be any extra work for you guys, unless you want to help."

"I change my vote," Paul said. "I'm going to help Starbird."

"I'm helping, too," said Devin.

V smiled widely at that. "I'll help," she offered, "if I can."

"I'm not coming out of the kitchen," said Sun.

"Yeah, me either," echoed Cham.

So it was decided. I was throwing the Free Family Café's first ever apple pressing.

25

When we finally closed up the café for real, a drizzly rain was falling outside, and the grassy patches along the concrete had turned into sopping sponges. Raindrops hung from every branch and streetlight. We walked past the grassy lot next to the café and then home.

As we got back to Beacon House, I called Gamma Lion on her cell phone, expecting a difficult conversation. I was disappointed in that. She was easy to convince.

"I've been wracking my brain for moneymakers this fall, and was thinking of adding another roadside stand. But you're right, Seattle is a bigger market. Still, this weekend is practically here. I'll have to talk to Iron and make sure the press can be moved easily enough, and maybe get Caelum and Indus to plan the hauling."

Hearing Indus's name turned my tongue to metal. Indus would come to Seattle. Indus would see me in my new element, maybe think of me as "really Seattle." Unfortunately, it would probably mean seeing Lyra Hay, too.

"You'll have to help call the Family members." Gamma was still talking. "A lot of people are already planning on coming to the Farm this weekend. Ephraim has a copy of the Book of Names, so just start at the top. Some people won't like that we're making it a commercial venture instead of a Family gathering, but just remind them it was a commercial venture to start with."

Gamma and I agreed that the apple pressing would be held on Sunday, giving the Farm until Saturday to collect and wash the apples.

"One more thing," I said before Gamma hung up. "Tell Iron to bring our ceramic mugs with him." It was a peace offering. He would know.

V was in the kitchen eating a late-night bowl of granola when I got off the phone. "I'll get you the Book of Names," she told me, "but I'm not sure it's been updated a lot since EARTH left."

The torture began at eight-thirty the next morning. With a hundred things on my plate already, Teacher Ted tried to add a spoonful of American history. How could I care about constitutional amendments when I was busy thinking about the list of things I would need Gamma to bring from the Farm? Luckily, we already had a nice setup for our roadside stand, including a white tent, tables, and hand-painted signs that said ORGANIC PRODUCE and FREE FAMILY FARM STAND.

When I walked into second period, Ben didn't look up or say hello. When we exchanged homework, the sheet he gave me back had my score of six out of ten but was otherwise blank.

The one I gave him back wasn't.

In the margin of Ben's homework (ten right out of ten), I drew a road. That was easy since it only required two straight lines with a dotted one down the center, and I had practiced drawing it the night before. The road continued down the page until it took a sudden right turn and headed horizontally across the bottom edge. At the turn, I drew an arrow and wrote, *BEN(d)*.

He smiled, on the edge of a laugh. I whispered, "Is lunch tutoring available today?"

In the cafeteria, Cham shot a few confused looks at me as I sat down with Ben, but he didn't approach us. I was opening my leftovers from the night before: pasta with foraged mushrooms and nutritional yeast. Ben had a slice of pizza and a soda. He stared at it like the pizza was talking to him and he was trying to understand the language it spoke. He stole a few awkward looks at me.

"I don't really need help on math," I said.

"You got six out of ten today."

"Well, I probably do need help, but really, I need your help with something else."

"You need the accountant's son," he said. "Okay."

"No, I want you to draw something for me. A tree, I'm thinking, with lots of apples."

Ben looked up. *Puddles.* He fished a notebook out of his backpack, and opened to a fresh sheet of paper. I had done some thinking after I talked to Gamma on the phone. I realized that if I was going to pull off the apple pressing in just a few days, I was going to need all the help I could get. So I decided to ask Ben and Rory. Even though they were Outsiders, they were the closest thing to friends I had. It's true that I was attracted to Ben, and I had practiced flirting with him, but I would make it clear to him that I just wanted to be friends. After all, Indus was coming to Seattle, and Indus was in my stars.

"You're not sitting with that curly haired, brooding guy today." Rory stood at our table with her tray.

"Oh yeah," I said, "he's my cousin. Here, sit with us."

"Who's this?" she said.

"Ben. He's drawing something for me. It's a work thing," I said.

"Hot." She sat down and started her ring removal ceremony. "Oh," she said, pausing on her pointer finger. Then she leaned over to me and whispered in my ear, "I think my period just started. Do you have a tampon?"

"A what?" I said back without whispering.

She looked at me, her eyes ringed in eyeliner like little

planets. She leaned in again. "A tampon, like, for your period." She held up two of her silvered fingers and made a sweeping motion.

"For your moon cycle?" I said, not whispering. Why would you whisper about that?

"Tell the world, please," Rory said, throwing up her hands.

Ben was sort of frozen with his pizza half raised.

"What's the big deal?" I said.

"I'm just not trying to advertise it," Rory said.

"Why do girls act so ducking weird about that?" Ben asked. "It doesn't make me uncomfortable or anything."

"Did you just say 'ducking'?" said Rory.

"I promised my mom I'd stop cussing," said Ben.

"Well, I'm glad *you're* not made uncomfortable by my ducking menstruation. That really puts my mind at ease," said Rory, throwing her napkin at Ben and leaving her tray as she ran to the bathroom.

Ben cleared his throat. "So, tell me more about this drawing."

When Rory came back, I asked her a bunch of questions about the harvest festivals that her mom was doing. Then I told them both about the apple pressing but was careful not to add too many details about the Family, just saying, "the café" and "the Farm."

"We can hang the flyers up at school," Rory said.

"It's not really a school thing. More of a neighborhood

thing," I said. I certainly didn't need a bunch of people from Roosevelt showing up and meeting vanloads of my relatives.

In every class I managed to get some aspect of apple pressing planned, even horticulture, where I discreetly mapped out a way to heat some of the cider in the café kitchen, so customers could have the choice of pasteurized or unpasteurized juice. I was starting to appreciate horticulture. Rory told Ms. Frame that I grew up on a farm and it turns out she did, too, and she asked me a bunch of questions about our crops that I couldn't answer because I never worked on the back lot. When she told me about her family's farm on Whidbey Island, her eyes got sad and faraway and it made me think of Fern. She said she would bring pictures of her family farm to show me.

Ben found me and Rory walking together after the final bell and gave me a stack of flyers. "They let me make copies in the office."

The image was a gnarled fruit tree sagging under the weight of fat apples, with the words *apple pressing* vining their way up the trunk. And in the sky above, a flock of dark birds passed, holding stars gently in their beaks.

"You're incredibly . . ." Rory said, snatching one of the flyers from the stack before I could say anything. "Incredibly talented."

"She's right," I said, staring at the flock of birds.

"No, you're, like, really good," Rory said. "Really ducking good."

Ben blushed and wrapped his right hand around his left arm.

Rory and I had to hurry to history club, which was nearly unbearable on such a busy day. At least I could research the history of cider pressing, and maybe get some good ideas.

Teacher Ted greeted me. "Starbird, did you have a chance to check out that book yet?"

"No." I glanced at Rory, who raised both eyebrows. "I've got something else going on."

Ted looked a little crestfallen. "School project?"

"She's doing an apple pressing and you should come." Rory grabbed a flyer off the stack I was holding and handed him one. "You should also tell your classes and your teacher friends."

Before I could protest, Teacher Ted scanned the flyer. "Hey, guys, check this out." He held it up to our group. "You can learn how cider is traditionally made. Extra credit if you're in my class."

"Oh, it's not really a school thing."

"It's no problem, Starbird," Ted said. "Okay, gang, let's write some questions."

That day, I found out that Washington state produces 42 percent of all the apples grown in the United States, that the apple is the state fruit, and that cider making was once a big business in the Northwest. And that secrets have a way of leaking out.

The Book of Names was actually a three-ring binder with a leather cover and the words *Book of Names* hand-painted on the front in cursive letters. Inside were at least fifty pages that had once been typed, but with many of the original details crossed out and handwritten in pen.

Each entry contained the following information: Name (cosmic names, about half of which I recognized), naming date, dwelling (Farm, B.C. Farm, Beacon House, or Bellingham Compound), contact information. There were other curious notes next to some names. They said things like, *Exiled 2008* or *On Mission, no return*, or some ominously read, *Lost*. Entries were organized alphabetically, and the entire book contained about two hundred names.

I sat in the kitchen of Beacon House with a little time to work before dinner. The book was in my lap, watching me screw up my courage to dial the first number. Luckily, since the names were listed alphabetically, the first ones were Adam and Adeona, both Farm dwellers. Gamma would talk to everyone on the Farm, so I could skip them. The third name was Adlai, from Story Night, whose dwelling was simply listed as *Seattle*, so I started with him. Adlai loved the idea of the apple pressing and said his whole family would help. He also offered to get flyers the next day and hang them at coffee shops in the neighborhood. I was off to a good start.

The fourth entry in the Book of Names was Andromeda Snow, whose residence just said *Bellingham*. I couldn't remember meeting Andromeda before.

"Andromeda?" I said when a woman answered the phone.

"Who's this?"

"I'm Starbird, from the Farm, well, Seattle, I guess, Beacon House, now, the café, you know. Anyway, we're having an apple pressing and we need—"

"Are you trying to get me back in the Family?"

"Back in the Family?"

"Don't tell me, let me guess," she said. "EARTH is back and he wants us all up at the Farm in a hurry for some big Translation. Listen, Stargirl, EARTH abandoned us and we've moved on, so you can cross us out of your Book."

"EARTH didn't abandon us, he's on a Mission."

"Open your eyes." She hung up the phone.

I still couldn't place Andromeda. She must have been one of the loose hangers-on, never really devoted to the Family. Adam said a lot of the pretenders left when EARTH did. I happily crossed Andromeda out of the Book of Names. In the space provided, I wrote *non-Believer*.

The next few names I could skip. Badger Ion and Bithiah were on the Farm, and Bathsheba Honey was with

EARTH and Mars Wolf on the Mission. I could also skip Caelum Stone, although it made my heart flutter to think about Indus's brother at the apple pressing. Next was Cham and then a Family member named Clay Omega, whose residence was listed as *Seattle*, with a slash and the word *café*, next to it.

"Hello."

"Is this Clay Omega?"

"Is this a joke?"

"No. I . . . my name is Starbird, I work at the café. We're planning an apple pressing—"

"You're pranking me, right? Do you know who I am?"

"This isn't Clay?"

"I was Clay long enough to be brainwashed into giving away my business. If you want to talk, why don't you tell EARTH or whoever he really is to give me back my café."

"The Family's café?"

"Who the hell are you and why the hell are you calling me?"

My mouth turned to stone. I hung up. Then I took the phone off the hook again so he couldn't call me back. I was staring at the receiver when V walked into the kitchen.

"I'm thinking noodles for dinner," she said, padding past me in slippers and a long dress. "How are the calls going?"

"That last one was . . . crazy," I said, my hand a safe distance now from the phone.

"You can't toss a potato at a Family gathering without hitting crazy," V said, opening a cabinet and taking out a water glass.

"Are you really a non-Believer?"

V paused with a cabinet door open. Then she closed it and walked over to me, putting her elbows on the kitchen island. "Sure you want an answer to that?"

I nodded.

"Venus Ocean, also known as Shelly Allen, was nineteen when she died on the floor of the barn, because EARTH said babies shouldn't be born in hospitals. She was three years older than you are now, and she died giving birth to me. Afterward, EARTH said that her death was the will of the Cosmos." V's hair draped down over her dress and onto the island. She held the empty glass in both hands and looked at it.

"Maybe she would have died in a hospital, too," I said.

"We will never know."

"Why didn't you leave?" I asked. "I mean, when you were old enough?"

"If I lived on the Outside and my mom died in childbirth and my dad went crazy and started living in a tree house, what would have happened to me? Ward of the state, foster homes? In the Family I had Ephraim, and I had community." V clutched her hair with one hand and pulled it back. "I told him about the apple pressing, by the way. He's proud of you." She turned to the sink and filled her glass.

I didn't know what to say to comfort V. I wanted to say that I was sorry about her mom, but I didn't think that would make her feel better. I wanted to tell her that Ephraim would be okay, but how could I know if he would be okay? I turned back to the Book of Names, looking down to the next Family member on the list. Unfortunately, that name was Douglas Fir, and in the box next to his entry, it just said the word *Lost*.

26

The next two days flew by in a frenzy of phone calls, plans, emergencies, and anticipation. Sadly, Ephraim missed all of it because his doctors wouldn't release him, and I was too busy for visiting hours. When I wasn't faking my way through school with half-finished homework, I was hanging up flyers, working at the café, cutting the grass in the empty lot, and working my way through all the phone numbers in the Book of Names.

After the distressing phone conversations of the first night, I was nervous about returning to my outreach, but a series of talks with joyful Believers picked up my spirits. A few volunteers offered to come from the Bellingham Compound and promised to bring handmade soap and tinctures to sell. Two Family members who ran a landscaping business in Seattle met me at the lot and helped me extract dandelions and edge the sidewalk, and Paul's friend at the co-op said they would buy any surplus pasteurized juice we didn't sell. Io got the day of the pressing off and volunteered to watch Kale and Eris, along with any other Family children who needed a nursery.

But even with all the support rolling in, it still didn't feel like enough. The café waitresses would be too weeded in the restaurant to make change for the cider sales, and most of our Family members didn't touch money. It wasn't an ideal situation, but I knew who I had to ask.

"Sure," Ben said at the lunch table.

"If Ben goes, I will," said Rory. They were both eating limp and watery broccoli from their school lunch trays. Why would someone torture a vegetable like that?

I felt okay asking Ben to help since he already knew about the Family and the café, and even our undocumented workers. I was taking a chance letting Rory come, too. But Ben couldn't take money by himself all day with no break. And I couldn't think of a way to tell Rory not to come without hurting her feelings.

"You should know what the people you're going to meet are like," I said. "We talk a lot about family."

I believe in telepathy. I caught Ben and Rory exchanging a silent communication. It was so quick I might have missed it, but I didn't.

"I want to meet your family," said Rory.

At least if they meet everyone, they will see that we're not a cult, I thought.

✻   ✻   ✻

On Saturday, I worked my usual brunch shift, staying late to make final preparations for the pressing, and then it was Sunday morning and the alarm was going off with brutal intent.

Even if you wake up before dawn, it's not easy to beat farmhands to work. When I arrived with V and Europa, the first Farm truck was already there, carrying the ancient apple press into the vacant lot. The person hauling the crank out of the flatbed was Indus Stone.

Red blotches held their own festival on my chest. Luckily, the apple pressing wasn't the only thing I had prepared for. I had given all my tip money to Io, asking her to buy me a dress and a scarf. The dress was a navy-blue knit with turquoise chevrons, tight across my abdomen and flaring at my knee. I wore it with the golden eagle jacket and my farm boots, because they were still the only shoes I had. A thin braid traveled from my part to the back of my ear, growing to a thick rope at my nape, and a tan scarf concealed my blotchy neck. Io had even loaned me some eye shadow, dusty pink.

V and Europa went inside, and I waited for Indus to put down the crank in the yard and turn around.

"Whoa," he said when he looked at me.

"Hey, Indus." Io and I had practiced for this moment. She played the part of Indus, and I practiced seven versions of what I would say.

He was wearing faded jeans with a sweatshirt pushed up to his forearms, and tan leather gloves. My ears got hot. Had the blotches traveled to my ears? "You've changed." He started to run his hand through his hair, seemed to remember he was wearing gloves, dropped the hand.

He might as well have said, *You're so Seattle, Starbird.* He might as well have said, *I want to kiss you.*

"How was the harvest?" I asked, which was not part of any of my practice conversations.

He leaned against the crank of the press. "Everyone's worn out."

"Where's Iron?" He must be nearby. Iron wouldn't trust anyone else with the press.

"He and Gamma had to go to Bellingham."

"They're not coming?" So much for my cool composure. "Iron *and* Gamma?"

"Don't worry. We've got this." Indus smiled and slipped a thick arm around my shoulder. "Caelum and I can manage the press, and you're pretty enough to sell a tanker full of apple cider."

Hello, sap. It started in my feet and rose all the way to my lips. I didn't care about the apple pressing or the café. Frankly, I didn't care if the whole Family went bankrupt and had to live in a tent in the vacant lot. I just wanted Indus Stone to press his body against mine until I was as empty as a juiced apple.

"Hey, Sister." Lyra Hay emerged from the café, wiping her hands on her long denim skirt, her hair falling in silky braids on either side of her face. Indus dropped his arm.

Lyra embraced me like I was a puppy under a Christmas tree. "Ooh, look at your outfit. It's so cute! Look, Indus, little Starbird is in high school," she said, turning me toward him.

Why did Ben have to show up early? He came loping down the sidewalk with his long legs, his eyes peering out from under his shaggy dark hair. He walked up while Lyra's hands were still on my shoulders. I shook them off.

"Hey, Ben," I squeaked. "Ben's going to handle money," I said to Indus.

"I meant to remind you that we should start with plenty of change," Ben said. "The vacant lot looks amazing. Do you guys both work on the Farm? We have a lot to set up before people come. I'm going to need that calculator from the office." Ben's bony hands were jammed in the pockets of his jeans. Standing next to Indus, he looked like a stunted tree, unable to grow because of the taller trees stealing all the sunlight.

"Yeah," Indus said, clapping his gloved hands together and looking Ben over. "Lots of work to do." Then he put a hand on my shoulder and said, "We'll talk later?"

I nodded while pushing Ben toward the café door. "How many Red Bulls today?" I whispered.

"Just coffee," Ben said. "Why?"

Behind me, I heard Lyra purr, "Young love." I nearly ripped the café door off its hinges.

V was too busy talking to Devin to notice when I took Ben through the beaded curtain and into the office. We collected the cash box, change, calculator, paper, and pens.

"Rory can help you with these." I handed him a book of paper receipts.

"She texted. She's running late."

"You guys text?"

Ben shrugged.

The next car to arrive brought Eve, Bithiah, Ursa, Pavo, and Fern Moon. When Ursa spotted me emerging from the café, she ran full speed in my direction, nearly causing me to drop the cash box when she hugged me around the middle. "Starbird, your hair!" She gaped at me. "Your clothes! Your dress is so . . . pretty."

"I'll give it to you when I'm done with it."

When Ursa released me, Fern Moon was there, exactly the same and so different from the woman I left on the Farm. Her hair was still lined with gray, and she wore the same saggy wool sweater, but standing on a sidewalk in Seattle, she looked fragile, like a child lost in the cornrows. She stared at me.

Of the two of us, facing each other in the chilly morning under the café sign, I was the first to hold out my arms. She fell into them and gasped for air like a woman drowning.

"You look so adult," she said over my shoulder.

How did I live without this? How did I forget that I needed a mother? I do want to go back to the Farm. I do forgive her for lying to me.

She pulled out of the embrace and held my arms down to my sides. "My girl." She smiled and the wrinkles around her eyes came alive. Had my mother gotten older in my absence? Then she frowned. "Is that eye shadow?" She took a finger and started to rub my skin under the brow. "You shouldn't be wearing makeup. I hope that's not V influencing you."

I yanked my arms away. "I'm not being influenced," I said. I glanced around, hoping that Indus couldn't hear us.

"You're sixteen and on the Outside. Of course you're being influenced," said Fern, trying to take my arms again.

I backed away from her. "I've got work to do," I said, and marched through the door into the café, forgetting to leave the cash box on the farm table. I had to turn around and walk back outside.

Despite the rocky reunion, I had to admit that Fern and the others did do the lion's share of the setup. They cleaned the apple press, arranged glass bottles for the finished product, set up the tent and signage. In an hour, the vacant lot was transformed into a functioning cider plant.

By seven o'clock, Adam and more Farm people arrived in a truck packed with apples and parked it out front. We opened the back and unloaded some for the press, leaving enough to sell bushels straight from the tailgate. Half an hour later, an old blue Cadillac with Canadian license plates pulled up and stopped in the middle of the street. A woman with white hair and gray robes emerged from the passenger door, held her arms over her head, and said, "Praise," as if she was talking to the sky. It was Saturn Salt and some other members of the British Columbia Farm. They had a picture of EARTH on their dashboard.

A VW bus brought three Family members from the Bellingham Compound who took stacks of Ben's flyers and staple guns and hit all the telephone poles in a five-block radius. When that was done, they stood on the sidewalk, inviting people who walked by to eat at the restaurant and come back when the cider was ready.

That's when my day stopped feeling like a plane on the runway and took off. Customers started arriving in large groups, filling in both sides of the street with cars. Soon, the restaurant was full and I had to start a waiting list, encouraging people to explore the cider press while in line for a table.

I helped Indus and Caelum load the first batch of clean apples into the mill, where we chopped it into a fine mush called cheese. When the cheese was ready, we packed it into wooden trays and let the kids watching help turn the crank that would press those trays down with the heavy metal arm. Within an hour, we had pressed our first batch, the precious juice running down through the trays and collecting in a pan where it was funneled into glass bottles. A crowd of thirty people gasped and clapped with their gloves on as the juice sloshed into the first jar. Then, as fast as that jar filled, someone bought it. Ben worked the sales table with Fern Moon.

Running the press was demanding physical labor, and the boys all stripped down to their T-shirts even though the morning was chilly. Lyra Hay was supposed to be arranging and selling pumpkins, but instead she was buzzing around Caelum and Indus like a fly on fruit. Even when we were working together on the press, I barely got to talk to Indus beyond "Hand me another jar" or "tell Adam we need more apples."

And if I thought the demands of being a waitress were bad, they were nothing compared with managing an event. *Starbird, where can I find a ladder? Did anyone make a sandwich board for the intersection? We're almost out of one-dollar bills. Tell the kitchen we need more hot cider, and where did you put the paper cups?*

Felicia was the worst. *Do you expect me to manage your waiting list while you make cider? Am I supposed to go outside and scream their names when their table is ready? There are too many people here for two bathrooms. Do people understand that only some of this is pasteurized? If the health department comes, I'm pointing at you.*

V started running interference, physically blocking

Felicia every time she tried to get to me. Once I heard V say, "Go count your tips again," and turn Felicia around toward the office.

And the crowds grew. As fast as I could weed names from the waiting list, more sprouted there. People walking past noticed the crowd and stopped to see what was happening, then ended up buying cider. We started a second pressing right after the first one, without even stopping to taste the product.

Ben was amazing at the cash box. Despite the throng of people that swarmed around him, the line never got longer than four families as Ben totaled merchandise and made change at an electrifying rate. Every time I came over to bring him small bills or take a collection of large bills back to the office, I overheard Farm women doting on him. If Eve wasn't bringing him a piece of apple bread, then Adeona was commenting on how smart he was. I heard Ben ask my mother if he could have another chai. "Thanks, Fern, I love chai," he said.

At ten o'clock, as I was flying past the farm table on my way to check the pasteurizing juice, I heard Fern say, "Ben, could you help these folks get two large pumpkins to their car?"

I was stopping to help him carry them when I heard Rory's voice from the sidewalk. "I'll help," she said, dropping her bag in the grass and running over to Ben.

"I got it," Ben said. Then he grabbed each pumpkin by the stem and hefted them onto his shoulders like they were filled with air.

Rory and I both watched him carry those pumpkins to the car. So much for Ben not being up to physical labor.

I gave Rory the receipt book and put her at the table. I didn't make it back to the cider press again after that because I had to answer the phone and run between the office and the sales stand. By noon, we had our first open café table of the day. By one o'clock, I was racing off to set up lunch for our volunteers in the small parking lot out back. Paul and Devin had fixed sandwiches and salads the day before, which Eve and I arranged on a folding table just outside the back door. Family members brought out lawn chairs and camp stools. The VW bus from Bellingham pulled its side door open and people climbed inside to sit and eat.

Whatever I was doing, I was always aware of my proximity to Indus. In the back parking lot, there were two doors and forty-seven footsteps between us. At the cash register, one door and nineteen footsteps. Standing at the sales table with Fern and Ben, Indus was ten footsteps and no doors away.

"You should take a lunch break now," I told Fern as she arranged the tablecloth under the gourd display. "We just put out sandwiches in the back."

"Ben should go before me," she said. "He hasn't stopped all morning."

"I'll go with Ben," Rory offered.

"Yeah, okay," I said.

As Ben and Rory walked off, Fern said, "Your Outside friends make a cute couple."

"They're not a couple."

"Well, maybe they're on their way."

A rose garden bloomed across my chest. *Jealousy.* I shouldn't be feeling that way about Ben, especially not when Indus was finally in Seattle, at the cider press, seven footsteps away. Not since Indus saw the way I had changed. I forced myself to feel happy for Ben and Rory. Let them fall in love and get married. Let them have smart, unusual babies. They were both Outsiders. They would be good for each other.

A man placed three bottles of cider and a loaf of zucchini bread on the table. I totaled his purchase and gave him change.

"You handle money now," said Fern.

I put a fistful of fives into their compartment. "It's no big deal."

We stood in awkward silence beside a pyramid of pumpkins.

"Are they feeding you well at Beacon House? Does V cook for you?" she asked.

"We all cook together," I said.

"You all cook? Could you imagine that on the Farm, the way we would all bump elbows trying to work?" Fern playfully bumped elbows with me. I stiffened.

"It feels strange to be working out here today. I've been working in the farmhouse kitchen for fifteen years," said Fern. "I didn't start there until after you were born, because it was too hot for me in the kitchen when I was pregnant with you. When I was pregnant with Doug, I worked as a waitress at a restaurant like this one." She turned to look at the facade of the cafe. "Can you imagine doing that job when you're waddling around with a huge belly?"

"You never told me you worked at a café." I felt guarded, afraid I would find out more things my mother had lied to me about, or just neglected to tell me. Fern rarely talked about her life before the Family, other than to say that EARTH had saved her.

"My mother had kicked me out." Fern fussed with the gourds on display, rearranging them as she spoke. "She said it was my own sin that had cast me into the darkness. The boy wouldn't admit the baby was his, even after I called his mother. I didn't push for a paternity test. I wasn't much older than you are now."

"Three gourds and two gallons of cider," a man said, handing me two twenty-dollar bills. I gave him change.

"I didn't tell the restaurant I was pregnant when they hired me, but after three months, big sweaters weren't hiding it anymore. A friend's parents agreed to let me stay in their guest room, but I had no idea how to pay for a baby. I guess I hoped my parents would come around. EARTH and Uranus came to eat at my restaurant and sat in my section. Isn't that a miracle?" Fern finally turned toward me, her eyes holding the question.

"Farm people are trying to do their own dishes and Sun is getting pissed," Felicia yelled from the café door, her arm pointing into the restaurant.

V was right behind her. "I've talked to them, it's all worked out. Table two wants bread," she said, pushing Felicia back inside.

"I was the third woman to give birth on the Farm with only a midwife in the room," Fern went on. "EARTH wanted to give my child a biblical name, but I begged him not to. So EARTH named him Douglas Fir, and gave us a place to live, work to do, a family." A red ring formed around each of Fern's eyes. "When Doug ran away, I thought I would go crazy. But I still had you."

"We finished eating, so you should take a break now," Ben said. He and Rory were suddenly behind me. I didn't know how much they'd heard.

I handed Ben the cash box and Fern followed me through the café and out the back door to the parking lot. Family members were sitting around eating, their legs hanging out of the bus door and windows. I turned to Fern.

"Why are you telling me this now?" I said.

"You're exactly the same height as me," she said, brushing my long bangs away from my eyes. "When did you get to be so tall?" A fat tear rolled down my mother's face and fell onto her sweater. Another followed it. Then her face was covered in tears, and so I started crying, too. And then we hugged each other, tears falling down our cheeks and onto each other's shoulders, and I was aware again of how much I missed my mother, whose room and sleep and thoughts I had shared for sixteen years of my life.

"I'm sorry I didn't tell you about the birth certificate," she whispered into my shoulder. "I was worried about you going Outside. How could I know you were capable of all of this?"

The awareness came suddenly. My mother was not just my mother, but also a separate human being, with a past and a future that didn't entirely involve me. She was my age once and pregnant. Did she love that boy who was Doug's father? Did she ever love any of the men on the Farm the way I loved Indus? Did she love EARTH? Did she love Iron?

Indus appeared from the café door, seven footsteps away. "Three o'clock total," he announced, "is two hundred gallons." People sitting around cheered, and a few hooted. Adam jumped up and clicked his heels together, and two men from Bellingham beat the VW bus like a drum. Those who didn't benefit directly from the café were cheering as loudly as those who did. "Crowd's thinning, but we've got apples left. We're going to press more for Family members," Indus said. That brought another cheer.

Then he walked over to me. "Want to take a walk?"

Indus Stone and I walked down the alley, away from the café. The event seemed to be handling itself for the moment, but more important, I was finally alone with Indus. It was happening. I was afraid my eyes were still red from crying with Fern, and I had to keep sniffling.

"How's Fern?" he asked. "You know she's been depressed ever since you left?"

"She has?" Guilt played around in my stomach.

"Yeah, everybody misses you," he said.

"Everybody?"

"Well, mostly the chickens." He smiled. We were several feet from the café now. The sun was a dim bulb in the sky and would stay that way until spring.

"You didn't say good-bye," he said.

"Yeah, I just . . . went." My tongue tied itself like a cherry stem. Indus was so close to me. The sleeves of his T-shirt stretched tight over his muscular arms.

"Lyra's right," he said. "You do look more grown-up."

I realized I was still wearing my café apron over the navy dress. I wished I had taken it off. I shivered.

We got to the place where rough alley met smooth road and saw the Farm truck parked on the street. Indus sat down on the rusty chrome fender. My heart was a mess of butterflies and net, fluttering and getting tangled in itself. I stood in front of him.

"You remember when Doug and I got our apprenticeships? That was your first Translation, right?"

"I was ten." I nodded.

"You were so cute, Doug's little sister," he said. "Those pink flowers in your hair."

"You remember my flowers?"

"I remember everything about that day." Indus's hair was shaggy and badly in need of a trim. I wished I had been there to cut it for him.

"Were you jealous when Doug got EARTH as a mentor?" I said.

"Are you joking? I was learning to fix tractors while Doug was stuck inside doing math. I felt bad for him." Indus put his hands on his legs and looked at his boots.

"You wouldn't have wanted to be EARTH's apprentice?"

"I'll put it this way. We've kept the Farm running for three years without EARTH. How long do you think we would have made it without Iron?"

I had never thought about it like that. "I've got Iron's last name now. It's Murphy," I said, folding my arms against the chilly air.

"No shit," Indus said. "Is he your dad?"

I kicked the truck's tire with my boot. "No one knows."

Indus studied my face like a painting. "I could see it. You remind me of him."

"It might be EARTH, though," I said. "It's possible."

Indus turned his head and didn't say anything for a minute. "I felt like it was my fault you left the Farm. That night you saw me with Lyra—"

"I shouldn't have walked in. It was my fault. We're not into ownership. Now that I've lived in Seattle, I get it." I was talking too fast, interrupting him. A panic was creeping up alongside desire.

"I don't think it's ownership to want to be with one person," he said. "To *want* to be faithful."

"I don't either," I said.

"I was pretty upset the night I kissed you. I couldn't stop thinking about what my mom told me, how my dad left because she slept with EARTH. And you were being so sweet and listening to me." Indus took both of my hands in his hands. His eyes were blue, not like Ben's puddle eyes. Indus's eyes were clear water in a pool at the bottom of a waterfall on a hot day when you've been hiking for hours. "Starbird, we've been so close my whole life." He rocked my hands back and forth with his and looked at my fingernails. "I want to be the kind of guy who picks one person. Who's devoted. I'm with Lyra. She's my girl-friend."

The truck might as well have come out of park, started moving, and rolled right over me. He wasn't trying to kiss me. He was squeezing the juice from my heart.

"I was wrong to kiss you. I'm too old for you. I should have been looking out for you like a little sister." He squeezed my hands. My heart butterflies were all caught and pinned to the wall.

I looked down and let my braid swing in front of my face. The tears tried to take control of my eyes again.

"You're so pretty and special and important to me." Indus reached one hand up to move my hair out of the way. Then he said, "Oh hey, man."

My head snapped up. I looked at Indus, whose eyes were looking at the alley. Standing on the sidewalk just beside the truck and staring at us from under his dark hair was Ben.

"Fern said you were here, and I wanted to tell you the total money you made, but I didn't mean to interrupt you. She said I should go while Rory watches the cash box, but I thought you were alone." He held a piece of paper out to me. It was his handwriting and had a dollar amount written in block numbers and a note that said, *Enough for all the big bills*. Then there was a drawing of a bird with a dollar bill in her mouth, perched on top of a pyramid like the one on the back of the money.

Indus stood up. "I'm going back—"

"I gotta go home," Ben interrupted him, and started walking backward down the sidewalk in the direction of his house. "I told my mom I would be home for dinner and she's making chicken and she said the chicken gets dry if you try to keep it warm, but Rory knows how to handle the cash box. Spam it, I wish I didn't have to leave, but I do."

"Wait—" I said, taking three footsteps after him.

"Sorry." He turned and ran a few feet, leaving me standing next to Indus, who tenderly took my hand and walked me back to the café.

"To Starbird!" Glasses clinked as cider was raised in all directions. It was nine o'clock and the farm stand was packed up, the cider press cleaned and loaded on the truck, and the restaurant closed for the day. Rory was surprised when I told her Ben had left, so she took out her phone and started texting. She left pretty soon after that. I didn't ask her if she was going to see him.

Everyone else had gathered in the restaurant's main room, all the visitors from the Farm and Bellingham and Family members from Seattle. Even Felicia stood behind the cash register, biting at her fingernails, and Sun and Cham stood behind the counter with their aprons still on.

"We should have enough for every person to take one gallon home," announced V, "and we doubled the best day we ever had at the restaurant." Applause broke out, along with many congratulations. Fern Moon kissed me on the cheek and Devin hugged me. Other members patted my shoulder or clinked their cups against mine. Lyra Hay wrapped Indus's arm around her shoulder and nuzzled into his chest.

"Say something, Starbird!" Paul yelled above the chatter.

"Yeah, a speech before we all go home," Adam said.

The room quieted and all eyes focused on me. I cleared my throat. "I'm more tired than I've ever been in my life," I started. People laughed and agreed, raised their glasses again. "And I wish Ephraim could be here." There were many sounds of agreement and more glasses clinking. "Thank you for everything you did. I always wanted to do something important for the Family, I always wanted—"

"I just got off the phone." Eve burst in through the beaded curtain from the direction of the office and cut into my speech. Heads turned toward her. "EARTH is coming back."

27

Like the moon moving in front of the sun, whatever moment of congratulations I might have enjoyed was eclipsed. A roar went up in the café that Ephraim could have heard all the way at Harborview. People were hugging one another, so cider was sloshing onto the floor, sleeves, and shoes.

"Perfect timing," Adam said to a guy from Bellingham, giving him a high five.

"It's a sign. We had to be successful on our own for him to return," Saturn Salt proclaimed, putting a hand over her heart. One of the Canadian Family members started crying.

"It's so fortuitous," Adeona said to Caelum, "EARTH has made all this possible."

EARTH was the name falling off of every tongue, when just seconds before it had been my name.

"Do you think EARTH will get here in time for Story

Night?" Europa was saying to V, who crossed her arms over her chest and did not smile.

Most of the Family members were talking excitedly and making plans. But Sun took off his apron and threw it on the floor behind the counter before slamming through the swinging door to the dish room. Felicia took her purse from behind the register and walked out the front door. I caught sight of Paul and Devin heading through the beaded curtain toward the office. And I stood in the middle of all of it wondering why I didn't feel happy that EARTH was finally coming home.

Indus and I said good-bye while Lyra stretched out in the passenger seat of the truck. When she said good-bye to me, she added, "I was so much wilder than you when I was sixteen. No way could I have been this . . . organized." She didn't make it sound like a compliment.

"I'm proud of you." Indus hugged me. Then he handed me a piece of paper from his back pocket. "I found this by the cash box when I was cleaning up the farm table. Looked like it was for you." He jumped in the truck with the cider press and drove off, Lyra Hay's bare feet dangling out the passenger window.

I unfolded the paper and found another one of Ben's drawings, this one decorating the margin of his scratch sheet, a doodle page full of numbers. The top half was all stars, made of sticks and chubby points and perfect triangles interlaced, all the different ways you could think of to draw them. And the bottom was birds, flying and perched, preening and singing from a branch, sparrows and blackbirds and falcons. It didn't look like Ben was thinking about Rory. And all I had been thinking about was Indus, just one constellation in a night sky full of them.

V and Devin locked up the café behind me. "You ready to walk home?" V said.

"I've got somewhere to go first."

V and Devin walked me two blocks to the house with the red door, so that I wouldn't be on the streets alone at night.

"I'm staying at Devin's, but still don't be out too late," V said, walking off before the door opened.

A woman stood in the doorway. She was wearing jeans and a red sweatshirt and a delicate gold chain with a cross on the end. Her brown hair was in a perky ponytail on top of her head.

"I'm sorry it's so late. I just got off of work and I was hoping to talk to Ben," I said.

Her smile flickered and her eyes dropped to my shoes. Ben popped into the hall behind her. "It's a little late for a visitor," she said, addressing him instead of me but still smiling.

"Just a few minutes," said Ben. "I can still be in bed by ten."

The woman looked me over before stepping aside and motioning me through the door. "You and your guest can sit in the living room. What's your name?" she asked as I stepped one boot over the threshold.

"Starbird."

"How unusual." She disappeared without introducing herself.

Ben led me to a room at the front of the house where a white rug was nestled beneath white furniture. I looked behind my every step, fearing muddy tracks would trail me in the shape of my boots. On every wall was a painting of a man dressed in robes, with flowing brown hair and a light circling his head. It might have been EARTH when he was younger, but I knew they were paintings of Jesus. We had plenty of Christian books on the Farm.

Ben sat down next to a Bible the size of my history text. "There is this kind of seizure that happens in the frontal lobe of your brain," he said, instead of hello. He leaned close to me on the couch, his voice barely over a whisper. "The people who have this kind of seizure experience a religious epiphany. They all report seeing God or sensing Him, even the ones who were atheists before."

"That's interesting," I said, awkwardly crossing my legs and sitting up too straight.

"It is. It could mean that a major religious experience is just caused by some spasm in the brain, a physical convulsion that makes us believe in religion. But someone else could say that God is the one causing the spasm in the first place, and that our brains were designed by God to have seizures."

"Oh," I said, nodding.

"My mom saw God when I was eight years old. She told me about it every night at bedtime for a year afterward. She had never talked about God before that. We didn't even go to church."

"You think she had a seizure?"

"We were at the park. She was sitting on a bench and I was standing on the top of the monkey bars. She says she wasn't paying attention because she was thinking about how she and Dad were trying to have another baby, and when she looked up, I was swaying dangerously on top like I was going to fall. So she jumped up, but then she fell over onto the ground. She says she looked up, and there was Jesus laying his hands on her head. She was filled with a warm light like liquid silver. She wasn't anxious anymore, or unhappy. Since then, the only thing she has wanted is for me to feel it, too." Ben swept his hair to one side so I could see his eyes. They looked brown and sad. Extra puddle-y.

"I came to tell you that I've been practicing flirting with you," I said.

"You're good at it."

"I mean, I've known Indus my whole life and I always thought that we—"

"He seems cool. I get it."

"He is, but we're not together. We were just talking."

"Oh."

"And I was practicing flirting with you, but I wasn't sure if I wanted to flirt with you because you're—" I didn't want to say it.

"I'm what?"

"You're not like me."

"I'm really sorry about saying that cult thing."

"No, it's okay. I mean, I'm not mad."

"Did you make a lot of money today?"

"You should know, you wrote it down."

"Oh yeah." He laughed.

"Do you think she had a seizure?"

"Yes, maybe. I don't know. When I was ten, I was being really bratty and terrible one day, and she locked me in a closet and said I couldn't come out until I saw Jesus. After an hour, I said I saw him and she made me sit at the kitchen table and describe exactly what he looked like before she would let me have lunch."

"What about your dad?" I peered behind me into the hall.

"I started having insomnia after the closet thing, so Dad insisted on a psychiatrist. But my mom said it had to be a Christian psychiatrist, and when I went to one, he kept steering the conversation back to my 'crisis of faith' and using Bible quotes." Ben twisted his thin arms together at the elbow as he spoke. I thought about him picking up the pumpkins. "So when I asked if your family was a cult—"

"EARTH's coming back."

"EARTH?"

"He's, like, kind of our leader. Well, not our leader. I mean, I don't follow him or anything. But he Translates for us. Anyway, he called the café tonight."

"Are you excited?"

"I think he'll be proud of me," I said, realizing it myself. EARTH was going to be proud of me. "Indus is just my friend. I wanted him to be something else for a while, but he isn't, and when he was touching my hair, we were just talking."

Ben, on the white couch, looked at me.

"Do you like Rory?" I said.

"No."

"I thought you did."

"I don't."

"But you guys text."

"Everybody texts."

"Benny?" A man in pleated khaki pants and a white button-down shirt appeared at the living room entrance. "Close to bedtime." The man smiled broadly and extended a hand toward me. "I'm Ben's father, Mr. Fisher."

I still wasn't used to handshakes. I tried to act natural as our palms touched.

"Good night, Dad," said Ben, and his father left.

"So, thanks again for your help today and with the flyers and everything." I stood on the snowy carpet.

"Sure, no problem. I like your family." Ben stood, too.

"So, I'll see you in math." I walked toward the door.

"Yeah, math." Ben followed me.

Just as I reached for the doorknob, Ben touched my arm, the right one just below the elbow. I turned to look at him and he did not kiss me. He didn't push me up against the wall or press his body against mine. He just touched me on my arm, and that's when I learned that touching a girl's arm can sometimes be more powerful than kissing her against a tree under the moonlight.

"You said I'm not like you," Ben said, holding my arm. "But I am."

I smiled at him. The butterflies struggled free of their nets.

I skipped one step for every three I walked on the way home. The sidewalk was like creamy slabs of oatmeal that strangely sparkled in the light of the streetlamps. *Ben. When. Then. Again.*

He still wasn't part of the Family and would probably never be a Believer, but he did draw pictures of my name and lift a thirty-pound pumpkin with each arm. I put my hand on the place where he touched me. Just hours before, all I could think about was Indus. Maybe the Family was right all along. Maybe it was possible to love more than one person.

It had gotten chillier in the hour since the café closed, and I pulled up the collar on my eagle jacket, thinking I would soon need the wool coat I had left packed away on the Farm. Or maybe Io could find me a new one to wear to school. School, where I would see *Ben, men, amen.*

I was still several blocks from home when I first saw the shadow flit between two trees near a house. *A dog*, I thought, *or someone taking out the trash*. I picked up my pace, putting my hands in my pockets.

One block later on the same side of the street, I noticed another one, a dark mass passing behind a truck parked in someone's driveway. Definitely not a dog, a little taller than me. I heard Io saying, *Don't walk alone at night. It's not like the Farm, there are more dangerous things than raccoons*. I crossed to the other side of the street, taking my time in the middle of the road, and keeping an eye on the truck behind me.

A few cars passed and their lights made my shadow stretch and then collapse. I was only five blocks from Beacon House when I saw it the third time. It was definitely a person, running across the street ahead of me, in a dark patch where the streetlights didn't touch. I remembered the homeless man yelling about God. This person had on a dark sweatshirt, the hood pulled up. Now it was on my side of the street.

I crossed again, considered going back the way I came, but didn't want to walk away from Beacon House. If I had a cell phone, I would have used it. *Can I shout loud enough for V to hear me? She's not even at Beacon House; she's with Devin.* There were fenced yards on my left side. I couldn't leave the street until the next intersection, and I didn't know the neighborhood well. I broke into a light jog.

I made it safely to the next cross street, now just two blocks from home. I wasn't close enough to see the porch light, but close enough to imagine that I could almost see it. I shouldn't have gone to Ben's house alone. I should have called V to come get me. *If I scream as loud as I can, they might be able to hear me. Would the Outsiders in these houses help me?* Just two more blocks to go.

That's when the shadow stepped right out of the bushes, a large form blocking my way, making me stop suddenly and gasp for air. I inhaled, preparing to curdle every house's milk on the block with my scream. But the shadow pulled down the hood of its sweatshirt and stepped into the light in front of me, and it wasn't a shadow. It was my brother, Douglas Fir.

28

"**I** thought it was you, but I had to make sure." My brother's voice was gruff. He put his hands on his head and said, "It's really you."

He took a step toward me and I stepped back. The man in front of me had oily hair hanging down to the collar of his limp and dirty sweatshirt. There were days of unshaven growth on his face, and he had a ratty pack strapped to his back. I was certain this man was my brother, but he felt like a stranger. I kept a square of concrete sidewalk between us.

"What are you doing?" I said. I might have meant, *What are you doing here?* or *Why did you leave? Why are you back?* or *Why are you coming toward me?* I meant all of those things at once.

"I was trying to make it to the Farm, but I hitched to Seattle first. I didn't even know you were here until I walked by the café today." Doug's voice was raspy, the way it used to get when he had a cold.

He took another step toward me and I stepped back again.

"Are you afraid of me?" Astonishment colored each of his words.

"No. I'm just . . . surprised. You look so different." But I did feel afraid. My heart was pounding in my ears.

"Yeah, I've changed a little." He gave a strained laugh.

"You abandoned us," I surprised myself by saying. "In the middle of the night, you ran away."

"You think I abandoned you? That's why nobody looked for me?"

"We did look. EARTH looked. Fern went to the Outside police. Where were you?"

"Fern went to the police? Did EARTH know that?"

"No, she did it behind his back. Where were you?"

"Did the cops come to the Farm? Did they investigate?"

"I never saw them. You're not answering me."

He looked up and down the street. There were headlights approaching each way. "We can't talk here. Come with me."

"No." I balled my hands into fists. "Tell me where you went."

"I will, but not here." One set of headlights reached us, panning their white light over Doug's grayish skin.

"You're going to creep up on me in the middle of the night and scare the life out of me and not tell me why you ran away, and expect me to follow you?" I stepped back again, feeling the heat in my belly. I always thought I would be ecstatic to see my brother. But I wasn't ecstatic. I was furious.

Doug threw up his hands. "He drove me to Oregon in the middle of the night saying it was a Mission, and then he said that if I came back or called, he would kill you and Fern. Homeless shelters and migrant worker camps, that's where I *ran away* to. Are you pissed I didn't send a postcard?"

"What are you saying? Who drove you there? Are you saying that EARTH did this?"

"Of course not. It was Mars Wolf. He left me in Eugene with no food or money, yelling after his truck in the street."

A streetlight near us flickered once and went out. Another one, closer to Beacon House, came on. I looked at Doug's outline, afraid he would disappear again in the dark. He was bigger than he was at sixteen, more bulk under his sweatshirt, and we were the same height now. Growing up I was always a head shorter.

"EARTH said you abandoned the Family."

"I don't know what EARTH knew. Trust me, I've had plenty of time to wonder."

"Mars said he would kill us?" No one in the Family even killed animals, unless they were sick or dying, unless it was a mercy kill. I was finding it hard to stand.

"Do you trust your brother enough to walk two blocks?" he asked.

Honestly, I wasn't sure if I trusted the man in front of me. But when he motioned for me to follow him through the intersection, I did. I walked a few paces behind him for half a block, past a row of fenced houses, and then off the street. We walked into an unlit neighborhood park, full of sharply mown grass and rusty equipment. Nestled in a carpet of soggy wood chips was a metal dome made of intersecting triangles.

"I saw Fern with you at the café. It's lucky you're both in Seattle. It's a lot easier than trying to get you off the Farm," Doug said, approaching the dome.

I could see the ghost of my breath as it hit the cold air, but my heart was beating too hard to feel it on my skin. "Fern went back already. What do you mean, 'get us off the Farm?'"

"Shit, she's back there?" Doug grabbed one of the metal triangles with both hands. "Shit."

"Why shouldn't she be?" The exhaustion of the whole day—getting up before dawn, the apple pressing, EARTH coming back, Indus, Ben, and now Doug—was making me sick. My stomach churned and I couldn't remember if I had eaten dinner. I leaned against the metal dome to steady myself and felt its cold bones press against my side.

Doug gripped the equipment with bony hands. I noticed how his clothes hung off him, how everything seemed too big. "At first I had a recurring dream that I came back and found both of you dead in the yurt. Sometimes there was blood on the door. That's when I was in the homeless shelter, sleeping with all my clothes on so they wouldn't get stolen. I had that dream every night for months." He let his head drop toward his shoulders. He looked like a wounded animal, bent over, protecting his injuries.

How could I have been so cruel? It was Doug, my brother; recovered, alive.

I pulled his arms from the equipment and put them around me. A real hug, a brutally real hug. We fell against the metal dome, one of the rods digging into my side. I felt Doug shudder with a raspy cry and then I cried, too, squeezing his shoulders.

"I thought you ran away from us," I said. "I was so angry."

"I thought you never looked for me."

He felt wiry and thin in my arms and smelled like he had been harvesting for a week with no shower. We squeezed each other till we might have caused bruises. The tears poured down my cheeks and my shoulders shook, and Doug sobbed and gasped for air. That's when I heard the footsteps.

"Hey there." A flashlight was walking toward us. I looked at the street and saw a dark police car with its door open. "This park closes at dusk."

"Sorry, officer." Doug dropped his hands from my

arms. He combed his hair with his fingers and stood up straight.

"What are you folks doing out here?" The flashlight shined into each of our eyes, causing me to raise a hand to my face. "Miss, do you know this person?" The light crawled up and down Doug's body, his muddy boots, his torn pants.

"He's my brother," I said, wiping the tears with the back of my hand.

The light rested on my face. "Where do you two live?"

"Three blocks that way." I pointed.

The light traced over each of us again, head to toe. "Park's closed, so I'm going to need you to move on."

"Yes, sir," Doug said. As we started walking toward the street, he reached out and took my hand. We were back on the sidewalk before Doug whispered, "He could have found my camp."

"You're camping here?"

"See that line of trees? Tent underneath."

"What would happen?" I glanced back over my shoulder at the police car.

"Arrest maybe. Probably just make me pack up and move. Tell me to go to a shelter downtown but not give me any way of getting there. That's the real Outside, Starbird. You're not allowed sleep in the grass under the stars, unless you own the grass."

✻ ✻ ✻

After walking on for a few blocks, we finally saw the police car drive off. Then we doubled back toward the other end of the park and came to a baseball diamond, where we sat in the darkness of a cement dugout, both looking out toward the pitcher's mound.

"How did you survive?" I pulled my knees up to my chest and wrapped my arms around them.

"I stayed at a teen center until I turned eighteen. Then some kids told me about the network for organic farm-workers. I didn't need a Social Security card and most of the farms have housing for migrant workers. I made my way up through northern Oregon."

"Why did you wait? I mean, why did you come back now?"

"Bathsheba Honey showed up a week ago on my farm. She was traveling north along the coast with network people because she had just left EARTH in California with Mars. She said he bought a house down there. I wish I had known he wasn't at the Farm. I would have come back so much sooner."

"Mars Wolf can't buy his own house. We only own property together."

"Mars didn't buy a house, EARTH did."

"EARTH bought a house for us in California?"

"He bought it for himself, under his Outside name. Sheba told me. She said he's buying things as Arnold Muller—a truck, a business. EARTH told Sheba he was going to share everything with her, that she could be his wife. But she got sick of the scene and took off."

"Arnold Muller?" I said. My brain was a camera that couldn't get focus. The repeating payment logged in the café ledger, the payment that Ben and I had never sent.

"Yeah, Arnold Muller. The reason Mars tried to drive me off." Doug snorted and turned away from me. He reached into his backpack and pulled out a rolled-up pouch that held crinkly strings of tobacco.

"You smoke?"

"Hanging out with migrant workers," Doug said. "Learned some Spanish, too."

"Tell me about Arnold Muller."

"What's funny is that the day I became EARTH's apprentice, I felt like a hero." Doug loaded two pinches of tobacco into the paper and rolled it into a thin tube, licking one end to seal it. "I can't really describe it. It was like not just being part of a cell, but being part of the nucleus of a cell. I got my own desk in EARTH's office, remember? He had fired that accountant from Bellingham and wanted to train me to do the books. He probably would have used Mars, but Mars could barely add. Do you know Mars never finished high school? He was a drug dealer when he met EARTH. I found out a lot in that office." Doug took a lighter from his jacket pocket and lit fire to the end of his cigarette.

"There was complicated math in those ledgers, lots

of money coming in and going out. I was only thirteen." Doug propped one foot up on the bench and took a long drag from his smoke.

"You know what job they gave me at thirteen?" I said. "The chicken coop."

"If I could go back in time, I'd do anything to get the chickens," Doug said, exhaling blue smoke through the dugout fence. "But no, I had to work for EARTH. He kept giving me harder paperwork and not explaining how to do it. If I asked too many questions, he would just tell me to go away until I felt like being useful. Soon I was writing checks, doing taxes, and I barely understood any of it. It's a convoluted corporation they set up to manage the Farm." Doug took another long drag from his cigarette and exhaled slowly. "And the CEO is Arnold Muller."

I remembered what Ben had pointed out. Sun's last name was Muller.

"Some Family members showed up with nothing, like Fern," said Doug. "But some came to the Family with money or property, like Jupiter, or the guy who owned the café. EARTH got them to turn everything over to the Family, said that nothing should be left under their Outside names."

"That's the only way we can be communal," I said. "We have to own everything equally."

"Exactly. That's why it was so weird when I found the Farm's monthly payments to EARTH's Outside name. He had bank accounts as Arnold Muller. Why would EARTH own personal property when no one else in the Family did?"

"Maybe he had to. It doesn't mean he did anything wrong just because the bank has his Outside name. V tells everyone her name is Felicia."

"Who's V?"

"A girl from Beacon House. Never mind. My point is, maybe it's just a legal thing."

"That's what EARTH said when I asked him about it. I knew I shouldn't, but we were in the office late at night, and Mars was there, too. The frogs were so loud by the pond that it sounded like a stereo was on in the room playing frog noises. EARTH didn't get mad. He actually sat closer to me so I could hear him over the frogs. He said that Jupiter, who he called Judas, was bringing a lawsuit against the Family to try to get back the money that he had willingly shared. EARTH said the only way to protect the Family was to put the money in a personal account. That was the same night that Mars Wolf told me we had to go on a Mission, all the way to Eugene."

"But that makes sense," I said. "If EARTH had to protect us from a lawsuit, why does it matter what name the money was under? I'm sure EARTH didn't know what Mars did. You didn't see how upset he was when you went missing. Fern and I sat with him all day." I remembered

EARTH, sitting on a pillow in his room the day we discovered Doug missing, the red veins showing in the whites of his eyes. "I can talk to EARTH when he gets to Seattle tomorrow. I can tell him what Mars did."

"EARTH is coming back?! Now?" Doug put his foot down on the cement and turned to face me. "Shit. Then there's no time." He stood up and tossed the end of his cigarette through the fence. "It took me a week to hitchhike from Bend, but we should be able to score a ride to Bellingham pretty fast. Getting all the way to the Farm is going to be harder, but maybe you could just call there and ask for Fern. They won't suspect you. Damn it. Why now? Just when I found out he was gone."

"Suspect me? Of what?" I stood up, too.

"We can't leave without her even if she wants us to. I'm sure it will be terrifying leaving the Family at her age. You know she's afraid of the Outside. But we can't abandon her to them."

"What are you talking about? I know Mars did something terrible, but we can't run away."

"Mars? What about EARTH? What about Arnold Muller and the house in California? Aren't you listening?"

"You're the one who isn't listening. EARTH said he had a good reason for using his Outside name. I'm sure he has a reason for the house, too."

"I know you've grown up in this." Doug gripped my

hand and squeezed it. "But it isn't what you think it is, Star. We can all go back to Oregon together. I can find us all work on the farms. We can make it."

"No." I wiggled my hand free from Doug's grip. "EARTH was looking for you in California. We just need to talk to him. He'll fix it."

"If EARTH was looking for me, I'm afraid to think why."

"You're wrong about him." I said. "I'm a Believer. I believe in EARTH."

Doug took hold of my upper arms. "I know this is hard, but you've been brainwashed."

I knocked his hands away and tried to push past him to leave the dugout. "Maybe you've been brainwashed by Outsiders."

"We don't have time for this." He grabbed my arm again to stop me.

"I'm not going to run away from my Family." I moved wildly like a fish on a hook, trying to wriggle out of his grip.

"*I'm* your family, Starbird. I am and Fern is." His voice quivered. He looked sad and cold in his thin sweatshirt and jeans. I was cold, too, and exhausted. I stopped struggling and he let go.

"I don't want to leave without you," he said.

"I need to think about this." He wasn't just asking me

to leave my Family. He was asking me to leave everything I had ever known. And the same day I might have saved the café, the very same day I became important. But how could I just send him away again, with no one to love him, alone on the Outside?

"I'll wait for you for one day. But promise me," Doug said, dropping his hands to his sides, "if you see EARTH, you can't talk to him about any of this. Don't even let him be alone with you. He has a way of convincing people of things."

Doug looked so lonely and strange standing in the dugout, no friends, about to sleep in a tent in the park. He looked like what the Book of Names had called him. He looked lost. "Okay. I won't say anything."

Doug walked me back to Beacon House, where all the lights were off and the house was quiet. I snuck some food from the kitchen out to him through the back door, along with a jug of new apple cider. He stuffed a roll into his mouth as soon as I handed it to him.

"Remember your promise," he whispered, disappearing into the wet darkness. "I'll come back tomorrow."

29

The next morning's alarm rang without mercy. It clashed around my head like three different shades of red. My thoughts jumped right to Doug, waking up in a tent in the middle of a rainy park, alone and hiding. I wanted to run there and take care of him. But if I did, I was afraid it would mean that I was agreeing to leave my Family and go with him. I wasn't ready to do that.

I had questions. *Is Doug telling the truth, and, if so, why did Mars drive him off the Farm? Did EARTH know? Why is EARTH holding money and property as Arnold Muller?* And the most pressing of all: *Have I been brainwashed?*

I closed my eyes again and tried to look inside my own skull. It still felt like my brain, like my thoughts. *What if it's the Outside that's trying to brainwash me by telling there is something wrong with my Family? Maybe Doug is the one who got brainwashed. Where is my actual brain in all of this?*

I thought about staying home from school, maybe playing sick. But then I would be surrounded by Family members all day with no room to think. That's when I remembered it. I reached under my mattress for something I had hidden there, careful not to make noise and wake Io.

I pulled out the book Teacher Ted had given me, *Looking for Utopia: Intentional Communities in the United States.* I turned it over in my hands. The book was from the Outside, probably written by an Outsider, but it was also a history of other communities like mine. Educational information or Outside propaganda? I peeked under the cover and then opened to the introduction titled "America, the Utopian Dream."

> *A commune is a group of people living together who share common interests or philosophies, and, in some cases, work, income, and jointly owned property. Members have emotional bonds to the whole group rather than to any subgroup.*

That sounded like my Family. Not our beliefs or our Principles, but the way we lived. It didn't call us a cult. I kept reading.

> *Attempting to build more equitable, sustainable, and loving communities outside of "normal" society*

has been a human endeavor since the Greeks and Romans. In the sixteenth century, Thomas More's book Utopia *became popular in Europe and led to a rash of communes—communities created to exclude tyranny, corruption, and private property. When North America was colonized by Europe, many of these alternative communities were looking for a new land, unsettled by the old power. Utopian societies sprouted like weeds in the so-called New World.*

So far, my Family sounded like a utopian society, and that didn't sound like a bad thing. Dispelling "tyranny, corruption, and private property" had to be good. I glanced at the clock and realized I would need to run for the bus. I shoved the book into my bag and got dressed.

I couldn't risk reading any more on the way to school because I was sitting next to Cham on the bus. But I did sneak in some reading during first period, hoping Ted wouldn't notice *Looking for Utopia* nestled in my history text. While the rest of the class read about constitutional amendments, I was skimming the first chapter, about an early American commune called Fruitlands, founded by Amos Bronson Alcott, the father of Louisa May Alcott, who wrote the book *Little Women*. At Fruitlands, people believed spiritual fulfillment was found in nature, not in a church. They lived and worked on a farm together near Boston, but their commune lasted only seven months. Some members said it was because Amos "held too much authority and demonstrated a stringency that limited the autonomy of the others."

A shadow fell across my desk. Teacher Ted was standing over me. His eyes traveled from the book to my face. He nodded and kept walking around the room.

In second period, I had to admit that I hadn't done the homework. I still graded Ben's paper (another ten out of ten), and he gave me a drawing on notebook paper of Earth orbiting the sun, and a banner that said, *Stars have magnetic pull*. I was forced to do math problems all period and couldn't find a subtle way to learn more about communes.

At lunch in the cafeteria, Ben said, "What book were you hiding in your lap in math? More homework you didn't do?" He smiled at me from under his hair. Rory was absent, so it was just the two of us.

"Not exactly," I said. "Do your parents call themselves followers?"

"Sure. Jesus is the Good Shepherd and all Christians are his flock."

"I just don't like that word, *follower*. It sounds sort of brainless, doesn't it?" I sipped the cider I had brought from home and picked at my portobello sandwich.

"My parents wouldn't say 'brainless,' they would say 'humble.' By calling yourself a sheep, you're admitting that your nature is sinful and that you need to follow Jesus to overcome your nature." Ben took a bite of pizza. "But I don't know. Karl Marx said religion is a drug that keeps people complacent and easy to control," he said with his mouth full.

"What do you think?" I asked.

Ben put down his slice and wiped his hands. "You know when someone seems desperate to make you believe something, and it just feels weird to you? Like, why do they care so much what you believe? It feels off to me, like someone is trying to make me wear a coat that doesn't fit, and they don't want to hear me admit that the coat's too small. They want me to say that it fits perfectly."

"Yeah," I said, shifting around on the cafeteria bench.

After lunch, I could no longer stand to hide my book in class. So I went to chemistry and presented my teacher with the crisis pass Ms. Harper gave me. This felt like the closest I would come to a crisis. Even though I was supposed to use the pass to go to the guidance counselor's office, I went to the library and found a little table behind one of the tall stacks. There I read about the Shakers at Mount Lebanon, New York, who led the largest and most successful communal society in North America. For a hundred and sixty years, they lived their ideals about the equality of labor, gender, and race, as well as communal property and nonviolence. They were led by Mother Ann, an Englishwoman who came to America with eight followers and used her charismatic personality to get them to give up their possessions and stop having children. That community died out for obvious reasons.

Our Family believed in communal property, too. At least, I thought we did.

I read about early socialist communes like Brook Farm, the Amana Colonies, and the Oneida Community. Most of them were concerned with creating a bond between intellectual and manual labor, giving everyone access to education, and promoting equality for men and women. Nearly all of them had conflicts with Outsiders. The bell rang. I hadn't stopped reading for the entire period.

I used the crisis pass again to get out of literature, then Spanish and horticulture, my whole afternoon of classes. I kept going back to the library and the same table behind a tall stack. Classes of students came and went, and occasionally someone would stroll past my table. But I was lost in the pages. I finally got to the chapters on modern American communes.

The author said there were tens of thousands of communes started in the 1960s and 1970s. There were "open land" communes where there were no leaders, just free space where people built structures and lived together. Most of these communes didn't last because of management conflicts and because they had no leaders to help find resolution.

I read about places like the Hog Farm and the Olompali ranch, where members made food and gave it for free to Outsiders, because they believed everyone should have something to eat. All of the communities seemed to start with such good intentions, such intense beliefs that the world should be a better place. But commune after commune failed, and lots of people went away feeling angry.

> One persistent reason communes dissolve is dis-
> agreements over authority and structure. A common,
> idealized notion in such communities is that no one
> should tell anyone else what to do, and directions
> are given by those with the most knowledge about
> a particular job. But strong personalities frequently
> step forward to take on responsibility, and there is a
> tendency toward the creation of mother and father
> figures. Communes with shared spiritual beliefs have
> proved to be the most stable and the most long-lasting.
> One of the largest and oldest of these is the Free
> Family Commune in Washington State.

I stopped. I read the sentence again. I slapped the book shut and looked around. The library had gone quiet, not one student left in the room. I didn't even see a librarian bustling around behind the circulation desk. With a shaky hand, I opened the book again.

The Free Family Commune was founded in 1970 by Arnold Muller, a first generation German immigrant and advertising salesman who purported to hear divine instructions from "the Cosmos." Renaming himself EARTH and his disciples after planets, he moved the group to the Murphy family farm in rural Washington State in 1975 where a faction of the group has lived for almost forty years. Although a splinter group in British Columbia worships Muller as a deity, most factions consider him a father figure. Some former group members report excommunication of those considered non-Believers and coercion to share property. Most notable among these is Ronald Sums (Family name Clay Omega), who deeded a property and restaurant business in Seattle to the Family during his membership in the 1970s, and Steven Cross (Family name Jupiter Sand), who gave a large sum of cash to the Family in 1981.

There it was in print: my life and my Family boiled down into five pathetic sentences written by an Outsider. This didn't capture my Family. It didn't sound like us at all. It did explain why Clay Omega was so angry when I called him about the apple pressing. My eyes wandered around the library, still quiet and student-free. Suddenly, I realized why. School had ended twenty minutes ago. I was late for history club, and it so happened I really needed the answer to a question today.

When I burst through the door of Teacher Ted's classroom, other kids were already at computers doing research. Ted looked up from his desk and said, "Starbird, you made it."

"Sorry I'm late." I was out of breath, the book gripped against my chest, its title hidden by my arm.

"Want some tea?" He reached for the electric kettle on his bookshelf.

"I have my question." I sunk into a chair near his desk.

"Okay." Ted poured hot water into a cup and handed me a tea bag. "Want to share it with me?"

I glanced at the other students in the back of the room. Their eyes were stuck to their computer screens. I didn't want to expose more secrets to Teacher Ted, but I needed help I couldn't get from my Family. I scooted my chair closer to his desk and lowered my voice. "How do you know if you're being brainwashed?"

Ted touched his beard before leaning toward me. "Starbird, before we go on, I need to tell you that if I believe you are being physically harmed or in danger, I legally have to report that to the state of Washington."

"No. I'm not in any danger." I paused. *Was that true? Did Mars really threaten to kill me?* I shook off the thought. "I'm struggling with my beliefs."

"Ah," said Ted and nodded. "That is a common experience for people from all backgrounds. Brainwashing is an interesting topic. There is plenty of debate in psychology and sociology about mind control." Ted leaned back in his chair again. "Research has shown that sudden changes in behavior, even core values, can be achieved through coercion and that all human beings are susceptible. Some neurology experiments indicate that conditioning the brain's frontal lobe can lead us to more black-and-white thinking indicative of mind control." Ted paused. "I'm getting too technical. Let's look at this another way. Have you ever noticed a situation where a bunch of people were all doing something strange, maybe even shocking, and it doesn't make sense to you?"

"I guess."

"Give me an example."

"Well, I don't get why women wear high-heeled shoes. They won't keep your feet warm or dry, you can't do physical work in them. You could twist your ankle. They don't seem to do what shoes are meant to do."

Ted started laughing. "Great one. Yes, high-heeled shoes are specific to certain cultures, and they happen to cause all kinds of muscular strain. So that's an example from our culture. To take it in a more serious direction, you could look at a case of genocide, like the one in Rwanda in the nineties. Neighbors who had lived next to one another for years suddenly started picking up machetes, going to their neighbors' houses, and killing everyone. Not just in one incident, but all over the country. The world was shocked. Now, there were complicated historical reasons that this happened, the most insidious and devastating being the effects of colonization, but the *way* it happened is that radio stations were running a constant program of insults against a certain ethnic group, calling them rats and calling for their extermination. Seemingly rational people picked up machetes and started killing their next-door neighbors because they heard on the radio that they should."

I wanted to cry. "But I would never do something like that just because someone told me to."

"That's what we all think. But what if you were being constantly fed a diet of terrifying information, someone telling you that those neighbors were going to steal everything you owned, take over your country, if you didn't go kill them?"

"I still don't think I would do it," I said.

"And many people didn't. It wasn't everyone in the country. Some people risked their lives to save others. The important question for us as people has to do with the difference between those two groups—those who followed orders and those who didn't. As a teacher, I influence students to act, dress, and speak in ways that are culturally acceptable in the U.S. Those rules would be completely different if we were in China or South America. The point I'm trying to make, Starbird, is that we all see ourselves as freethinking individuals, but each of us is a product of cultural rules and information that guide our beliefs. It is very difficult to tell the difference between that and mind control."

I dropped the book into my lap and leaned against the back of the chair. Teacher Ted's examples were making me feel hopeless.

"Oh man, I went there again, didn't I?" Ted put both hands on his head. "You came here to talk about your life and I went all history teacher on you. It drives my wife crazy. She wants to talk about chores, and I start a discussion of the shifting gender roles in the industrial age. You said you were having a crisis of faith?"

I did need to talk to someone, but it was so hard to tell who to trust. How could I know what to think if I was being influenced by everything I heard? "People are telling me things," I said, "and I can't tell who I should believe."

"I see." Ted laced his fingers together and put his hands on the desk. "That can be very difficult, but the fact that you're asking these questions is a good sign," he said. "It shows that you are questioning, thinking critically. The ability to think critically seems to be the one way we're able to distinguish between culture and our individual decisions. The world is a complicated place, and sometimes that makes people want to follow a leader or a set of principles that makes the world look simple, black-and-white, right and wrong. Do you mind if I give you some advice?"

"I don't mind."

"Keep asking questions. Listen for what resonates as the truth within yourself, but think critically." Ted made a fist and put it against his chest. "Don't look for absolute rights and wrongs. The world rarely provides them."

30

After history club, I ran to the bus stop. I wanted to get home so I could sneak some food to Doug before dinner. EARTH was coming tonight. EARTH would be at Beacon House for Story Night. I should have been elated. This was the moment I had been anticipating for three years. But no other emotion could trump my anxiety. If dogs can smell fear like they say, then every pooch on our block must have known I was coming.

I raced up the steps of Beacon House, flung open the door, and nearly screamed. Standing right inside the foyer and peering into our hall closet was an older, thinner, and more wrinkled Mars Wolf.

My face probably showed the terror I was feeling, so when I attempted a smile, I must have looked demented, smiling and sad at the same time.

Mars Wolf looked at me and he smiled, too, but more like a satisfied cat. "Starbird, I've missed you," he said, opening his arms to offer me a hug.

I dropped my backpack on the floor and stepped toward him like he was a diving board and I didn't know how to swim. How do you hug a man who threatened to kill you?

Through the door to the kitchen, I could see V chopping onions at our island. She was watching us.

"Starbird!" A warm, full voice came booming from the living room and filled the hall, rescuing me from Mars. It was a voice I loved. It was EARTH.

I moved with relief into the front room. Seated in the overstuffed chair where Ephraim usually sat, with Kale on his lap and Europa perched on a short stool next to him, was our Translator and Guide. His beard was whiter than before, long and full. He was a thinner version of Santa Claus, wearing a cashmere sweater and jeans instead of a fur-lined suit. He also wore black leather slippers and had a large silver ring on each hand.

EARTH handed Kale to Europa and gestured to me. "I've got some serious questions to ask you," he said. "Come here and stand in front of me."

My hands became fists. A gang of red blotches ran roughshod over my chest. Did he know about Doug, or about my conversation with Teacher Ted? Did he know about my bringing Ben into the café, or that I knew about Arnold Muller? Would I tell the truth or lie? "Okay," I said, walking over to a spot on the rug in front of his chair. I tried to hold my head up.

"What did you do with the little girl I left at the Farm? You've replaced her with a beautiful woman." EARTH's blue eyes sparkled and the sweet wrinkles around them multiplied. His shoulders had a slight hunch where he sat in the chair, but his presence was huge in the room. Even seated, he might have been ten feet tall.

The fortress I had spent my day constructing fell to pieces. EARTH was back. All the stress, sadness, and concern drained out of me. I sank down on the rug at his feet. Everything that had been wrong—Doug, Mars, the Farm, the café—it was all manageable. EARTH could fix it. We could do it together. I could feel my love for him fill up my chest. How could I have doubted him? He loved me.

"Eve and I framed your letters," I said, resting my head against his knee and wrapping my arms around his calf.

"I wish I could have written more." He stroked my hair. "We were so busy. Wait until you see everything we've been doing for the Family."

Tears of relief and joy came fast and unexpected. It was warm and dry in our house, and the smell of dinner cooking was rich, and EARTH was back and everything was going to be okay.

"I was just saying to EARTH that we should start home-schooling again, that you and Cham should stop going to public school," Europa said.

Cham walked in from the kitchen carrying a cup of tea and handed it to EARTH. EARTH took the tea with his left hand, but reached for Cham's hand with his right. "The first thing we need to do is get Ephraim home from the hospital," he said, staring at Cham. "Then we can get him healthy again."

I looked up at Cham's face to see it breaking apart. His lip was quivering and his eyes were red. He put his free hand over his face and his shoulders buckled.

"The Cosmos told me he will heal," said EARTH, squeezing Cham's hand.

Cham sucked in a sudden breath and pulled his hand away. He turned to the basement door and disappeared into the lower level.

"He'll be okay," said EARTH. "We'll all be okay." He took a sip of the tea and put it down. "Tell me, Starbird, about our wonderful success at the café. Europa says you've been very helpful." EARTH put his hand under my chin and looked into my face. I felt like I hadn't been looked at in a long time. Or maybe I'd been looked at but not seen.

"I've tried to be useful," I said.

Europa made a little snorting noise.

"That's what I hear. I know about the apple pressing. I know how profitable it was. We need more entrepreneurs in the Family."

A prideful sparrow started singing in my belly. *Entrepreneur.*

"So, was it just the apple pressing, or did you help with more of Ephraim's work while our brother has been ill?"

I looked down at EARTH's slippers. "I did some bank deposits, too," I said, which wasn't untrue. Then I added, "I'm pretty good with numbers."

"Yes," EARTH said, his eyes squinting almost imperceptibly, "so I've been hearing. You did deposits, and did you pay some bills as well?"

"I did pay some bills," I confessed. "I know it wasn't my job, but there were so many marked *final notice*, so I just paid those. And I did the payroll." The more I told EARTH, the lighter I felt.

"What an amazing girl. You figured that all out on your own?" EARTH's eyes moved through each of the four quadrants of my face, a searching gaze.

I nodded slowly. He looked a little longer, then said, "Well, our financial worries are over. I've got some exciting news to share tonight. I would like you to sit next to me at dinner, Starbird, and during Story Night as well."

Europa stood abruptly and lifted Kale onto her hip. "Come on, Kale, let's make ourselves *useful*," she said, disappearing out of the room.

I practically skipped into the kitchen to help V finish the meal. I had waited three years for this. EARTH never meant for me to work in the chicken coop. He called me an entrepreneur. He saw me as important, the way he saw Doug Fir.

Doug Fir. I suddenly remembered I hadn't brought him dinner. My brother was out there in a park hungry, and I was in a warm kitchen, filled with food and Family. The thought made me furious. Why did he have to leave in the first place? Why did he have to snoop into EARTH's affairs? That's why Mars Wolf threatened Doug—he was just protecting EARTH and the Family. I had managed to help with café bills without getting in trouble. Why did Doug have to ruin it? I couldn't leave the house now. *Doug will just have to fend for himself,* I thought, but guilt nagged at me as I gathered silverware to set the table.

"We visited Ephraim today in the hospital," said V, cutting slices of warm bread. "EARTH and Mars went, too. His cough isn't getting any better, despite the steroids. They're going to do more tests."

"I bet he was so happy to see EARTH there," Europa said.

"Yeah, in between coughing fits, he was just ecstatic," said V.

We put an extra leaf in the table, and EARTH sat at the head with Mars Wolf at the other end. Europa put out a white tablecloth and candles and the loveliest of our mismatched china. As everyone started to sit, Europa put her hand on the chair to EARTH's right. EARTH stopped her. "I want Starbird to sit here," he said. "You move one down."

Europa made a big production of moving Eris's high chair toward her new seat. I took the chair to EARTH's right and Cham, who had reemerged from the basement for dinner, sat on his left. Throughout the meal, EARTH gave most of his attention to me. He asked me about Fern Moon, about my apprenticeship in the chicken coop, and about school. He asked me about the general mood on the Farm and how people had been behaving in his absence. I told him about the fistfight between Firmament Rise and Spring Meteor and how lots of people left us after that.

"Yes, I felt strongly that I had to leave the Farm for a while. Like the storm that shakes the tree and loosens all the dead limbs, the Farm needed to lose some non-Believers," said EARTH. "You're one of our true Believers, aren't you, Starbird?" EARTH's eyes seemed to open the door to my thoughts and walk right in.

"Yes," I said, but it didn't sound the way it had sounded when I said that in the past. "Yes," I said again, inserting more conviction.

"Good." EARTH patted my hand. "I'm going to need you in the exciting days to come. But first, I've got something I need to tell you."

EARTH put down his fork, so I put mine down, too. He leaned closer to me, his blue eyes losing the reflection of the candlelight and turning dark. His voice quieted so no one else at the table could hear.

"I wasn't able to locate your brother," he whispered, taking one of my small hands into both of his large ones. My hand felt protected and safe in the space made by his.

"We looked for him, in California and Oregon. We asked for news from all the travelers we met. Then Mars heard some rumors." EARTH sighed and his eyes flicked away to the candles and then back. Could he feel my heart beating through my hand?

"This will be hard to hear," he continued. "We believe that Doug has been living in homeless shelters and taking drugs that may have deluded his thinking. We heard that Doug is a non-Believer now, spreading falsehoods about the Family. I fear he may be gone for good." EARTH's eyes shone like wet rocks. He put a hand on my shoulder.

My conversation with Doug from the night before came echoing back—the gruffness in his voice and the desperation, the tobacco he smoked in a rolling paper, how haggard and unkempt he looked. He did say he had been living in a homeless shelter. Was my brother addicted to drugs? Is that why he said that Mars Wolf threatened to kill me? Did Doug invent that story to get me to leave the Family? I glanced down the table at Mars, who was spearing a piece of asparagus with a steak knife. He was smiling a greasy smile and talking to V, who didn't seem that interested in what he was saying.

"But why would he run away in the first place?" I asked. "He wasn't doing drugs on the Farm."

EARTH looked down at his dinner plate. "Many nights I have blamed myself for that," he said. "I don't think your brother was ready for such a challenging apprenticeship.

The work was hard, and I was a demanding mentor. I'm not perfect, Starbird," he said toward his plate.

I squeezed EARTH's hand. Who comforts EARTH when he's busy comforting all of us?

"I tried to make him an accountant when I should have let him be a boy. Doug was pretending he could handle all the work, but he started showing signs of stress, strange paranoia. He was having fantasies, conspiracy theories that I was stealing from the Family, that Mars was some sort of evil henchman. In the end, I think he just snapped." EARTH shook his head sadly, picked up his fork, and put it down again.

I couldn't make eye contact with EARTH. He knew everything that Doug was saying. Doug, a paranoid drug addict? He wasn't acting normal when I saw him in the park. He was scaring me. But then, he was scared himself, hungry and homeless. After a minute, I managed to speak. "Can we help him?" I asked, tears interrupting the words.

EARTH's voice was dry. "No, my sweet girl. Doug is lost."

"Thank you for coming together tonight, Family." EARTH's voice radiated through the living room where twenty Family members had gathered for Story Night. From Beacon House, V, Cham, Europa, Kale, and Eris were there. Penniah and Adlai had brought Dathan and a starstruck Sapphira, and other Family members from

Seattle had gathered to welcome EARTH back to town. A few who weren't even at the apple pressing came. By the time we were all seated, every chair in the house was in use, and most of the floor space on our rug, too. But Paul and Devin had yet to show up. Io was missing, too, since she had to work late at Red Light.

I sat next to EARTH in a chair from the dining room. Mars Wolf sat on his other side, with a large poster board cradled under his arm.

"I want to hear stories about everything that's happened to my Family since I left for my Mission." EARTH stood in front of the windows as he talked, all heads looking up at him. "But first, I have an important story of my own."

A thrill went through the room at the thought of EARTH telling a story. Sapphira squealed, causing everyone to laugh. Then the room became so quiet, someone might have told an ant walking across the carpet to stop making so much noise.

"Three years ago, I left to go on a Mission. I told you all that the Cosmos instructed me to go, but I didn't tell you everything the Cosmos said. Our Farm is destined to fail," EARTH looked up toward the ceiling. He seemed so tall standing in the living room, and his words were haunting. "Our café will go bankrupt, too. The Cosmos told me that our businesses would barely survive five years, much less see us safely into the future." The silence in the room turned tense. I could hear the refrigerator in the kitchen hum. A few people exchanged panicked glances.

"The Cosmos instructed me to leave my Family and journey into the wilderness, although it pained my heart every day to be away from you. I was told to go to California, and promised I would find a new paradise there. After these three long years, the Cosmos has provided. Behold, the California Mansion."

At these words, Mars Wolf stood and revealed the image he was concealing on the poster board. He held it up over his head in front of the room and turned slowly so we could all see. It was an aerial photograph that showed a sprawling multistory house, with a white stone facade and circular driveway. The backyard held a swimming pool, tennis court, and a pond with a fountain. The only evidence of nature were some palm trees and several beds of flowers.

Gasping in surprise, hands clasped over their mouths, people seated on the rug got up on their knees and everyone leaned in closer. A few people stood up, blocking other people's views. "Fourteen bedrooms and plenty of space for a yurt village," EARTH was saying. "The kitchen has restaurant-grade appliances, the living room has vaulted ceilings, and the basement is the same square footage as our barn. It even has an indoor movie theater and water pressure you won't believe."

A few members laughed. One woman seated on the floor started to cry.

"And here is my most exciting news." EARTH smiled. "Have a look at some of your new Family members."

Mars turned over the poster board in his hands and revealed another photograph on the back. There were five young people, two men and three women, arms linked, sitting next to a bank of computers.

"These are the lost ones the Cosmos sent us looking for." EARTH motioned toward the photo. "They have worked hard and shown themselves to be true Believers. They are ready to welcome you to California and train you all in the new Family business, information technology."

V, who had been leaning against the archway to the dining room, disappeared into the kitchen. Other Family members turned to one another and began talking. I'll admit, the photo of the mansion was stunning, especially the bright sun that seemed to bathe the walls. From our crowded living room in Beacon House, where the rain was whipping itself against the windows in splatters, it was hard not to be swept away by the dream of California. But it was also hard to shake the feeling that something wasn't right. We weren't the kind of people who lived in mansions.

"What about farming, and being back to the land?" a Family member named Branches asked.

"I've been seeking out farmland near our Mansion where we can grow food to sustain ourselves. But small farming as a business is nearly impossible to maintain in this age. We must acknowledge the changes in the modern world, and the Cosmos has instructed me to build our future on computers."

Some of the men in the group nodded, but many of the women looked uneasy.

"How will we find the money for this?" Adlai asked from his seat on the carpet.

"I'm glad you asked that, Brother," said EARTH. "It's the reason I've come back to you now. It's time to sell the Farm and use the proceeds to finish payment on the Mansion."

EARTH's words tore through me like a sword, cutting me right in two. The farmhouse, the chicken coop, the apple orchard? The back lot? What about Iron's cabin? What about Iron's ancestors? Would Iron be able to live there until he dug a hole near the fir trees to bury himself? I couldn't picture Iron in the California Mansion. I couldn't picture any of us there, except EARTH.

"Change can be difficult and frightening. When Moses led his people out of Egypt, they were terrified. But the faithful went with him, in search of the Promised Land. I have come back to ask this of my Family." The room was no longer silent. Penniah and Adlai were whispering to each other. Other people were talking in small groups.

EARTH held up his hands for quiet. "Mars and I will go to the Farm tomorrow morning, with the faithful in tow, to hold a Translation and announce the plans to the Family. I hope you will all go with me."

For some reason, my dumb mouth synthesized all my questions and concerns into one utterly inane query. "What about my chickens?"

EARTH looked almost startled for a second when my voice came at him from his elbow. He turned and stared at me, examining me for a moment in silence. Then he started to laugh, a big, full-bellied laugh.

"What a wonderful child! Starbird asked about the chickens. We'll get new chickens, with a larger coop, more sunlight, and fresh air in California." Then he paused and looked at me. "But I don't think you will be working in the chicken coop anymore, Starbird. Stand up here, next to me. I have another announcement to make."

I pushed myself out of my chair. I hadn't even processed EARTH's first announcement yet, and he was about to make a second.

"In honor of Starbird's work in organizing the apple pressing and helping the Family stay financially solvent during my absence, I am assigning her to a new placement." EARTH paused and looked around the room. "Starbird will be working with me, in our offices in California on all things related to our new business. I will be grooming her for an important role in the future of our Family. She is uniquely suited for the job"—EARTH paused again and looked at me—"because Starbird is my daughter."

31

The clamor inside my head was unreal. "Of course, that makes so much sense," I heard someone say. "I can see it now, in the eyes," said someone else. Sapphira broke free of Penniah's arms and ran over to me singing, "EARTH's your dad. EARTH's your dad," and then Kale joined in, too.

EARTH did not draw me into his arms and hug me. Instead, he gave me a gentle push into the center of the room, where Family members could pat me on the shoulder, congratulate me, and clasp their hands to bow.

Europa said, "Starbird, how wonderful," before turning away and stomping into the kitchen. Cham gave me a halfhearted bow. Venus was nowhere to be seen, but other Family members closed in to praise me. "She was such a strong leader during the apple pressing," I heard Adlai say, "I'm not surprised to see this."

This is what it feels like when all your dreams come

true. There are twenty hands touching you, but you don't feel them. The congratulations swell into your heart the way seawater rushes into a sand castle when the tide comes in. And then the water leaves again, and your sand castle is flatter, looking a lot like sand.

"Thank you," I said to the people around me, "thank you so much." The congratulations continued until EARTH finally quieted everyone again and called for the true beginning of Story Night with a song.

I barely heard any of the festivities that followed. *EARTH is my father.* Those were the only words I heard ringing through every song and repeated in each story. *My father* sung to me in so many voices.

The last of the Family members left around ten. Europa bustled around cleaning up the living room. "V's coat is gone. I bet she went to spend the night with Devin again," said Europa, shaking her head. "I can't believe she left me to clean up alone."

"I'll help," I said, moving the living room chairs back in place.

EARTH remained seated in the overstuffed armchair, talking quietly with Mars Wolf while we cleaned. Europa took a tray of tea mugs back to the kitchen, and I moved to follow her when EARTH said, "Let me speak with you for a moment. Alone."

Mars Wolf exited the room, leaving me with a mug

in each hand, staring awkwardly at the man who called himself my dad.

"Have a seat, Starbird." EARTH motioned to the floor in front of him.

The only promise I'd made to Doug Fir was that I wouldn't talk with EARTH alone. But Doug was possibly a drug addict. And if EARTH was my father, then when Doug Fir insulted EARTH, was he insulting me? What bond is more important, father or brother?

I put down the mugs and walked over to EARTH, sitting down before him on the rug.

"Did you always suspect that I was your father?" EARTH looked down at me, his blue eyes dancing the way Ephraim's did.

I nodded. *Suspected and hoped.* "Why did you wait until now to tell me?"

"I will need my most trusted allies next to me during this next phase. Plus, you're old enough to bear children now, so you should know what genes you carry." EARTH smiled and folded his hands in his lap. "Starbird, there were some payments that Ephraim was making each month before he went into the hospital. Do you know anything about that?"

It was a yes/no question. I couldn't tell a half-truth. I bobbed my head up and down, *yes.*

"Yes. Europa told me you had been looking into the books at the café."

How did Europa know that?

"Do you know who the payments were being made to?" he asked, still smiling.

"Arnold Muller," I answered, "but I didn't know who that was. Until I figured out it was you."

EARTH closed his eyes. "That was my Outside name," he said. "Sometimes we have to use our Outside Names when we do business with Outsiders. Ephraim was making payments to help us purchase our Mansion, and we have made the down payment on what will be our new home. Do you see how necessary it is to the future of the Family? Do you see that we can't sustain ourselves just from our little Farm?"

It all sounded logical. Why shouldn't money from the Family's café be used to buy the Family's new house? And he was right. The Farm was failing, and we had to have a new plan. We were lucky EARTH was watching out for us. I nodded.

"Is there anything else you're curious about?" EARTH said.

"The new mansion, it belongs to all of us right? It wasn't just purchased in your name?" I regretted asking it immediately. I had been infected with Doug's paranoia. It wasn't my place to question.

The crow's feet around EARTH's eyes formed a series of tiny Vs. "Where did you get a question like that?"

"Nowhere," I said too quickly. "I shouldn't have asked."

EARTH studied me. "Of course it belongs to the Family," he said without blinking. "Why would it be any other way?"

I let out a slow, even exhale. Then everything was settled. It would be sad to lose the Farm, but we would all be moving together. I was sure Family members would love to get out of the damp cold of the Northwest and go live in sunny California. Ursa wouldn't have to work in the chicken coop. Fern wouldn't have to bake all day in the kitchen. Iron could adapt to California, I told myself. All he needs is time. But Doug. What about Doug?

"Go on up to bed now, Starbird," EARTH said. "Tomorrow's a big day."

"Good night, EARTH," I said, turning toward the staircase.

"Starbird," he called to me, so that I turned back. "Call me father."

"Good night, Father."

It wasn't the alarm clock that woke me up. It was an arm shaking me. I was startled to open my eyes and see Mars Wolf.

"Quietly now," he said. "EARTH needs you."

I looked at Io's bed and saw her sleeping soundly. The clock said 2:30 a.m.

"In the middle of the night?" I pulled my blankets up to my neck, wishing I could just roll over.

"We're leaving for the Farm in the morning, so it has to be now."

"I'll get dressed," I said.

"Try not to wake anyone."

I met Mars Wolf in the foyer, expecting EARTH to be with him. "EARTH is at the café," Mars said. "He needs your help paying the bills for September."

"I can try," I said, "but I'm not sure I'll be much help." I didn't want Mars or EARTH to know I had shown the books to Ben. I got nervous thinking about EARTH in the office, looking through the books alone, and hurried to put on my shoes, wool hat, and gloves.

Outside it was misting rain, and the streets shone wet like black rocks on the beach. Winter was circling us, preparing to close in.

Mars and I walked to a shiny new truck, which was parked on the street in front of the house. As I touched the handle to open the passenger door, something occurred to me. "I'm not authorized to sign the checks," I said. "We have the money from the apple pressing, so all EARTH needs to do is take the bills to Ephraim and get his signature."

"EARTH needs you to explain some things about the books," Mars grumbled and added, "just get in."

Something about the way he said that, "just get in," made my heart tremble. Teacher Ted had told me to listen to my inner voice. Something inside me was yelling. My hand still on the passenger side door, I looked through the window and my blood stopped flowing. Sitting on the seat of the truck was the book Teacher Ted had given me, the one that had been in my backpack.

"Why were you in my backpack?" I said, taking a few steps back from the passenger door. "Where are you trying to take me?"

"To EARTH," replied Mars Wolf, stepping away from his open door and walking toward the back of the truck.

"Did you drive my brother off in the middle of the night? Did you tell him you would kill me?"

"Crazy rantings of a drug addict. I wonder where you heard those?" Mars moved quickly around the truck, faster than I thought he could.

"I'm EARTH's daughter. You can't do anything to me," I said, panic rising like an elevator inside me, rocketing to the top floor.

"Just get in the damn truck."

I turned back toward Beacon House, thinking I could scream and wake everyone up. V wasn't home, but the others would help me. And that's when I saw the sight that squeezed my heart till it bruised. Standing in the hall, with the little green door open, watching the whole scene, was Europa. And as I took two running steps toward the safety of Beacon House, she stepped back into the foyer and closed the door.

I looked back at Mars, who was paused at the truck's

tailgate, one foot held off the ground. I sprinted. I had two feet on the sidewalk before Mars Wolf had one, and broke hard down the street, in the direction of the café.

I could hear Mars Wolf's steps after me, all the way to the end of the block. Then I heard him say, "Shit," and stop abruptly. After several feet, I turned to see if I had lost him and saw his driver's side door slam as the truck lurched down the street. I cut left at the intersection and then right between two houses toward the alley. A dog collided with his chain-link fence as I passed, barking ferociously. I could hear the truck's tires squealing, turning around toward the alley.

I doubled back, out between the same two houses and the barking dog, and across the street to some bushes. I knew where I had to run, but I couldn't lead Mars Wolf there. Luckily, no dogs were out on the next block, and I made it to another alley and then a yard without hearing the truck. I came out on a familiar sidewalk, and ran down it all the way to the park with the baseball diamond. I checked both directions before making a break for the trees at the north end and ducking into them to catch my breath.

The sound of my heart and the rain were what everything in the world was made of. Then headlights turned down the street near where I squatted, crawling slow and menacing down the road. I tucked myself low behind a trunk, making sure no white piece of clothing or reflective bit of jacket was visible to the street.

The headlights passed. I sat for a few minutes before pulling my hat away from my ears to listen. The park was dark and quiet again.

I didn't stand but hunched over, staying low as I moved. Doug said his tent was near this row of trees, so I figured I could creep from trunk to trunk and find it. How hard could it be to spot a tent pitched in a park?

I walked through the grass and over roots, head down, for several feet until I felt a surprising pain near my right ankle. My foot slipped and I tripped into the wet leaves, my cheek smashing into the ground.

"Get up," said a voice above me, thick and ferocious. Mars Wolf had found me. He was going to drive me off in the night to deposit me at a teen homeless shelter somewhere in Oregon, or maybe he would just kill me. "Get up," he said again.

I rolled over and looked. It was Doug Fir, poised over me with a baseball bat, ready for a battle. I held my arms over my head. Was he high on drugs? Would he hit me?

His arms went limp. "I set up trip wires so no one could sneak up on me," he said.

Doug didn't have a tent at all, just a dark-blue tarp secured between two bushes with a sleeping bag underneath. He had booby-trapped it on every side with some stakes and a wire that was invisible in the dark. It was hard to imagine a drug addict would think to do that. He helped me up.

"Mars Wolf," I said, feeling myself start to lose it, "he tried to drive me off." Then I was crying for real, crying like I cried when Doug left, like I hadn't cried since EARTH went on his Mission, like I was thirteen again.

"I would have come to find you," said Doug, pulling me into a hug, pressing his hands against my back and neck. And I hugged him back ferociously inside the square of trip wires.

"I'm sorry I didn't bring you dinner."

"I've been fending for myself for a long time," he said into my hair. Then Doug pulled away and started to untie his tarp from the bushes. "He's still out there looking for us. We should probably move."

"And go where?" I said. "We can't go to Beacon House. We can't go to the Farm because they're going there in the morning to have a Translation."

"What if Mars tries to do something to Fern?" Doug was rolling up the tarp now, into a tight ball, his eyes scanning the street.

"Doug, are you using drugs?"

He shoved the tarp into a canvas bag. I couldn't make out his expression in the dark. "I smoke pot sometimes. Did mushrooms once. Why?"

"No reason." It was true, Doug was using drugs, but did that make him a drug addict? EARTH smoked marijuana, too, but EARTH said that not everyone could handle it. One thing was clear: Doug had been telling the truth about Mars Wolf kidnapping him.

I grabbed one of Doug's bags, and he hoisted a pack onto his back when the camp was broken. We started walking toward Paul and Devin's house. That's where V would be, and it was the only place I could think of to go. There was Ben's, but I couldn't imagine his parents being too happy about a late-night visit.

We tried to take smaller streets. I didn't know the way very well and I kept getting confused. We decided to use major arteries and duck into the bushes whenever a truck passed.

"Do you think these guys will drive us to the Farm? If we can get there before EARTH, we can talk to Fern alone," Doug said as we walked. "Maybe we can even get her out of there before he arrives."

"We can't just grab Fern and go," I said. "What about everyone else? What about Iron and Ursa? What about Indus? We need to go expose Mars Wolf. We need to tell EARTH what he's been doing."

"Tell EARTH about Mars Wolf?" Doug stopped walking. "What about Arnold Muller and EARTH owning property?"

"He has good reasons for that," I said, stopping, too. "The Family was being sued and he had to put the money someplace safe. And he bought the Mansion for all of us."

"Oh, the leader of the cult's bank account is somehow safe from legal action?"

"Don't say that. Don't use that word."

"You talked to him alone, didn't you? What did he tell you, Starbird? How did he convince you not to listen to me?"

"Why should I listen to you? You already told me you're using drugs. Are you an addict now, is that why you're trying to break up the Family? Is that why you're here?"

"*Drugs?* Are you serious? Is that what he told you? I'm here because *you* are my family. I don't have anyone else in the world but you and Fern, and now you're going to choose EARTH over *me?*" Doug was yelling, no longer cautious about the passing cars. "You know what? Keep it. Keep EARTH and the Family, and good luck in California!" He grabbed the bag I was carrying for him out of my hands, turned away from me and started running.

"Doug, no!" I screamed. But he didn't stop. I tried to run after him, but he was faster than I was, even wearing a pack. He must have had a lot of experience running. He passed under one lamppost and into the darkness, and then he was gone again, out of my life just like before.

I was hardly aware that I was walking after that. I trudged along the sidewalk, occasionally ducking into a yard if approaching headlights appeared to belong to a truck, but almost too tired to care anymore. *Let Mars take me to Oregon*, I thought. *Maybe it would be easier that way.*

32

Paul wasn't happy to see me in the middle of the night. I got to his place a little before four a.m. It was dark and still outside the tiny house he and Devin shared with their mother, Seta, and with Sun.

"I'm working the open shift," Paul said when he saw me standing on his front porch. "And you are destroying my last half hour of sleep right now."

"I'm really sorry." I stepped through the door into the hallway. "Mars Wolf tried to kidnap me."

Paul flicked on the hallway light. His dark hair was standing up straight where his pillow had shaped it.

"What the hell?" Devin appeared from another door off the hall, wearing pajamas. V was right behind him.

"Doug came back from Oregon, but then he left again. EARTH's going to sell the Farm and café to buy a mansion in California." I sounded like a patient under hypnosis. I kept talking without emotion.

Another door opened at the end of the hall. Seta was

pulling on a cotton robe over her nightgown. She said, "Someone make some coffee. Starbird, come in the living room and sit down."

Paul woke Sun, who looked angrily at the clock in the hall and immediately went into the kitchen and started pouring a bowl of cereal.

The rest of us gathered in their tiny living room, crowding around the coffee table. I sat on the sofa between V and Seta, with Paul in an armchair and Devin on the floor. V stroked my back in little circles. I told them about Doug's reappearance, what he said about Mars Wolf, how he came back after he ran into Bathsheba Honey.

"I worried about Bathsheba when I heard she went on the Mission," Seta said. "EARTH chose me to go on a Mission once, when I was young. He can be quite captivating."

"Good word choice, 'captivating.'" Sun walked into the living room with cereal and a pot of coffee, which he put on the coffee table for all of us. He sat on the floor against the wall.

Then I told them about the payments to Arnold Muller at the café, and about Mars Wolf trying to get me into the truck.

"I've heard rumors about Mars before," said Seta. "Clay told me he finally stopped trying to get his café back because of Mars's constant threats."

"You've talked to Clay?" I remembered his angry

voice on the phone asking, *Do you know who I am?*

"We joined the Family at the same time," said Seta. "He had his café and I had my divorce settlement. We both signed over what we had to the Family willingly. It's hard to turn around and change your mind after that. But Iron never had the choice. He shouldn't have to lose his inheritance."

"EARTH's a con man," said Sun, "a classic scam artist."

"Don't talk that way about him," said Seta, scolding him like he was her child. "Think of all the people he's helped. We wouldn't have found each other if it wasn't for the Family."

"You left the Family, too," said Sun.

"EARTH's not perfect, but no one is. He just has no head for business. He's a dreamer."

"And what about Mars, is he a dreamer, too?" Sun tossed his spoon into the empty cereal bowl and put it on the floor.

"We can't let him sell the café. Where are we going to work?" said Devin.

"Some other café, I guess," said Paul. "It's not like we're gonna fight EARTH."

"It's easier to say you can just find another job when you have a birth certificate," said Devin.

"We would lose Beacon House, too," said V. "Ephraim signed everything he had over to the Family."

"Wouldn't any of you move to California?" I said.

There was a strange silence in the room. "I left the Family because I wasn't a Believer anymore," Seta finally said. "I don't think that EARTH is a terrible person or a con artist, but I just don't believe that he hears the voice of the Cosmos."

"I, however, think he's a con man," said Sun.

"What about you, V?" I said.

"Frankly, I don't buy the Cosmos crap," she said, pouring herself a cup of coffee. Devin put his hand on her leg. "But this is my Family, so what do I do?"

"I just don't want a leader," said Paul.

"Same here," said Devin.

"So, no matter what happens now, it's going to break up the Family." I thought about Doug Fir, out there in the dark with his duffle bag. Maybe I should have gone with him to get Fern. Wasn't there anything I could do to keep the Family together?

"I really need a ride to the Farm," I said to the room. "I can't just sit around and let this happen."

Sun finished off his cup of coffee. "Let me grab my keys. I think I finally got my Calling."

Sun put on his shoes and coat and went out to start his van.

"Do you need help getting dressed, Momma?" said Paul, helping Seta out of her chair.

"No time to waste," she said. "I'll go see EARTH in my pajamas."

"You're coming with me?" I said.

"I want Iron to keep his farm," said Seta. "My word probably holds no weight with the Family these days, but I still want to try."

"I'll go with you," said Devin.

"So will I," added V.

We were packed into Sun's rusty VW van by four-thirty a.m. and cruising up I-5 toward Bellingham by five. As the lights of Seattle and the congested businesses of Everett passed, the land was swallowed up again by trees. Evergreens lined both sides of the highway, their thin, pointy tops reaching futilely for the stars. We fell into a sleepy silence with the sound of the van's engine working hard on every hill and turn.

"What time do you think EARTH will leave for the Farm?" said V. "If we can beat him there, maybe we can talk to people before the Translation."

"They probably called ahead," said Sun. "Family members are probably in the barn as we speak, sprinkling rose petals on EARTH's pillows."

I imagined Caelum and Indus rushing to move their beds out of the barn, Fern rising in the dark to brew coffee. Would Iron even be there for this Translation, or would he be in his cabin or harvesting the back lot while the homestead of his ancestors was sold out from under him?

"EARTH doesn't have to convince everyone in the Family to sell the properties, he just has to convince the board of directors," said V, her head resting on Devin's shoulder in the rear of the van. I sat in the middle with Paul, and Seta was in the passenger seat.

"He may have already convinced them," said Paul. "Most of them will do anything EARTH says. Saturn Salt would walk to Mexico on her hands if he told her it was her Calling."

"I have to tell you guys something." I had to stop the shame burning a little hole in my belly. "I still love EARTH. I'm still a Believer. He told me he's my dad."

The sound of the road ate up the silence.

"I wouldn't take that too seriously," said Sun. "EARTH says a lot of things."

"But he wouldn't lie about that, would he?" I said, trying to dispel my own doubt.

"Well, if it is true, then it sounds like it's time for you and me to have a sibling chat," said Sun. "Haven't you guessed it by my name yet?" He looked in the rearview mirror at me. "I was seven years old when my dad came home and told me and my mom that the Cosmos was speaking to him. Can you imagine how that sounds to a seven-year-old?"

Sun checked his side mirror and changed lanes. The van struggled to keep highway speed. Of course, *Sun*. It didn't occur to me before. I had never heard it talked about on the Farm that EARTH had a child before he was EARTH.

"My parents were only nineteen when they had me. Dad had to start working, buy a house, try to be responsible. But then he got laid off when I was six and spent a year on unemployment. At first, he spent his days calling about jobs, taking his résumé around, but after a while, he started just watching television. My mom was the one who suggested he get a hobby." Sun laughed after he said the word *hobby*.

"First, he took these self-improvement classes through this group called EST, and from there he got into motivational speakers and then sweat lodges and fasting. His biggest obsession was a woman named Kathy who was channeling spirits. He took us to see her right after I turned seven. She sat onstage and closed her eyes, and when she opened them again, her voice sounded Russian or something, and she talked a lot about death and the other side. I got scared and started crying, and my dad got so angry, he took me out to the car and spanked me. A few days later, he started talking about the Cosmos."

"At first, Mom seemed to be humoring him, like she would say, 'That's so interesting Arnold, maybe you can tell us about it over dinner.' She and I even laughed about it one time when he was out. She said, 'The Cosmos said you should help your mom fold laundry.' But one night I heard him yelling at her in their room, and when she came out, her eyes were red and she never joked about it again. When the meetings of the Planet Elders started up in our living room, she changed her name to Uranus Peak. I remember the day my dad sat me down and told me that I couldn't call him dad anymore, that I would have to call him EARTH."

Sun grabbed his travel mug from its holder and took a sip of coffee. "So, I became Sun because that's what the whispering Cosmos told my father to call me. I don't know at what point EARTH told my mother that he wanted an open marriage, but I saw how he acted with Neptune and Venus. When he moved to the Farm two years later, he left Mom and me in Seattle. Did you know that I basically grew up at Beacon House?"

"No," I said, but that was the least of the things I didn't know. I had never wondered about EARTH's life before the Family because I had been taught that what we did in the World Outside, before the Family, didn't matter. But it mattered to Sun.

Sun looked at me again in the mirror. "Sorry, Starbird. You never heard that version on Story Night."

"So why did you move out?" I asked. "You never come to any Family gatherings anymore."

"Why did I choose to leave the Family? I didn't. Mom and I were at the Farm for a Translation when I was about your age. My mom had been struggling to raise me among the crowd of strangers that kept moving in and out of Beacon House while my dad lived in his palatial room at the Farm, constantly with different women."

"In EARTH's defense, we were all doing that, not just him," Seta said gently from the passenger seat.

"Not my mother. She wasn't doing that," he said.

Seta nodded.

"I actually wanted to be like him at first," Sun said. "I thought I might be the one Translating someday. I used to sit in my room and try to listen to the Cosmos." He laughed and shook his head. "I guess the Cosmos didn't choose to speak to me."

I was glad for the night because it meant Sun couldn't see me going pale. I thought about how badly I had wanted EARTH to be my father.

"Anyway, at that Translation, EARTH told us he was leaving for a Mission to eastern Washington, and that he was taking Mars Wolf and a woman named Eclipse Pine. And, right in the middle of the Translation, I lost it. I stood up and said, 'Why don't you take my mother on a Mission? Why are you always with a new woman?'

"I'll never forget his eyes when he looked at me. He didn't seem surprised at all. He said, 'Like Thomas the Apostle, my son has been infected by doubt. The Cosmos warned me this would happen. How many of you in the congregation also thought Sun would question his faith?' Hands sprouted up all around me, almost every person there. Not my mom, though; she didn't raise her hand. But then EARTH called her out.

"'Uranus Peak,' he said from the platform, 'do you feel

that I have forsaken our love?' My mom stood in front of everyone and said no without looking at me. So EARTH asked her, 'Do you feel I have put you aside for other women?' She said no again. And then EARTH turned to me. 'You are sixteen now, a man, and I won't keep any man in the Family against his will. I grant you my permission to leave us for the World Outside if you find that you are not a true Believer.'

"*I grant you permission.* Can you believe he said it that way? It's pretty hard to find a place to go when you're sixteen," Sun said.

Seta reached over from the passenger seat and patted Sun's shoulder. He drove with his left hand and pushed the cigarette lighter into the dash with his right. I thought about Doug being forced out into the world at sixteen. Had I lost my brother again? Why did I let him run off? A painful twist started in my belly. Everything was wrong. Everything.

We drove on in silence for a while, people looking out the window or dozing. It was another half hour before we took the exit off I-5 toward Bellingham.

The sun was lifting a lazy eyelid over the Cascades as we rolled into town. We turned onto the country road that would lead us to the Farm, and our little van started stirring with activity as people yawned and stretched. We passed the spot for our usual roadside stands, the sign that said FREE FAMILY FARM, and turned right onto our land.

Sun jumped out to open the gate that kept our goats from wandering off.

"It's locked," he yelled back toward the van.

The gate was never locked. It didn't even have a lock. I climbed over Paul's legs and jumped out of the van's side door. Sun was holding some sort of chain with a padlock on it. Devin climbed from the back of the van with an iron bolt cutter.

"I had a feeling they might beat us here," he said, handing the tool to Sun.

"This isn't going to be easy, Starbird. You should not underestimate my father. Or maybe *our* father." Sun placed the bolt cutter's mouth on the metal chain and brought down the teeth with a snap.

We crept slowly along the gravel drive, trying to make as little noise as possible. Sun didn't continue all the way to the farmhouse or even to the Sanctuary. Instead, he cut the engine, turned off the lights, and rolled quietly to park near the woods by Iron's cabin.

We all piled out of the van, with Devin helping Seta. Six sets of feet crunched over the gravel in the early morning light. It was chilly out and fall had settled everywhere on the farm. I shivered with cold and exhaustion. Chocolate crowed by the coop, followed by Bad Boy, like they knew I was there. Everything I loved about mornings on the farm presented itself. I felt all the joy and sadness of coming home.

"Do you have a plan?" Sun walked next to me. We were getting closer to the barn and passing a number of cars and vans, even a bus with a Canadian license plate. Apparently, word of EARTH's Translation had spread quickly. No one was standing outside and the Sanctuary door was closed. They had started already. EARTH must have left Seattle in the middle of the night.

"Plan? Me?"

"If EARTH sees me, he's going to know something's up. He'll send Mars Wolf out, or he'll turn the congregation on me. Same thing with Paul, Devin, and Seta. They all left the Family and they weren't called to the Translation. Either we go in there with our guns blazing for a fight, or you go in there quietly alone."

"I could go," said V. "It would make sense if I drove Starbird here."

"You've only been to a handful of Translations in your whole life," said Devin.

"I say we all go in," said Paul. "We call Mars Wolf out immediately and make EARTH explain about Arnold Muller."

"Then we give EARTH the advantage. He'll have some great explanation ready and make us look like non-Believing troublemakers. It's not like we have many allies in there," said Sun.

"But maybe EARTH does have good explanations," I

said. "I want to expose Mars Wolf, but I don't want to do battle with EARTH. I just want to convince him to keep the Family together."

The others exchanged silent looks around the circle, except for V who looked at the ground.

"I think she's too susceptible to him," said Sun. "I don't think we can trust her in there."

"Don't act like I'm not here," I said. "I know about mind control."

"Knowing about it doesn't mean you can resist it," said Sun.

"You're not giving her enough credit," said V.

"Maybe she's right," said Paul. "Everyone knows she's a Believer and they all love her since the apple pressing."

"They do?" I said.

"Keeping the Family together can't be our only goal here. EARTH wants to keep the Family together, too, and look at all the terrible shit he's done to accomplish it," said Sun.

"Yeah, but you'll never be able to kick EARTH out of the Family," said Devin. "EARTH *is* the Family. We should focus on what we *can* do, which is try to save the Farm."

"I don't want to get rid of EARTH," I said. "I want us to stay together, and keep the Farm."

"You think you're going to get EARTH to give up Mars Wolf and California?" said Sun. "Not going to happen."

"She's got to try," said Seta. "That's why we came here."

I looked around at my little team, who looked at one another.

"We'll be right outside the door," said Seta.

"I should go to Iron's cabin," said V. "We have to make sure he knows."

I wanted to beg them all to come, but I knew I had to go alone. None of them really wanted what I wanted. I turned around and started walking toward the Sanctuary.

The hinge on the barn door squawked when I opened it, but only a few heads turned to look. The back of my hand where I had scraped it against the wood was now completely healed; there wasn't even a scar. People inside were quietly concentrating their attention toward the north wall. I didn't see our usual seating assignment for the Translations. Instead, over a hundred people were scattered about on the rugs or standing, forming a human wall around the perimeter. There were faces I didn't recognize, and children were in the room, too, even ones too young to be at Translations.

I squeezed in between two tall men standing at the edge of the crowd and caught sight of members of Beacon House leaning against the wall near the platform. Cham was there, along with Europa, Eris, and Kale. At the opposite wall were Saturn Salt and some of the Canadians from the apple pressing.

In the middle of them all, seated on the dais where the early light from the window in the hay loft shone down on him, was EARTH. He was sitting on a stack of pillows and looking at his knees. Mars Wolf stood behind him, holding up the aerial photo of the California mansion.

"The voting will take place today," Mars Wolf was saying, "with all members of the board of directors who are present. Family input is valuable, but EARTH's Translation from the Cosmos has given us clear direction."

Fern Moon was the first to notice my presence, as if some maternal instinct guided her eyes to the back of the room. She was seated on the floor to the left of the platform, and when she saw me, she waved at me to join her. I was picking my way through the crowd when a few others caught notice. Eve reached out to touch my hand, Bithiah waved, and Indus gave me a warm smile as Lyra tucked herself under his arm and leaned against him. I heard a person whisper, "That's her." Gamma didn't look up from her seat near the dais, but when Ursa spotted me, she squealed "Starbird!" loud enough to attract EARTH's attention.

He turned to Ursa's voice and followed her gaze to me. A puzzled look crossed his face, as if he was working out a math problem. Then he smiled widely and at the same time, a ray of sunlight came through the window and lit up the barn. "Starbird," EARTH boomed. "Your presence is a great gift."

I froze midstep, just two feet from Fern Moon. All heads turned toward me. I was so close to my mother, I almost kept walking to her. I wanted to hug her, to tell her about Doug. I wanted to ask her for advice and help, but the whole room was watching. Fern seemed to notice my confusion and she frowned, clasping her hands together.

"During my time in Seattle, I received a message from the Cosmos about the future of our Family." EARTH addressed the whole room now, still seated on his pillows. "Child, please come here to the dais."

I looked at EARTH and then past him to Mars Wolf. Mars's whole body seemed to betray his shock at seeing me. He lowered the photo of the Mansion and nearly dropped it. I considered accusing him right there, pointing my finger and saying, "He tried to abduct me." But what would happen next? He would say he was just trying to drive me to the café. I would look paranoid and crazy. I could try to tell them about what happened to Doug, but Doug had disappeared again. No one could back up my story except Europa, and I couldn't trust her. I remembered my conversation with Teacher Ted. *Listen for what resonates as the truth within yourself, but think critically*, he told me. *Don't look for absolute rights and wrongs.* I glared at Mars Wolf, keeping my gaze on him as I walked all the way to EARTH's side.

A few more people said hello as I passed—Caelum and Pavo, a few others from the apple pressing. Finally, I arrived at the platform and turned to face my Family.

"The Cosmos instructed me to make an announcement, to tell you that Starbird has a special place among us. Those of you who were at the apple pressing saw what a leader Starbird has become. She is also my natural daughter."

I watched Fern Moon's mouth fall open. Other voices wove together in a pattern of praise and jealousy. Ursa clapped her hands in glee. I noticed Europa whispering something behind her hand to Cham, and Lyra, who had turned her back to the stage, was kissing Indus on his cheek and neck.

I looked at EARTH. His blue eyes glistened with joy but also sparkled with another emotion: fear. I tried to search his expression. Did he know what Mars tried to do to me?

I thought of the group outside the Sanctuary, Sun and the others, waiting in the dark. I thought about Doug somewhere on the streets of Seattle with no food or shelter. Inside the barn it was warm and right, and I was finally being recognized. I was special and seen. Everything I had always wanted was spread before me.

Maybe it *was* the right choice to sell the Farm and move to California. After all, the Farm was failing financially and what did I know about business? What if I convinced the Family to keep the Farm and then it bankrupted us all? Plus, if I were a Family leader, maybe I could be the one to fix everything—punish Mars Wolf, get Doug to come back, make the finances work. Maybe I was what the Family needed. Maybe this was my Calling and the way we would stay together.

I turned to survey the congregation again. *I could lead them in the right direction*, I thought. *If they trust me, if they believe I'm EARTH's daughter, then I could keep us all together.*

That's when I saw Iron. He had poked through the wall of taller men at the back and was standing behind the last person seated. His arms were folded over his chest, and he was not looking at EARTH. He was staring right at me.

Iron's ancestors sawed through giant northwest conifers and dragged their roots out of the ground using horses. They built the log cabin and the cider press. They worked the land for a hundred years, removed rocks for the ploughs, started the apple orchard. Iron would never move to California. Iron wanted to die on the Farm. Behind Iron, Venus had also slipped into the room. She was supporting her father, Mercury Ocean. I glanced over to see if EARTH had noticed them, too. He had.

Mars cleared his throat and resumed talking. "The vote will take place in the Sanctuary after this meeting. Plans for moving Family members to California will begin today, along with inventory of Farm property to be sold at auction. See me if you want to join the inventory group.

This evening, we will have a Feast to celebrate EARTH's return and our move to California." He leaned the aerial photo of the property against the wall and moved to the edge of the dais.

I hadn't spent much time onstage in front of the Family before. I noticed how easily I could read their reactions. Some shared worried looks with partners or children. Many whispered or stood to talk to members in different parts of the room. Others seemed thrilled, their eyes already full of palm trees and sandals. Lyra looked eager, sitting up on her heels and straining to get another look at the photo.

Caelum was the first to speak up. "What if we don't want to go to California?"

EARTH smiled. "Members who want to continue farming and living in the Pacific Northwest can join the Farm in British Columbia. Members who want to stay in Seattle can find work with Outsiders. But there is room for everyone in California."

Adam stood next. "What if the board votes not to sell the properties?"

EARTH's voice was easy and deep. "The Cosmos tells me that won't happen."

"How soon would it happen?" Eve asked, holding her swollen pregnant belly.

"We hope to sell the Farm quickly, within the month," answered Mars.

That brought more chatter into the room, and more concerned looks.

"Some of us have Outside family who live near here," said a man I didn't know.

"The Free Family is the Family we have chosen," said EARTH. "Love holds us together through many changes." Standing so close to EARTH, I could see his wrinkles changing with each expression on his face. His smile seemed to require effort. "But if you choose to be with your Outside family, we must respect that and sadly part."

"Will we be near the beach?" asked Lyra Hay, smiling coyly at EARTH.

EARTH cocked his head toward her, and I remembered that she joined us after he left. He had probably never met her. "Very near," he said, "and California beaches are sandy and warm. Californians don't wear raincoats to the beach."

I looked back at Iron, still standing near the back wall. He was chewing the edge of his thumbnail and looking left and right around the room.

Mars Wolf stepped to the center of the platform again. "The Translation is now ended. Everyone but the board of directors will wait in the courtyard until the vote is finished. Then we will celebrate our move and begin planning our auction."

Ending so fast? There was no more time to ask questions and think, no more time to consider? People started to stand and move toward the door. Everyone started talking. EARTH rose up from his spot on the cushions and stepped down off the stage. Mars Wolf was making his way toward the back of the room. Iron didn't move, still chewing his nail and staring at me.

"This Farm is called the Murphy Farm," I said toward the crowd of people before me. No one seemed to notice. I had waited too long. People kept talking and moving around. The board of directors had started forming a circle around EARTH to the left of the platform, and Mars was urging people toward the back door, which was open and letting in the sun. "Wait," I said, but again no one heard me. Caelum and Indus had made their way over to Iron and were talking to him with their heads bent together. Fern was still seated on a rug and looking down at her hands. Where would Fern decide to go? I felt how all of our lives were about to change forever. "Wait!" I yelled. "It's called the MURPHY FARM!"

People quieted and stopped moving toward the door. Mars Wolf spun around toward the stage. EARTH turned too and stared at me. "Iron John's ancestors homesteaded here; they built the farmhouse and this barn," I said. "I don't think we should make John leave this place when his mother gave it to our Family to take care of."

"The Translation is over," Mars growled from the congregation, his eyes attempting to bore holes into my skin. "No comments till after the vote."

352 ✳ karen finneyfrock

"Wait, Brother Mars," said EARTH in his richest tone, stepping back onto the dais and putting his arm around my shoulder, towering over me. "Starbird has made a thoughtful remark. She gives us all so much with her childlike wisdom." I looked up at EARTH, who smiled at me the way you would smile at a baby.

Mars Wolf moved back toward the dais, hovering near it.

"This property has been a good home, as Callisto wanted when she gave it to us," EARTH said, squeezing me to his side. "I've loved it for forty years. But family farms are going bankrupt every day. We must face the modern world, and the way forward is computers. Change is frightening, but if we stay together, the Cosmos will take care of us. We must *stay together*, even if that means exodus."

There were many approving sounds. Saturn said, "Praise." A few of the Canadians clapped their hands.

"I want the Family to stay together, too," I said, wiggling out from under EARTH's arm. I had to make both hands into fists to keep them from visibly trembling. Red splotches erupted over my chest and neck. I raised my voice to make sure the whole room would hear me. "But selling the Farm doesn't feel right."

Something broke lose in the crowd. "Who are you to question him?" Europa yelled from near the wall. "You don't speak for the Cosmos," said a Canadian member.

EARTH held up both hands for silence. Standing

over six feet in his white robes, a gold cord at his waist, EARTH seemed to hold all the sound in the palm of his empty hand. "Sometimes our hearts are conflicted," he said, eyeing me with tenderness, "especially when we are young. Starbird doesn't know the trials of the Outside that brought us together as a Family. We haven't done a good enough job of teaching our children what our lives were like before we found each other."

"Before *you* found *us*, EARTH," said a man with a gray beard.

"I won't go back to the Outside," said the woman sitting next to him.

"Starbird, we need each other," said Adam. "You know that."

"I do need you. I want the Family to stay together," I said, guilt and shame starting to erode my courage. "I just feel like we all need to make a decision together instead of blindly obeying."

That's when the anger erupted. Saturn Salt walked through a group of people and spit on my boot. "Heretic," she said, pointing a finger at me. A man in the back yelled, "Sit down, Judas!" Then Fern stood up, yelling back, "You're the Judas! Don't yell at her!" "Shut up," someone else said. Others joined in, the tension rising alongside the sun.

"It is natural to have questions." EARTH's voice grew firmer and louder. "Faith is the only cure for doubt. But our human discussions won't change the will of the Cosmos."

"I wish I had listened to my questions," a man's voice said from the back of the room.

Mercury Ocean walked away from V and into the circle of those still seated. He looked dirty and tired, like he had just climbed down from a red cedar, like he was having trouble standing. "I listened when the Cosmos said our babies should be born on the Farm and not in the hospital. When you told me that, EARTH, I listened to you. Then she died. Venus Ocean died right on this Sanctuary floor." He made the word *sanctuary* sound unholy. "The Cosmos never wanted that."

"Death is a part of life and birth. We cannot control the will of the Universe," EARTH said. I was close enough to watch EARTH's eyes turn red and swell. "I wanted to save her, Mercury. You know I did. I was there too. I didn't want her to die."

"What about Mars Wolf? Can you control him?" Another voice broke through the crowd near the door. "Or is driving kids off the Farm part of the will of the Cosmos?" Pushing toward the stage was someone I never dreamed of seeing at the Farm, or maybe ever again. It was Doug.

EARTH looked as if a specter had entered the Sanctuary, declaring itself to be alive. "Doug?" he said to the ghost.

"Doug?" my mother called, turning around. She stood up and stepped on people as she pushed her way through the congregation toward my brother.

"You knew, didn't you, EARTH, that Mars drove me off in the middle of the night? That he tried to do the same thing to Starbird?" Doug kept his eyes trained on EARTH's even as Fern collapsed into his arms, sobbing on his shoulder and clutching him.

EARTH looked from Doug to me. Some horror seemed to be occurring to him. But when he spoke, he said, "Praise the Cosmos for this miracle! Our prodigal son has returned to us at the hour of our greatest transformation." He held both arms out toward Doug. "We know you've been through many trials on the Outside. But you've come back to let us heal you. Welcome home, Douglas Fir!"

As EARTH was talking, Mars Wolf had been inching closer to the door at the north end of the Sanctuary again. That's when I saw that Sun and the others had entered the barn after Doug. They stood in the crowd behind him.

A few women said, "Welcome, Douglas," and "Welcome home," but the tension in the room was unbroken.

"I was driven off the Farm," said Doug. "when I was just sixteen. I lived in homeless shelters. I was hungry and scared and stolen from. I had to hitchhike all the way back to the Farm, and I'm standing here because I want to know if *you* knew." Doug held an arm out toward EARTH, his finger pointed, his hand shaking.

Despite EARTH's obvious surprise at seeing Doug, EARTH never looked at Mars Wolf.

"Let Fern Moon take you to the Farm house and feed you," said EARTH. "We can talk about everything when you are rested."

"Doug deserves answers." Sun pushed into the crowd and crossed his arms. "Mars Wolf needs to tell us what he did."

The sun had now fully risen outside, a rare sunny morning in the early fall. Beams of light shone through the window of the hayloft and illuminated Mars Wolf standing amid the congregation in the barn. It was like turning over a rock and seeing the bugs that live in the darkness underneath. Mars looked like he wanted to scurry back underground.

"He ran away," Mars said, his voice thin and angry. "I had nothing to do with it."

"What about last night when you tried to drive away Starbird?" said Doug.

"I offered to drive her to the café to see EARTH," said Mars, tucking his long, dark hair behind both ears.

"You're lying," I said.

"You're the liar!" he yelled. "I serve EARTH," Mars spat at me, "not you."

EARTH held up his hands for quiet. He kept them raised until everyone was still. "Mars Wolf, are these accusations true?"

The veil hiding Mars Wolf's fury fell away. "Are you questioning *me*?" he said, bewildered. His greasy hair hung limp in the sunlight, and the cord on his robes was pulled tight around his thin figure.

"Do these young ones accuse you rightly?" said EARTH again, crossing his arms in front of him.

"I have done everything I was instructed to do," stammered Mars. "You know that. You know that."

"I never instructed you to do these things," said EARTH. "From where do you claim to be getting your instruction?"

Mars looked confused. His eyes darted around at the congregation, then back to EARTH. "I was your first Believer. You named me after the planet next to you," he began. Mars seemed small, then, not dangerous but feeble.

"Mars Wolf, you must leave this Family," said EARTH. A stunned silence reached every corner of the barn.

"What?" Mars whispered, clutching the cord on his robe.

"You have transgressed against Family, including my natural daughter, and the Cosmos instructs me to banish you from our company. You might return some day after restitution is paid."

"You can't. I did nothing wrong. I have nothing. Where would I go? You can't!" Mars looked around at the congregation. No one spoke for him.

"You can leave in the truck you drove here, but take nothing else," said EARTH, majestic and commanding in the light of the sun. He motioned to Adam and another man who went to Mars, each taking him by an arm.

"I'll apologize." Mars pulled away and tried to walk toward EARTH, but Adam stopped him. "I'll make amends. I can't be sent away."

"As you sow, so shall you reap," said EARTH.

"I can't survive out there," Mars pleaded. "Doug, I'm sorry. Starbird, I'm sorry!" He turned toward me. I felt a pang of sympathy.

"The Cosmos has spoken. You must leave," said EARTH.

"You planned this," Mars growled, suddenly furious and finding his strength. He struggled with Adam and the other man holding him. "He orchestrated this." He said to all of us gathered. "He's the one who told me to do it!" The men pulled Mars toward the back door of the barn. "Ask him about the bank accounts!" he yelled. "Ask him about Arnold Muller!"

Mars was dragged out of the Sanctuary by the two men, and we could hear his yelling grow more distant as he went.

That's when Sun spoken again. "Yeah, EARTH, tell us about Arnold Muller."

EARTH was like a rooster surrounded by foxes. A part of me wanted to defend him, wanted to run to his side and beg them to stop. But I needed to know what he would say next. I had to hear it from him.

"I have used my Outside name to raise funds for the purchase of the Mansion. It's nothing more nefarious than that," he said calmly.

"Really," said Doug. "Because I've seen the bank statements and it looks like you own money and property under the name Arnold Muller."

"Do not insult me by using that name in my Sanctuary," EARTH said, his voice gathering power in his lowest register. "I will not be questioned in my own house or scolded like a *dog*. I've given my life to you."

"You didn't give it to me when you kicked me out at sixteen," said Sun.

"Do you think I did all this for myself?" said EARTH, his voice audibly trembling with anger. He turned around and squared his shoulders to Sun's. The resemblance was stunning. "You have the nerve to act like this was all for me?" He paused and stood straighter, seeming to grow again in height. He took two steps closer to Sun. "Do you think it's easy keeping a Family of two hundred people fed, loved, and safe for forty years? Do you think that's a simple thing? Do you think I haven't had a life of sleepless nights and bank accounts and court cases to keep this Family together, while they were all free to eat and love each other and never touch money? Who do you think had to touch the money and risk corruption? Everything we needed for forty years, I found it. I found Beacon House, the Farm, the café. Do you think that the Outsiders don't dog our every step, don't hang over us like a cloud? Do you think you could do it?" EARTH paused, glaring at Sun. "And my own son questions my every motive. The person I needed beside me the most."

Sun's face turned red. His voice came out sounding small, like a boy's. "You should have been my dad. You should have been Arnold Muller."

"STOP USING THAT NAME!" EARTH's fury hit the barn like a flash flood. I took several steps back. "Do you think I *need* any of you?" He turned to address us all. "Do you think I couldn't go to California on my own? With my skills, you don't think I could have everything? I am giving you the CHANCE to come with me, to ride on my coattails, and you offer me questions and doubt? ANY OF YOU who wants to leave me and join the wide, desperate world of non-Believers should go. GO NOW! GET OUT!" EARTH pointed furiously at the door. His white hair was alive and his fury gained him even more in size. He was huge in the middle of the stage, and I was tiny and quiet and terrified.

"I guess we could argue about the will of the Cosmos all day." It was Iron's reasoned voice that snaked through the crowd and bit the stage. "But EARTH can't tell anyone to get off this property, because the future of the Farm won't be decided by the board of directors' meeting today. Gamma and I already filed the paperwork. Ownership of this place will be decided by the courts."

33

Talk erupted from every corner of the barn, but it quieted when Iron spoke again.

"There are laws protecting people who aren't in their sane minds when they change their will. My mother signed away the farm when she was consumed with grief. If it's given back to me, I'll let any of you who wants to stay live here and work the farm," he said. His arms were crossed and he barely moved when he spoke. It was like he was standing on the deck of a ship in the storm, braced against the roiling sea.

EARTH's gaze landed on Gamma, who had been quiet. I saw fury in his eyes that I had never seen there before. "You went to Outsiders." His voice dripped with disgust. "You went to lawyers."

"The Farm and café have been mismanaged." Gamma stood in front of the room and crossed her arms in front of her tiny frame. Her gray hair was in messy curls on her head. "The Family," she went on, glancing at EARTH, "has never had a head for business. And there was borrowing against the value of the Farm that wasn't approved by the board."

"What are you talking about?" Neptune Fox stood up. "Who borrowed against the Farm?"

"Arnold Muller," Gamma said.

"Stop saying that name!" Saturn screamed. Then she walked toward Gamma, still yelling, berating her inches from her face. Bithiah turned to Iron and slung a stream of insults in his direction. Sun defended Iron by going after Bithiah, and then everyone was yelling.

Family members pointed fingers, demanded answers. Children started crying, and several people tried to make their way toward the exit. Europa was toe-to-toe with Doug Fir, who had Fern Moon backing him up. At the head of it all, standing on the edge of the stage looking out over the Family he had founded, was EARTH. And standing next to EARTH was me.

"Look at all you've achieved, Starbird," said EARTH, motioning to the chaos in front of us.

"This isn't what I wanted." Watching the Family pitted against one another, I felt like my own heart was ripping in two. *What have I done?*

"Forty years I've kept us together, and you managed to break us up in one morning." His voice was caustic, accusatory, not fatherly.

"You didn't keep *all* of us together," I said.

"If one person, a malcontent, a disruptive element, threatened the preservation of the whole group, what would you do?" he said.

"I don't know," I said. "But I know I wouldn't drive a kid off in the middle of the night and abandon him with nothing."

The look that flashed over EARTH's face was difficult to name. It was a mix of recognition, remembrance, and regret. There was no self-righteousness left. There was sadness. Mars was telling the truth. EARTH had known.

"Are you really my father?" I asked.

"If I am, then both of my children have turned against me."

"You didn't answer my question."

EARTH looked at me, smiled sadly, didn't respond.

"You told everyone you were my father. Why?"

"Look at you up here on the stage, so fierce, so destined for leadership. Don't you feel like my daughter? Haven't you always wanted it?"

EARTH's blue eyes went past all my defenses, looked right into my heart.

"I did want it," I said, "my whole life. But I don't now."

The fighting continued around us in the barn while EARTH looked at me. "Family." EARTH's voice was a raindrop in a thunderstorm. He still watched me. "Family," he tried again, turning to the room, raising his hands and shaking them. Then, "FAMILY!" His voice shook the beams of the old barn until they rattled.

The room took a few minutes to quiet. But, eventually, even Saturn silenced her fury.

"We shame our love for one another with this vicious-ness," EARTH said, the last word hitting like a whip. A mix of shame and defiance was visible on all the faces. Many arms were crossed and only a few people were still sitting. "I never wanted to see us torn to pieces." He sounded tired, like he had been carrying something heavy and was finally setting it down. "Our Family has had no luck in business. Valuing love over money has made life"— he looked around on the stage below him—"difficult for us in the World Outside. Maybe that's my fault."

Saturn Salt whispered, "No, no it's not," clinging to another Family member from Canada.

"I was twenty-six years old, and I had a wife and a child. I had been working as a salesman, living in a house, chasing money, chasing new things to buy. My name was Arnold Muller and I thought, *This can't be all there is to life. This can't be what life is about.*"

For the first time ever, EARTH looked old to me. From where I stood on his right, his spine seemed to curve slightly toward the ground, and I felt that someone should offer him a chair. We had nothing but pillows.

"When I first heard the voice of the Cosmos, it was like a whisper riding the wind. It was sad and sweet and soothing. It comforted me. It told me that the Universe is not a cold, unfeeling place; it has shape and intelligence. I don't know why it chose to speak to me, or if it speaks to all of us if we listen. But when I started telling people what the Cosmos said, they wanted me to tell them more. I didn't ask people to join me; they asked me if they could join."

"I opened my home. I opened my marriage. Everything I did was for the Family. And I haven't done everything right. Maybe I made choices that were . . . harsh, but I did it for us. Everything I did was to keep us together." EARTH's head dropped toward his chest. He was hurting. I could feel it.

"Don't let our Family end like this," he said, and swept his hands in a low arc around the room. "We've loved each other for so long."

People turned back toward the dais, and some who had been standing sat again. My resolve broke into pieces and I sank down onto the stage, too. This couldn't be the end, could it?

"Since Iron John and Gamma have filed their paperwork and taken our Family into the courts, there's no point in fighting over their right to do it." EARTH smoothed down his robes and adjusted his rope belt. "Instead, we will declare our allegiances and decide our fates. The Sanctuary is now divided in two. All true Believers who wish to follow the Cosmos and go with me to California or remain with our Family in Canada should move to the right side of the Sanctuary. All brothers and sisters who wish to stay and work the Farm with Iron should move to the left. I see no other way."

There were a few scattered protests. One woman yelled, "Don't break up the Family! Gamma, stop this."

A few others claimed, "We shouldn't have to choose" or "Love holds us together."

But several people walked quickly to one side of the barn, many having already chosen a side.

Iron, of course, walked to the left, followed protectively by Paul and Devin. Fern was clutching Doug Fir like she thought he might disappear again. They both followed Iron. Seta, Venus, and her father, Mercury, joined them, too.

Saturn Salt went to the right side of the room, her hands clasped in front of her body and her chin raised. She looked tense, like a snake coiling to strike. Adam went to her side, along with Bithiah, Neptune Fox, and Europa, holding Eris and leading Kale. Eve walked slowly, holding her round belly as she went, motioning for Ursa and Pavo to join her. I watched Ursa drag her feet to the group on the right side of the barn, looking back at Iron as she went, then looking up at me. She grabbed Pavo's hand and held it against her worn skirt. I had to pinch the inside of my arm to keep myself from running to her. Was this a terrible dream?

There were still many people in the middle of the room. Gamma went to Adeona, the woman EARTH had rescued off the street in Spokane. They stood whispering together in the center of the floor, and touching arms, before Gamma, shaking her head, walked over to stand with Iron. Adeona went to the right side of the room and stood near Eve.

Cham seemed to hang back, watching the events unfold, studying each line of people. He finally went to EARTH's side, standing next to Europa.

Caelum was locked in a heated discussion with Indus and Lyra. Several times Lyra grabbed her braids or punched Indus on the arm. Finally, she backed away from the group in a tearful run and darted across the room to EARTH's side. She tossed herself dramatically into Cham's arms and started sobbing.

Indus threw up his hands and followed Caelum to Iron John's side of the room.

Sun stood near the south door with his arms folded, staring at his mother, Uranus Peak, who seemed to be frozen in her spot on the rug. She finally melted, dropping her head toward her lap, before standing and walking slowly toward EARTH's side. She never looked at Sun, but Sun watched her go like she was the only person in the room. His eyes followed her all the way across the Sanctuary, and I was sure he would go to her and try to drag her to his side. But he didn't. He made his way toward Iron's group, where Seta put her arm around his waist and kept it there.

The remaining Family members took their sides, most

of them heading toward EARTH's half of the room. Then Adeona suddenly broke free from her place near Eve and moved to the middle of the room. She stood looking at EARTH from the floor of the Sanctuary and put her hands together at her heart before hurrying over to Iron's side and folding into Gamma's arms.

That's when I realized that I hadn't moved yet; I was so hypnotized by observing the strange and solemn dance before me. I didn't want to, but I made myself turn to face EARTH, the man claiming to be my father, his blue eyes dripping with disappointment. I knew then that even if EARTH decided not to go to California, even if he moved back to the Farm again, I couldn't think of him the same way. I couldn't let him tell me what the Cosmos wanted for me. My own inner voice was getting louder by the minute.

I got up and walked to Iron's side of the barn and stood with Fern Moon and Doug Fir, who were holding each other tenderly. I was heartbroken. I was scared of the future and how we would manage now that we were splintered. I was afraid of life without EARTH, and afraid of following my own voice. I reached out and found Doug's hand and squeezed it hard with mine. He took Fern Moon's hand in his other. Fern reached out for Indus, who extended his free hand to Caelum. Each person in the group reached down the line for someone else until we were all linked together, one to another. My free hand reached out to Iron.

34

EARTH and the people traveling with him left that same day for Seattle and eventually California. Buses and cars were packed with items, stripping the house of most of its utensils and bedding, but leaving all the farm equipment for us. There was surprisingly little bickering as items were divided up, as if people were just too sad to fight over throw pillows and cheese graters.

Sun and Doug stayed with Iron near the farm equipment, in case anyone tried to start conflicts or damage property. I wanted quiet and isolation, so I tucked myself into the chicken coop where the chirping of the flock blocked out other noise.

I was alone for a few minutes before Ursa rushed in and collapsed into a crying heap in my lap. "She can't make me go! It's not fair. Why should my mother pick for me?" she said between sobs. "I hate California."

I held Ursa's shoulders as they shook. "California is sunny all the time, even in February," I said. "No more walking through the rainy mud to the chicken coop. You'll go to the beach every day."

"But I want everyone to come, and not everyone is coming," Ursa said into my sweater.

I felt so responsible. Everything was fine before I got my Calling, before I went to Seattle and discovered Arnold Muller.

"I'm so sorry," I said, starting to cry myself. We just stayed there, on the plywood floor surrounded by clucking chickens, crying and crying.

There were more wretched scenes before the caravan pulled out. Saying good-bye to Adam and Eve was mortifying. Hugging Kale and Eris made me start crying all over again. My Family was breaking up, and I was the one who broke it.

I watched Lyra stuff jackets and several pairs of shoes into the back of a VW van, her silky braids sweeping over the taillights. When Indus tapped her on the shoulder, she turned and gave him a cold look, crossing her arms over her chest. He attempted to hug her, but she kept her folded arms between them. Then she walked over and put her hand on Cham's back as he closed the hatchback on a car.

Sun carried Uranus's bags for her and helped her into the passenger seat of a van. I watched him kiss her cheek, his mouth a thin, flat line.

EARTH said his standard good-byes, bowing, hugging, and laying his hands on member's heads. When he got to Iron, he offered him a handshake. "Are you sure you want to do this?" I heard him say.

"Don't seem to have much choice," Iron said back, shaking EARTH's hand.

When EARTH got to me, he said, "Daughter," and opened his arms. I fell into them, allowing myself to feel it one last time, the protection of his shelter and his love. But it didn't feel the way it used to. His arms felt just like the arms of a man—bony, peculiar, and aging. I didn't feel any safer than I did hugging Fern Moon, or anybody.

"There will always be a place for you in California," he said, touching my head with his hand. It was a nice thing to hear, but I was sure I would never go.

As the caravan pulled out along the gravel drive, I stood watching, just the way I had watched EARTH leave for his Mission three years earlier. Some people waved, some cried, others were just angry and silent. EARTH was in the last vehicle, a van driven by Adam. Both of them waved. Doug sat on the front porch with Indus and Caelum, rolling his tobacco. Gamma and Adeona disappeared into the house. Iron stood in the gravel with me and Fern. As the last vehicle drove out of sight, Iron put his hand on my shoulder.

Epilogue

Our last day together on the Farm, I wondered when I would ever see EARTH again. It happened much sooner than I expected. Two months later, he came back to Seattle for Ephraim's funeral. Ephraim died of pneumonia, exacerbated by the weakness of his liver from alcoholism. I spent a lot of time with him in the hospital during his last weeks. Cham delayed going to California to wait for his dad, and he's the one who told Ephraim about the breakup of the Family.

I wish he hadn't. Ephraim talked about it incessantly, first demanding to be transferred to a hospital in California near EARTH and then begging us to sell the Farm and keep the Family together. "EARTH saved my life, Starbird," he said with oxygen tubes traveling into each of his nostrils. "He saved a lot of us. None of this money stuff matters."

I felt a familiar guilt, nagging questions about my role.

"We're just changing," I told Ephraim. "It's not like we will never see each other again."

That was the last time we talked.

V was inconsolable after. She spent all her time with Devin or alone. Since Ephraim left Beacon House to the Family in his will, we would have to wait and see what would happen with our living situation. But before he passed away, Ephraim asked V to take his position on the board of directors, the position vacated by her mother, Venus Ocean. So at least Venus would have a vote in what happened to the property.

A van full of Family members came up from California for the memorial service and Story Night at Beacon House the following Sunday. It was mostly elders who had known Ephraim for a long time.

A caravan from the Farm came, too. Doug Fir and Fern Moon held hands a lot, and whenever they were in the same room, she was hugging him around his waist. She was the happiest I had seen her in ages. Doug still looked haunted, but he told me he was beginning to relax with the familiar sounds of the Farm all around him. His color looked better from a healthy diet, and he cut his hair and shaved his face clean. He and Iron were spending a lot of time together, he told me, and he was learning to play the banjo. He took my old cot in the yurt and was living with Fern Moon.

"It's funny. I couldn't wait to get out of the yurt when I was fifteen," he told me. "Now it feels comforting to wake up and know my mom is right there."

When I took Fern upstairs to see my room, she cried. She cried again when Io showed her some of my new clothes. During a heart-to-heart on my bed, Fern told me that EARTH couldn't possibly know if he was my father. She said that she didn't even know.

"Do you believe the Cosmos could have told him?" I asked.

"I don't know if I've ever really believed that."

"I did," I said. "Now I don't know what I believe. But I think I feel okay not knowing," I said. "Right now, I'm mostly into asking questions."

"Are you doing okay in school?" asked Fern.

"I'm getting an A in math. And I really like my horticulture teacher; she grew up on a farm. My friend Rory and I are planting a medicinal garden in the school's P-Patch for our midterm project."

Fern cried again.

Indus came from the Farm, too. He sat on our couch and played the harmonica with his muscular hands. He told me he had met a girl in Bellingham, a yoga teacher, and that they had been dating for a month. I didn't really feel jealous when he told me. I mostly just felt happy for him. *Indus is too old for me*, I thought. *I'd much rather date someone my own age.*

Sun actually came to the memorial and sat in the same room with his father and mother. He must have cared very deeply about Ephraim. Even Felicia showed up, cried off all her mascara, and left before the speeches were made.

That Story Night was full of instruments and stories, giant platters of food, and only people who called themselves Ephraim's Family. It was just what he would have wanted. We all gathered tightly into the living room, and EARTH said many stirring things about Ephraim, standing by the mantel. He talked about how much Ephraim had given to the people he loved, how generous he was and how full of light. At one point, EARTH's voice gave out, and he had to stop speaking while he took some breaths. He told us to keep loving one another, and then he walked away into the kitchen and we heard the back screen door open and close.

EARTH left for California that evening after paying for Ephraim's burial plot. Cham went with him, taking all the possessions of his and Ephraim's that he wanted to keep. I gave Cham the navy-blue dress I wore for the apple pressing and asked him to deliver it to Ursa. Before leaving, EARTH told us again that there was room for us all in the California Mansion. He didn't display hard feelings toward Iron. When he left, he shook Iron's hand and said, "I'll see you again in February for court."

"Starbird, can I talk to you on the back porch?" Iron asked as Family members collected dirty plates, moved food into the kitchen, and put the furniture back into place. I got my coat and followed him out back through the screen door.

It was getting dark out, so Iron lit two candles sitting on the cement steps that led down to the grass. It was late November, and cold air knocked the wind chimes around above our heads. I could see the wet mist in the air when I looked toward the streetlight.

"We don't know how this court case is going to go," he said, sitting down on the last step and making room for me beside him, "but the lawyer thinks we have a good chance to show mental stress on the part of my mother. If we win, ownership of the Farm will revert to me."

"What if we lose?" I said.

"You can't cross a river until you reach it," Iron said with a sad grin. "If I get the Farm, I'll let the remaining Family live there. I'll manage the harvest and hope enough people stick around to help. Fern Moon wants to stay and so do the boys. Gamma and Adeona will be there, a few others. I'm still a young man, and I hope to live another forty years, but Ephraim was young, too, and you never know."

We sat quietly for a moment. I was thinking of Ephraim. Our collective future seemed to keep changing like the hands of a clock.

"Your legal name is Starbird Murphy. According to the records, you are my only heir and closest relative. If I get the Farm back, it would eventually be handed down to you."

I hadn't considered that before. *Personal property? The whole Farm?* I had never even owned a dresser.

"If and when that happens, you can decide what to do with it. Sell it, keep it, give it back to the Family. It will be up to you."

"That's a lot of responsibility," I said.

"That's what ownership is," said Iron. "If you want to come back, you can have any job you want. You don't have to go back to the chicken coop. Doug's taken it over for now."

"I think I want to stay in Seattle," I said, "and keep going to school."

"It's up to you," said Iron.

I heard the gate to our chain-link fence rattle. It was my boyfriend, Ben.

"Sorry I'm so shucking late," he said. He had on an ill-fitting suit with sleeves that were an inch too short. He walked over to where we were sitting. "I had church and then I had to do some work for my dad today and then I went home to change clothes and I thought I should dress up because it was a memorial, but I guess I kind of got here too late because it seems like everyone's leaving and I kind of missed it." He looked at Iron and reached out to shake his hand, but then pulled it back and put his hands together in prayer position and bowed. "Hello, sir."

Iron studied Ben for a moment, looking at Ben's suit and his hands pressed together in front of his heart. Then he started to laugh. It came out slow at first, a light chuckle that grew into a howl. I had never heard Iron laugh like that. He laughed until little tears sprouted from the wrinkled corners of his eyes, and he stomped his boots on the wooden porch steps.

"Hello, there," Iron said at last, holding his hands together over his heart. He was still chuckling as he went back inside the house.

"Why was he laughing?" Ben asked.

"I'm not totally sure," I said. "Maybe it was the suit."

"Should we go inside?" Ben asked. "I mean, I know I'm late, but maybe I should say hi to your mom."

I stood up to lead him into the house but suddenly changed my mind. "Come with me," I said.

I took Ben's hand and led him across the grass, toward the back of our property near the alley. The wind lifted up my hair and pulled it across my face, so I had to brush it out of my eyes as we walked. The grass was tall and wet, making the toes damp on the pretty brown boots Io had found for me. When we reached the evergreen that provided us privacy from the neighbors, I turned around toward Ben and kissed him.

It was sweet at first, like a quick good-bye kiss you might have in the parking lot after school. But then I wrapped my hands around his neck, threading my left fingers into his mop of dark curly hair, and I kissed him deeply, the way you kiss in a car when you're being dropped off after a movie. He put his hands around my waist and pulled me toward him. Then I pushed him on the shoulders to make him step away from me, his weight shifting until his back was up against the tree. And we kept kissing there as the wet air turned our cheeks red and the pinecones crunched under our toes and the moon rose over us like a fat, white egg up in the sky.

Acknowledgments

Many people and organizations helped me create this story. For generously sharing their own incredible stories, I thank Won Isreal and Vashti Whissiel-Wren. Organizations that made this book possible include: Hedgebrook Writing Retreat, 4 Culture, the City of Seattle Office of Arts & Culture, Richard Hugo House, and the Helen R. Whiteley Center. I'd like to thank my editor, Kendra Levin, and my agent, Dan Lazar, for their keen guidance. Writer friends make everything better. Thank you Peter Mountford, Kevin Emerson, and Brian McGuigan. Thank you Rachel McKibbens and writers of Pink Door. Thank you to the young writers of Nathan Hale High School and Teacher Ted Lockerly, the perfect choice for a mentor. Thank you Sunlight Café for the best cup of yogi tea in town. Thank you to my family, my grandmother, Helen Freeman, the best reader I know, and Joe Paul Slaby, who hears all my ideas first.